P9-CKX-543

Cat & Cat

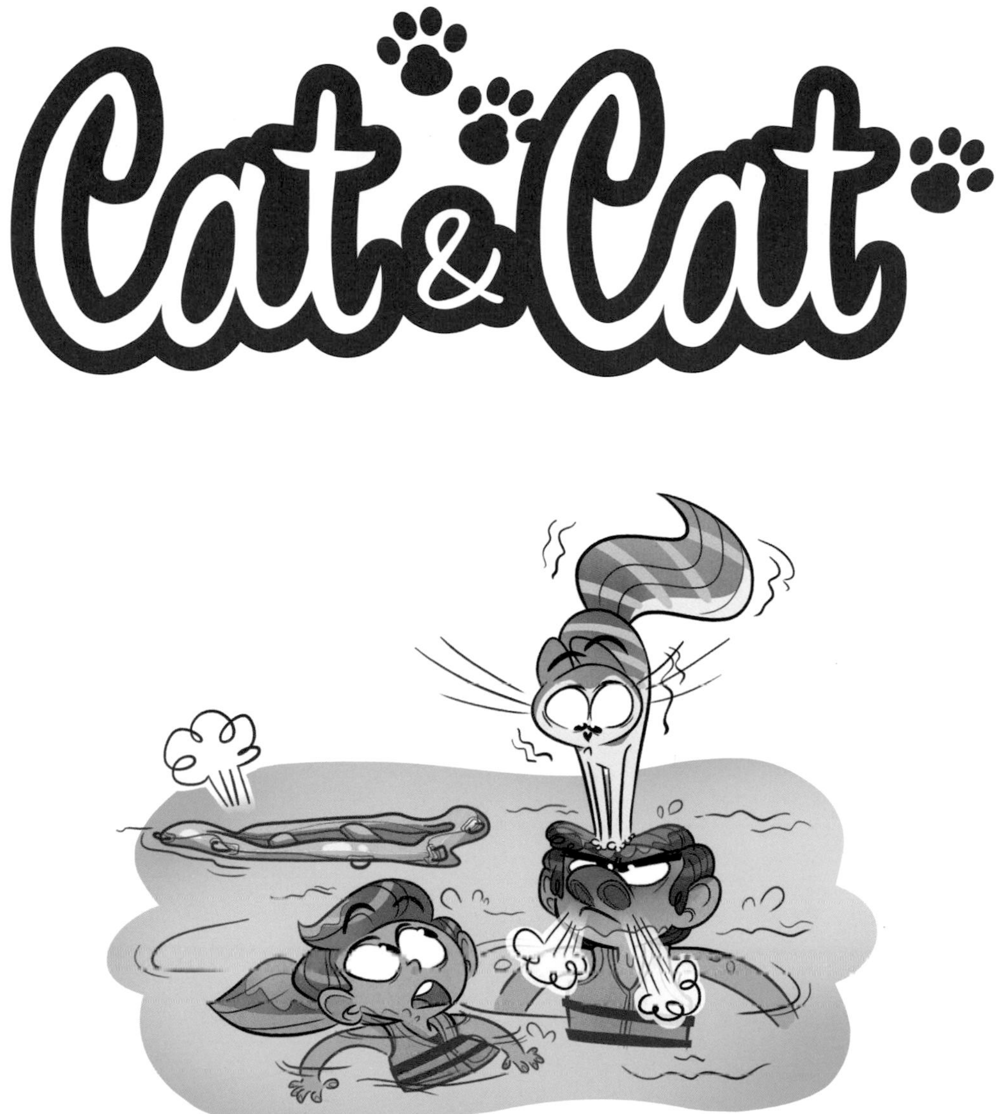

PAPERCUTZ

MORE GREAT GRAPHIC NOVEL SERIES AVAILABLE FROM

PAPERCUTZ™

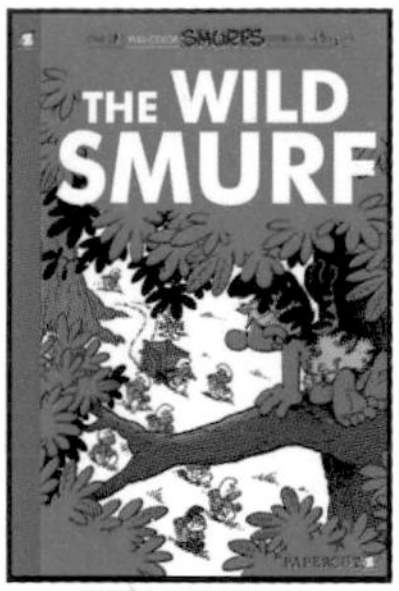
THE WILD SMURF
PAPERCUTZ
THE SMURFS

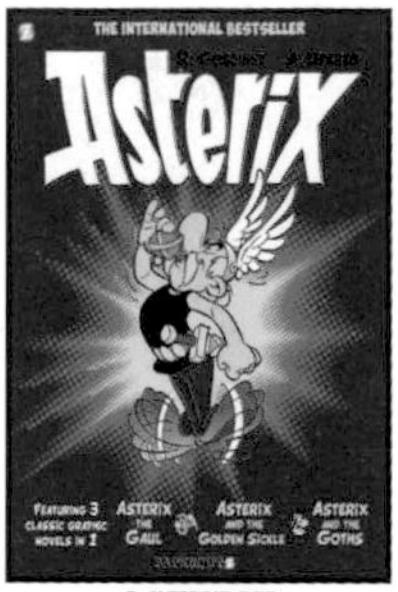
THE INTERNATIONAL BESTSELLER
Asterix
FEATURING 3 CLASSIC GRAPHIC NOVELS IN 1
ASTERIX THE GAUL
ASTERIX AND THE GOLDEN SICKLE
ASTERIX AND THE GOTHS
ASTERIX

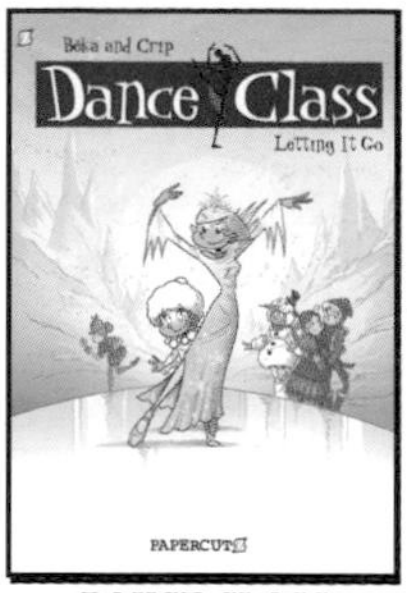
Béka and Crip
Dance Class
Letting It Go
PAPERCUTZ
DANCE CLASS

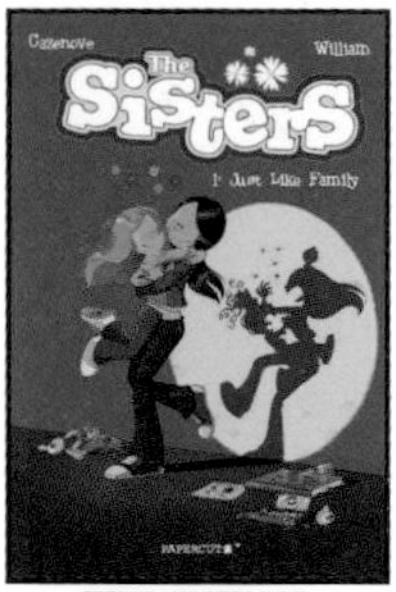
Cazenove
William
The Sisters
It Just Like Family
PAPERCUTZ
THE SISTERS

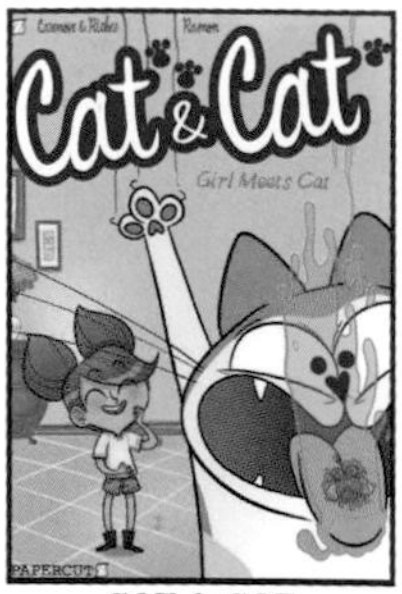
Cat & Cat
Girl Meets Cat
PAPERCUTZ
CAT & CAT

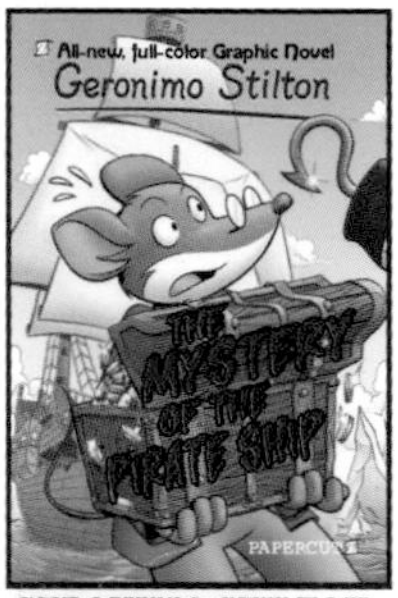
All-new, full-color Graphic Novel
Geronimo Stilton
THE MYSTERY OF THE PIRATE SHIP
PAPERCUTZ
GERONIMO STILTON

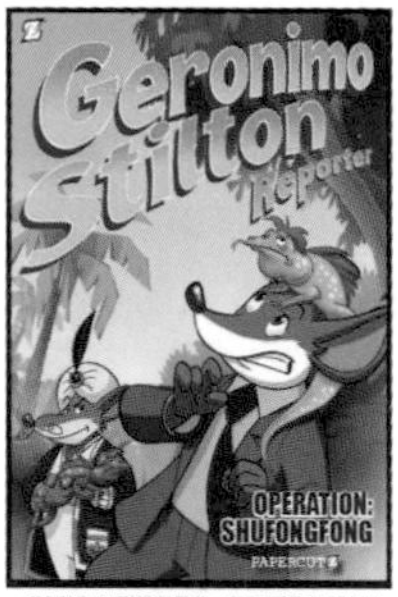
Geronimo Stilton
Reporter
OPERATION: SHUFONGFONG
PAPERCUTZ
GERONIMO STILTON REPORTER

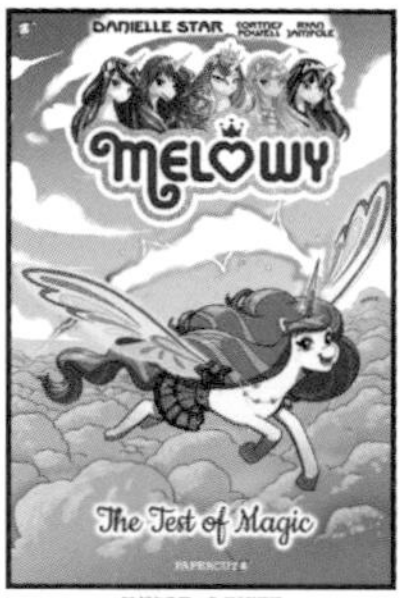
DANIELLE STAR
MELOWY
The Test of Magic
PAPERCUTZ
MELOWY

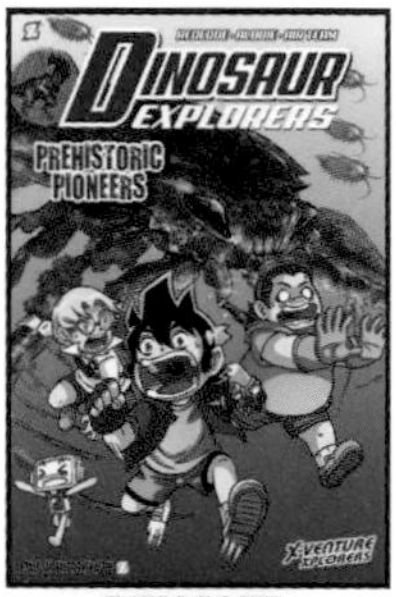
DINOSAUR EXPLORERS
PREHISTORIC PIONEERS
DINOSAUR EXPLORERS

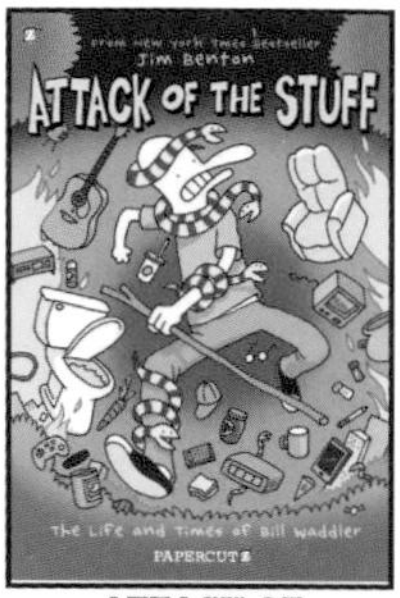
Jim Benton
ATTACK OF THE STUFF
The Life and Times of Bill Waddler
PAPERCUTZ
ATTACK OF THE STUFF

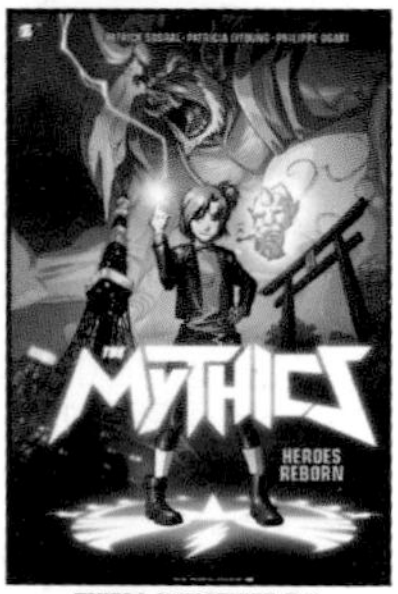
THE MYTHICS
HEROES REBORN
THE MYTHICS

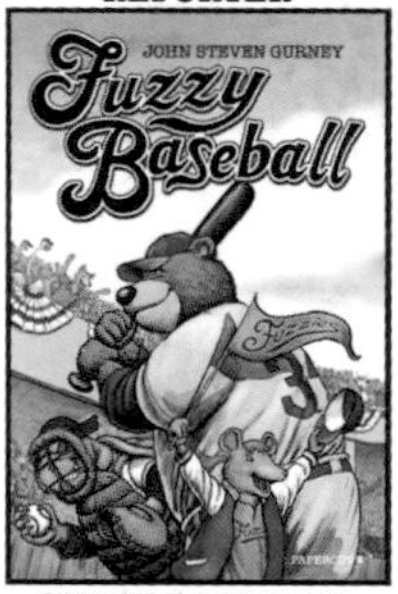
JOHN STEVEN GURNEY
Fuzzy Baseball
FUZZY BASEBALL

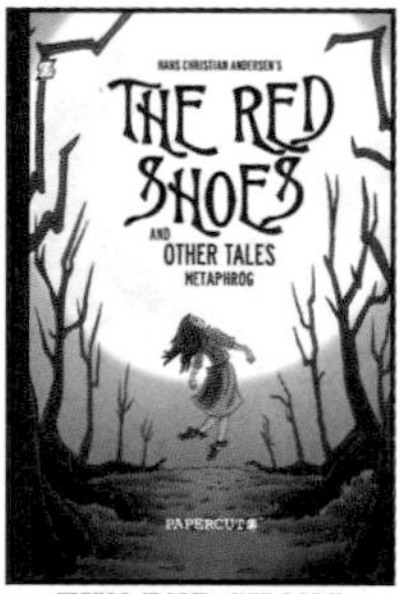
HANS CHRISTIAN ANDERSEN'S
THE RED SHOES
AND OTHER TALES
METAPHROG
PAPERCUTZ
THE RED SHOES

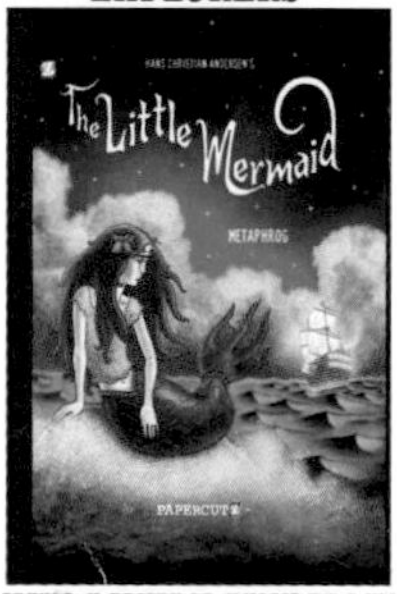
HANS CHRISTIAN ANDERSEN'S
The Little Mermaid
METAPHROG
PAPERCUTZ
THE LITTLE MERMAID

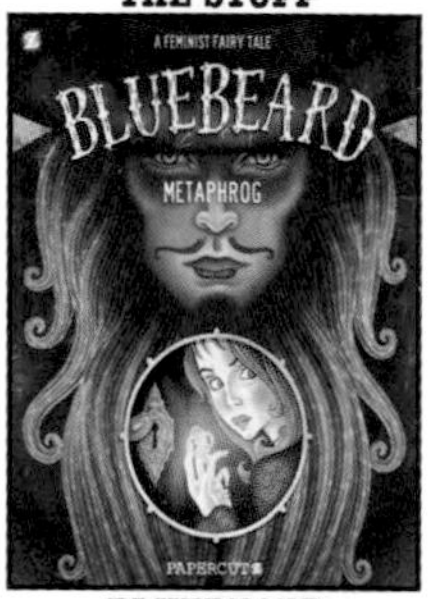
A FEMINIST FAIRY TALE
BLUEBEARD
METAPHROG
PAPERCUTZ
BLUEBEARD

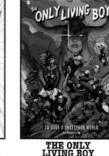

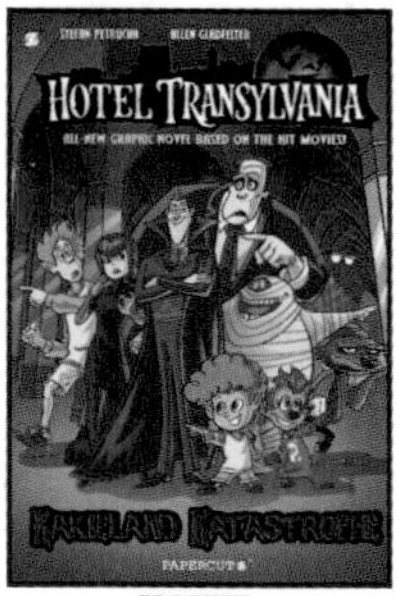
HOTEL TRANSYLVANIA
PAPERCUTZ
HOTEL TRANSYLVANIA

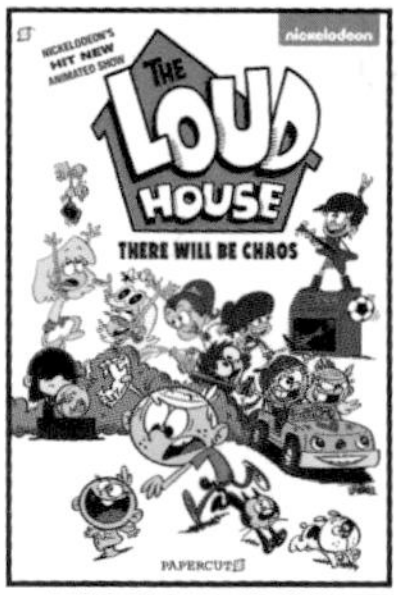
nickelodeon
THE LOUD HOUSE
THERE WILL BE CHAOS
PAPERCUTZ
THE LOUD HOUSE

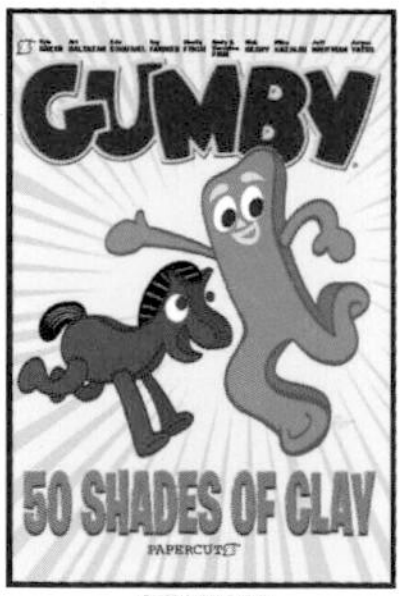
GUMBY
50 SHADES OF CLAY
PAPERCUTZ
GUMBY

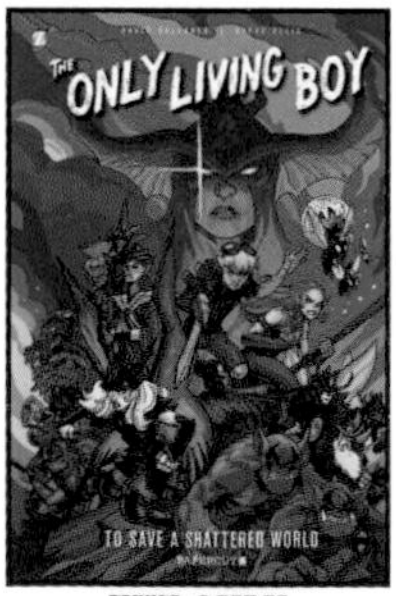
THE ONLY LIVING BOY
TO SAVE A SHATTERED WORLD
THE ONLY LIVING BOY

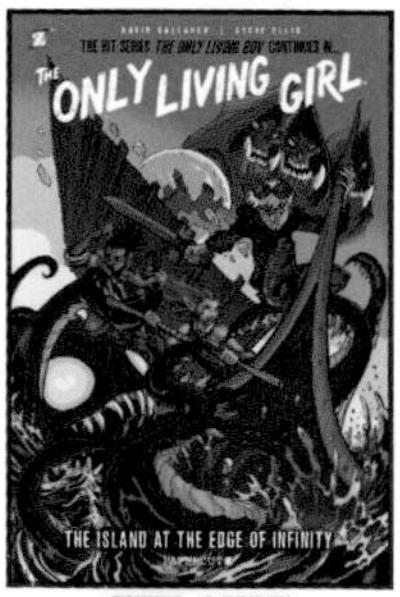
THE ONLY LIVING GIRL
THE ISLAND AT THE EDGE OF INFINITY
THE ONLY LIVING GIRL

Go to papercutz.com for more information

Also available where ebooks are sold.

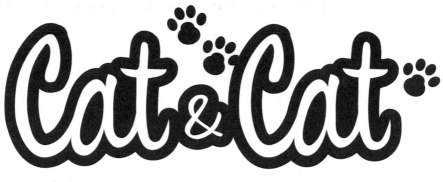

Cat & Cat

2. CAT OUT OF WATER

MiiiiAAAWW
POK
POK
POK

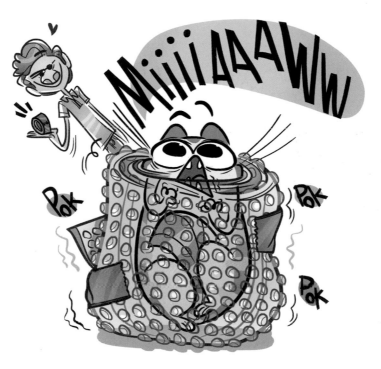

CHRISTOPHE CAZENOVE
HERVÉ RICHEZ
SCRIPT

YRGANE RAMON
ART

PAPERCUTZ
New York

To my parents,

To Kali, Patate & Pitou, Toudougras,
To Qwerty & Crokopik,

To Pioute, Eliott & Ness, Lola, the little keg, Mimi38,
To Croustiflette, Verveine, Tortue Géniale, Baboin, Symétrie, Igloo, Moquette, Sablier, Faux-filet, Capuchon, and
all the other cats I renamed in my town, from not knowing their real names.
To Bamboo, Timmy, Tyrion, June, Arwen, Mya, Lily, Socket & Cendre, Canaillou, the ferret with positive waves.
To every gang of purrers, to all loving beasties.
To those who look after animals.
To the late Kiki, my rabbit, who crunched his last dandelion bloom this year.
To Sarujin & Olivier Plazas for their prepping help for colorization for this book.
To the friends & readers who bring life to this series.
Thanks to Sarujin & Olivier Plazas for their prep work help for colorization of this book.
Thanks!
– Yrgane
www.yrgane.com

And always to Céline…
– Hervé

#2 "Cat Out of Water"
Christophe Cazenove &
Hervé Richez – Writers
Yrgane Ramon – Artist
Joe Johnson – Translator
Wilson Ramos Jr. – Letterer

Special thanks to Catherine Loiselet

Production – Mark McNabb
Editor – Ellen S. Abramowitz
Managing Editor – Jeff Whitman
Editorial Intern – Eric Storms
Jim Salicrup
Editor-in-Chief

Papercutz books may be purchased for business or promotional use. For information on bulk purchases
please contact Macmillan Corporate and Premium Sales Department at (800) 221-795 x5442.

Hardcover ISBN: 978-1-5458-0478-0
Paperback ISBN: 978-1-5458-0479-7

Printed in Lithuania
July 2020

Distributed by Macmillan
First Papercutz Printing

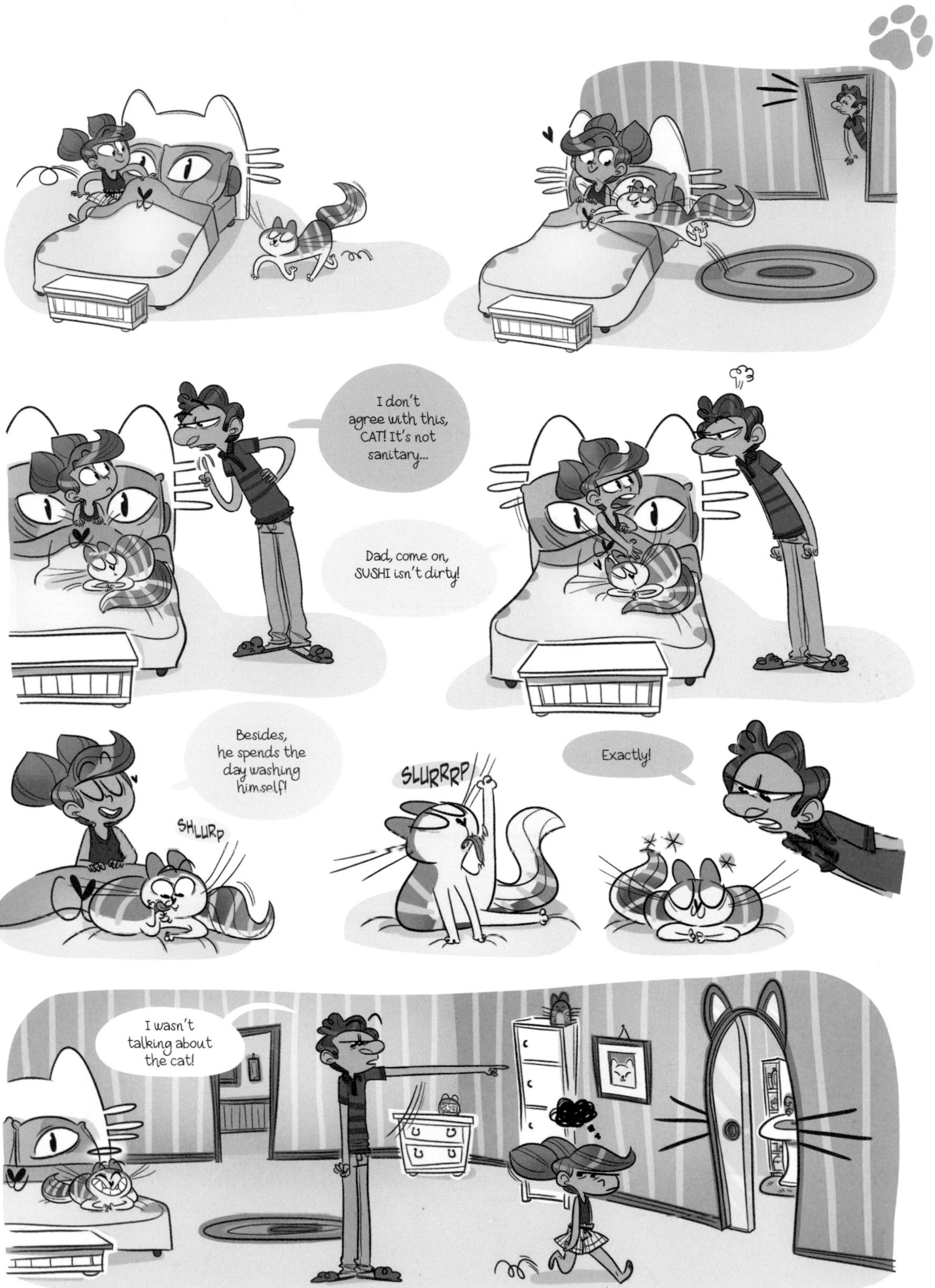
I don't agree with this, CAT! It's not sanitary...
Dad, come on, SUSHI isn't dirty!
Besides, he spends the day washing himself!
SHLURP
SLURRRP
Exactly!
I wasn't talking about the cat!

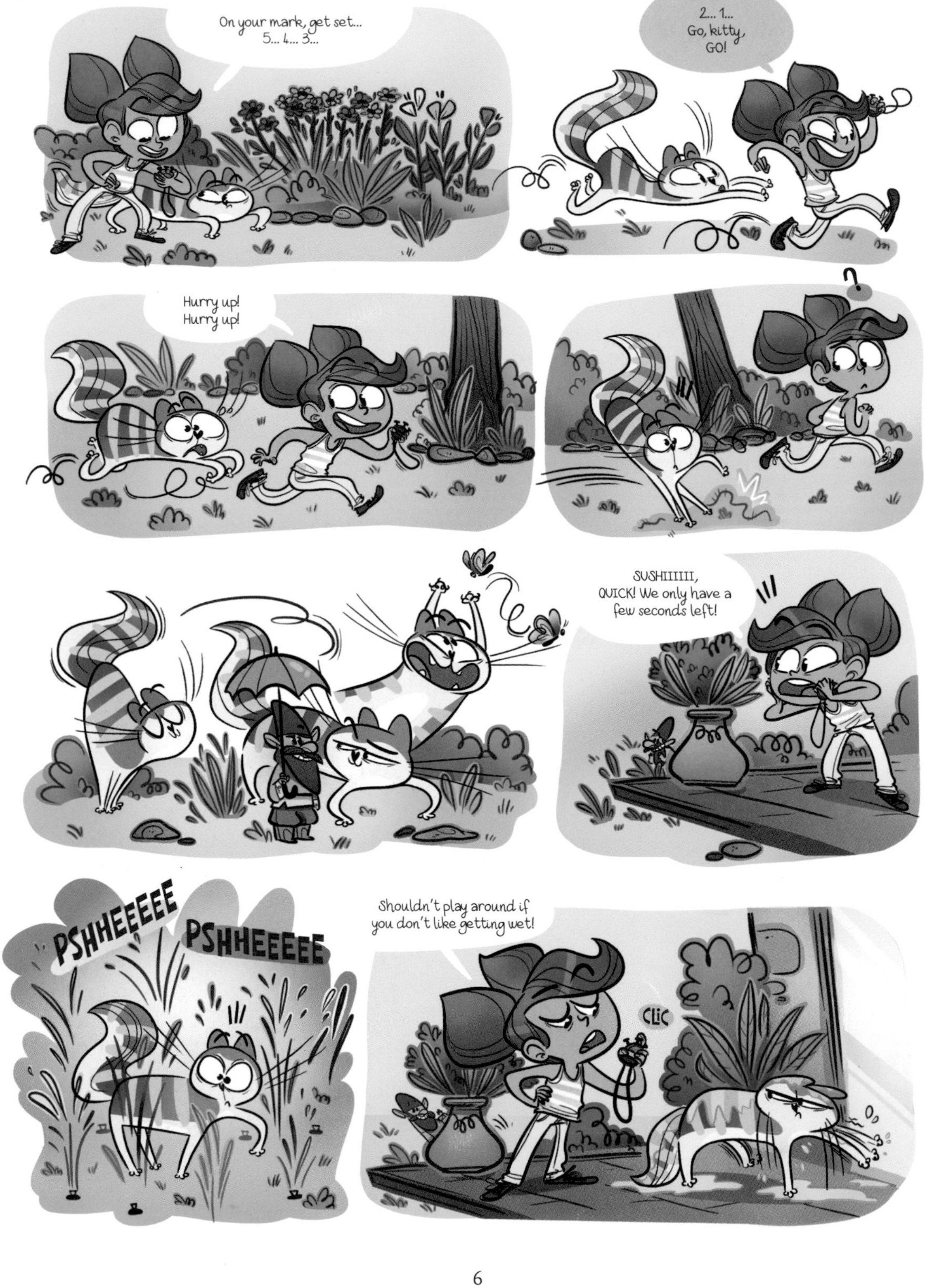
On your mark, get set... 5... 4... 3...
2... 1... Go, kitty, GO!
Hurry up! Hurry up!
SUSHIIIIII, QUICK! We only have a few seconds left!
PSHHEEEEE
PSHHEEEEE
Shouldn't play around if you don't like getting wet!
CLIC

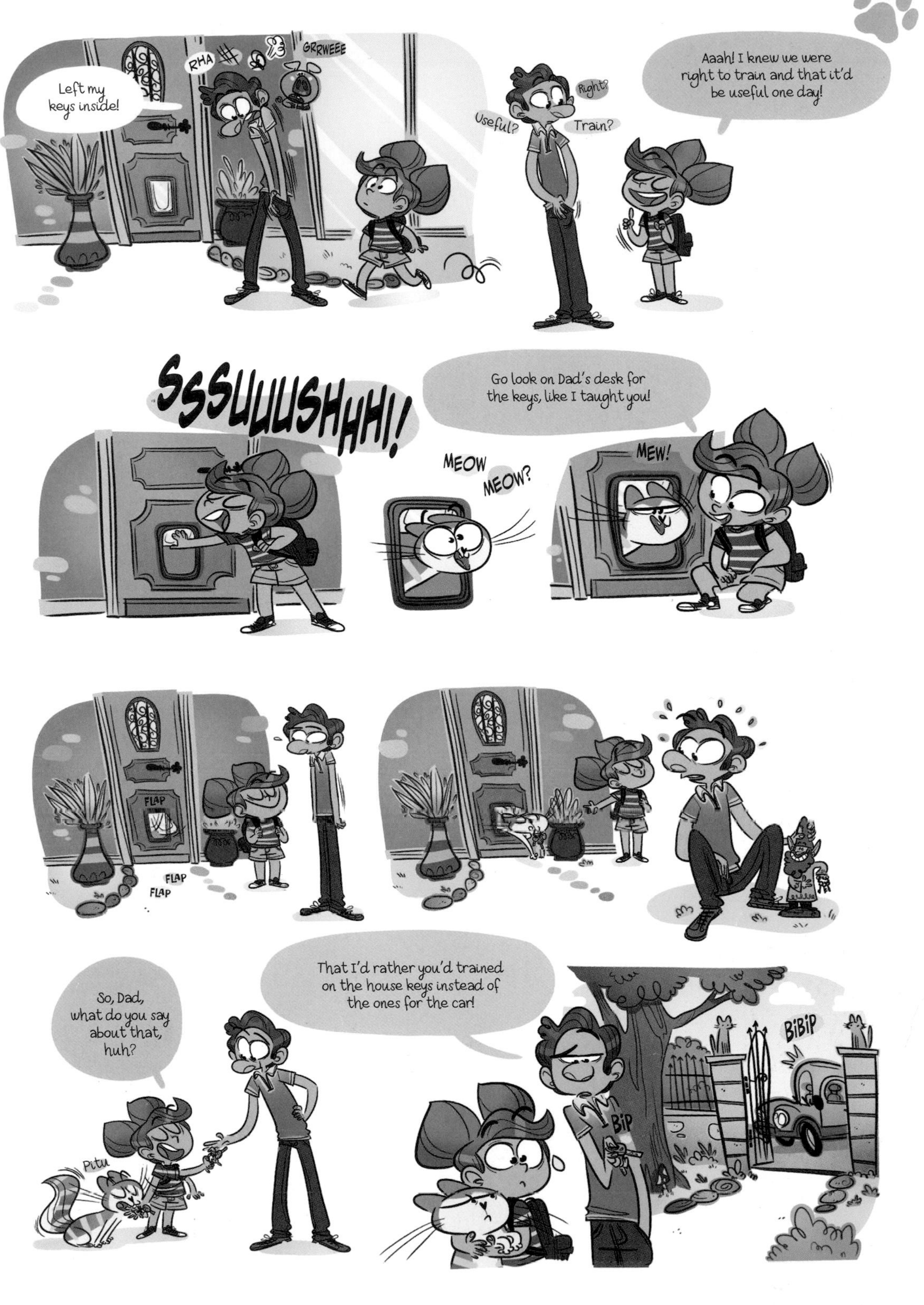

Left my keys inside!
RHA
GRRWEEE
Useful?
Right?
Train?
Aaah! I knew we were right to train and that it'd be useful one day!
SSSUUUSHHH!
Go look on Dad's desk for the keys, like I taught you!
MEOW
MEOW?
MEW!
FLAP
FLAP
FLAP
So, Dad, what do you say about that, huh?
Pitu
That I'd rather you'd trained on the house keys instead of the ones for the car!
BIBIP
BIP

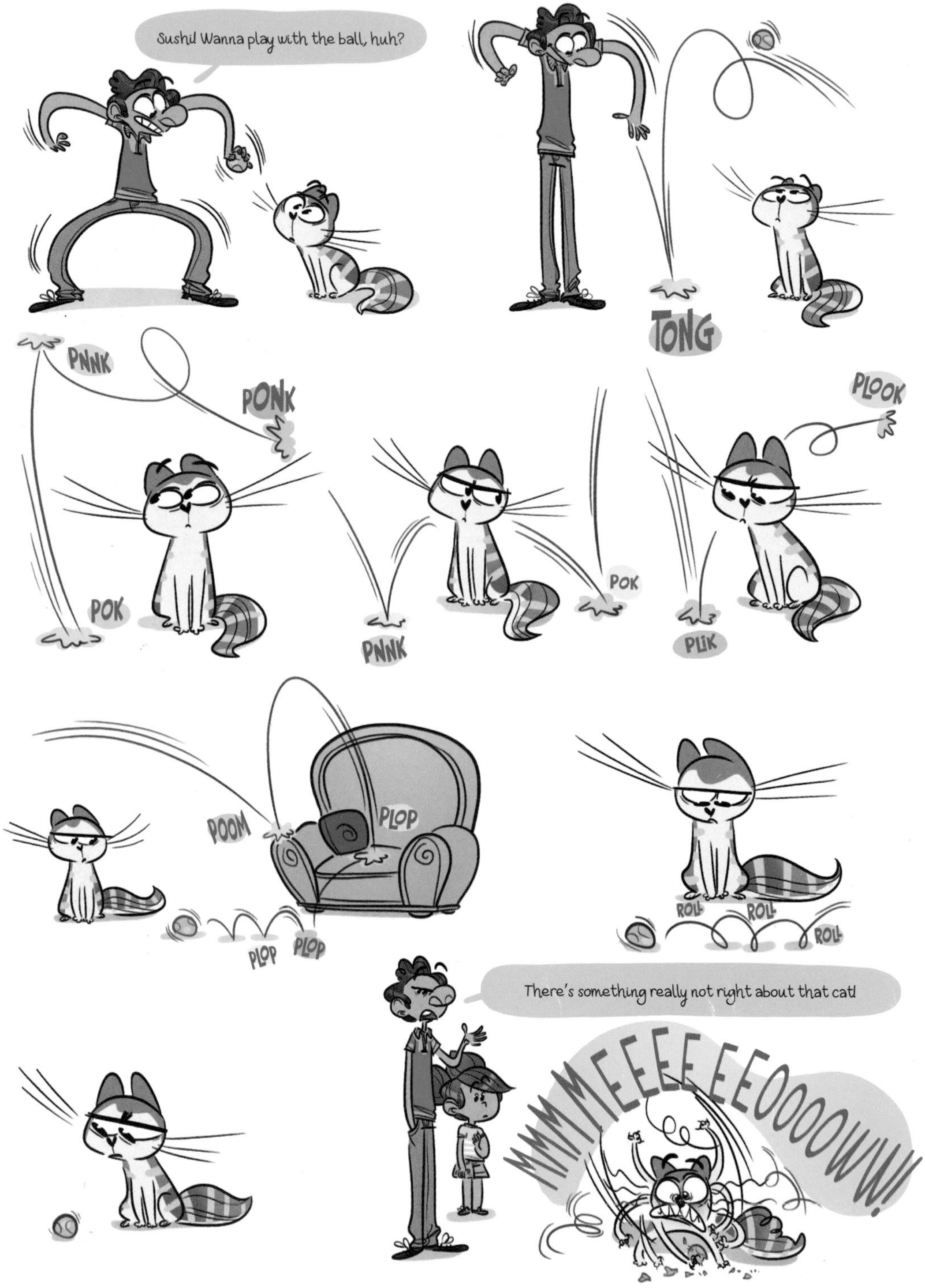

Sushi! Wanna play with the ball, huh?
TONG
PNNK
PONK
POK
PNNK
POK
PLOOK
PLIK
POOM
PLOP
PLOP
PLOP
ROLL
ROLL
ROLL
There's something really not right about that cat!
MMMMEEEEEEEOOOOWW!

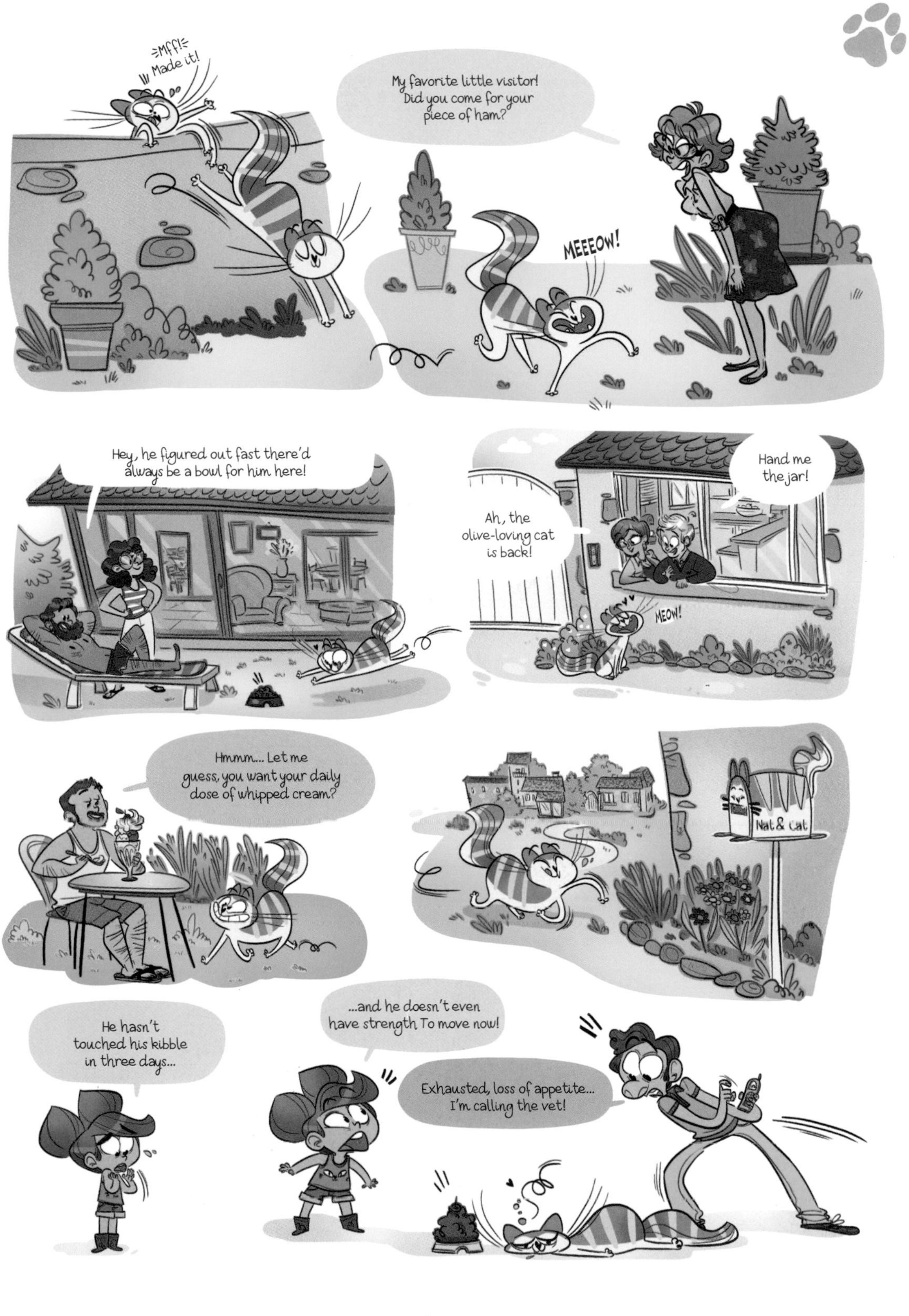
Mff!
Made it!
My favorite little visitor! Did you come for your piece of ham?
MEEEOW!
Hey, he figured out fast there'd always be a bowl for him here!
Ah, the olive-loving cat is back!
Hand me the jar!
MEOW!
Hmmm... Let me guess, you want your daily dose of whipped cream?
Nat & Cat
He hasn't touched his kibble in three days...
...and he doesn't even have strength To move now!
Exhausted, loss of appetite... I'm calling the vet!

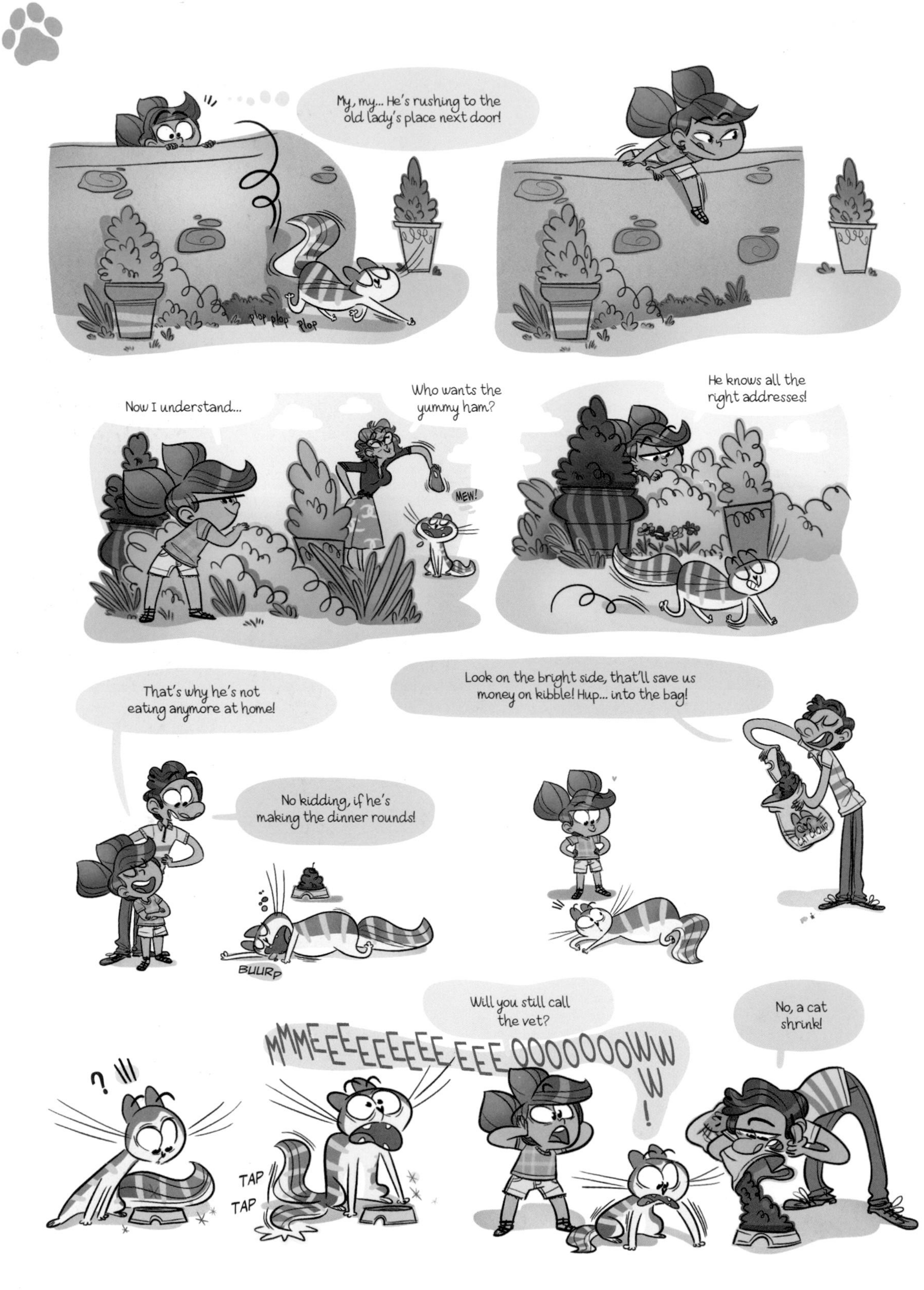
My, my... He's rushing to the old lady's place next door!
plop plop plop
Now I understand...
Who wants the yummy ham?
MEW!
He knows all the right addresses!
That's why he's not eating anymore at home!
No kidding, if he's making the dinner rounds!
BUURP
Look on the bright side, that'll save us money on kibble! Hup... into the bag!
CAT CHOW
TAP
TAP
MMMEEEEEEEEEE EEE OOOOOOOWWW!
Will you still call the vet?
No, a cat shrink!

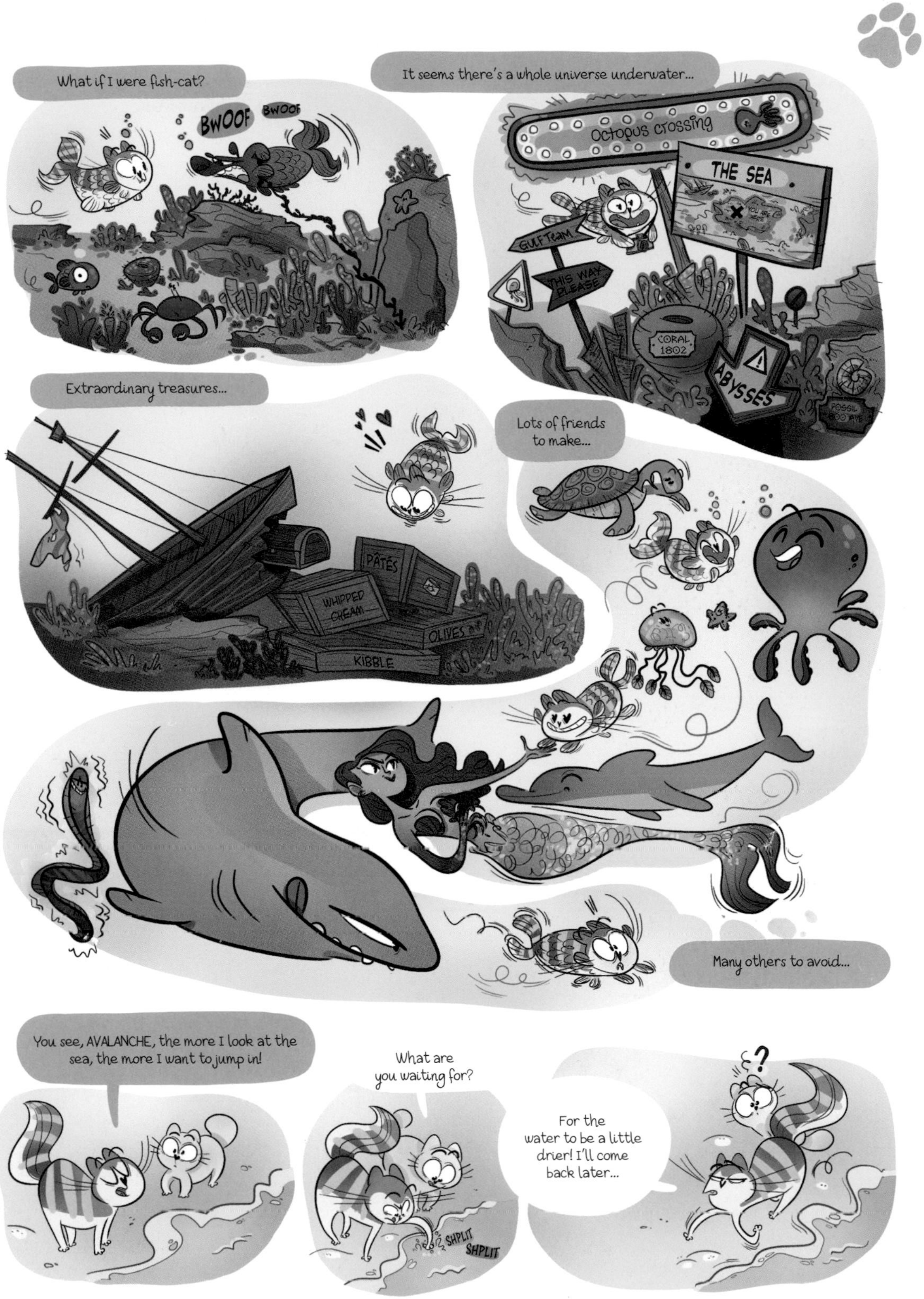

What if I were fish-cat?
BWOOF
BWOOF
It seems there's a whole universe underwater...
Octopus crossing
THE SEA
GULF Team
THIS WAY PLEASE
CORAL 1802
ABYSSES
Extraordinary treasures...
PÂTÉS
WHIPPED CREAM
OLIVES
KIBBLE
Lots of friends to make...
Many others to avoid...
You see, AVALANCHE, the more I look at the sea, the more I want to jump in!
What are you waiting for?
SHPLIT
SHPLIT
For the water to be a little drier! I'll come back later...
?

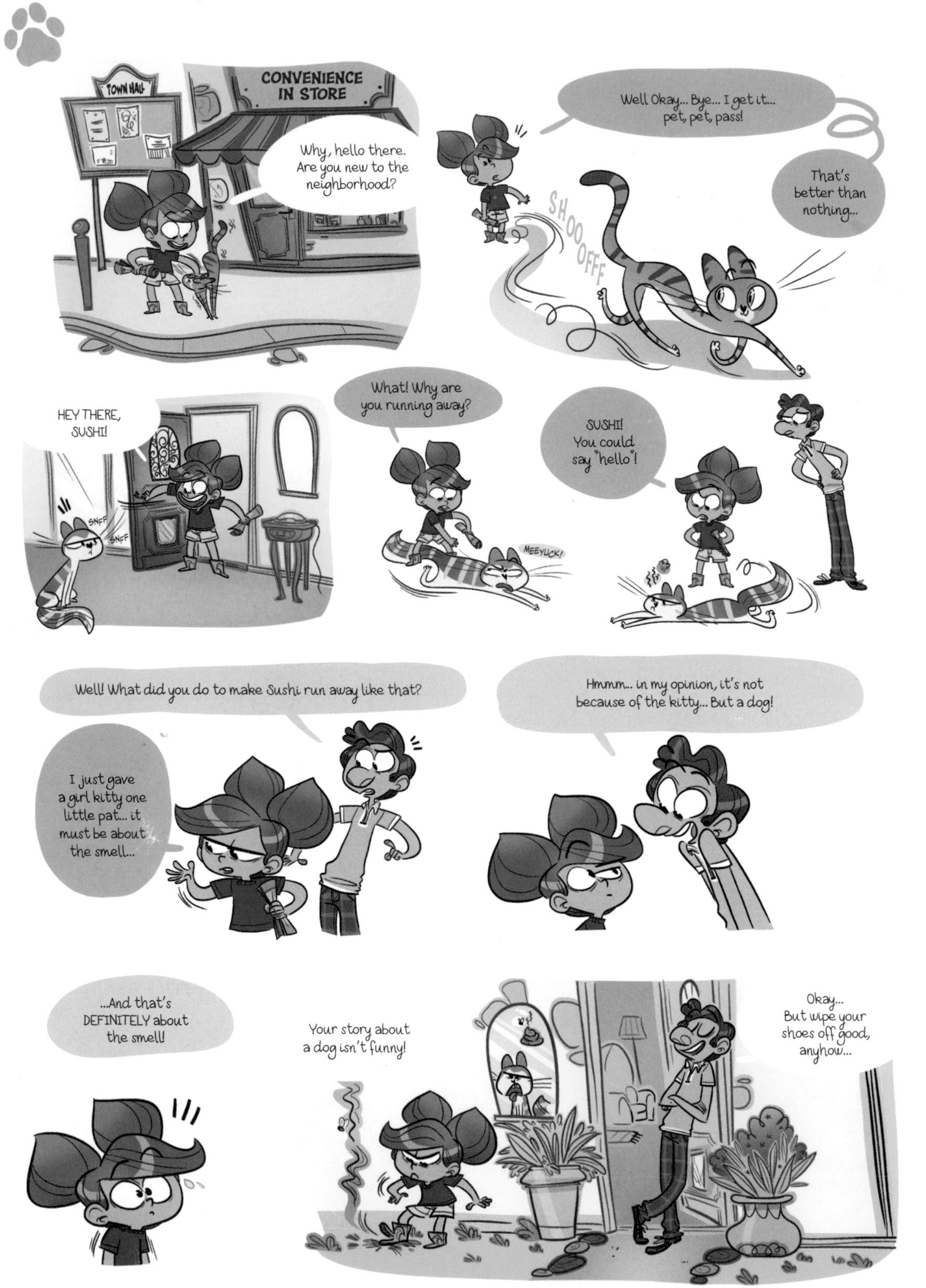
TOWN HALL
CONVENIENCE IN STORE
Why, hello there. Are you new to the neighborhood?
Well Okay... Bye... I get it... pet, pet, pass!
SHOOOFFF
That's better than nothing...
HEY THERE, SUSHI!
SNFF
SNFF
What! Why are you running away?
MEEYUCK!
SUSHI! You could say "hello"!
Well! What did you do to make Sushi run away like that?
I just gave a girl kitty one little pat... it must be about the smell...
Hmmm... in my opinion, it's not because of the kitty... But a dog!
...And that's DEFINITELY about the smell!
Your story about a dog isn't funny!
Okay... But wipe your shoes off good, anyhow...

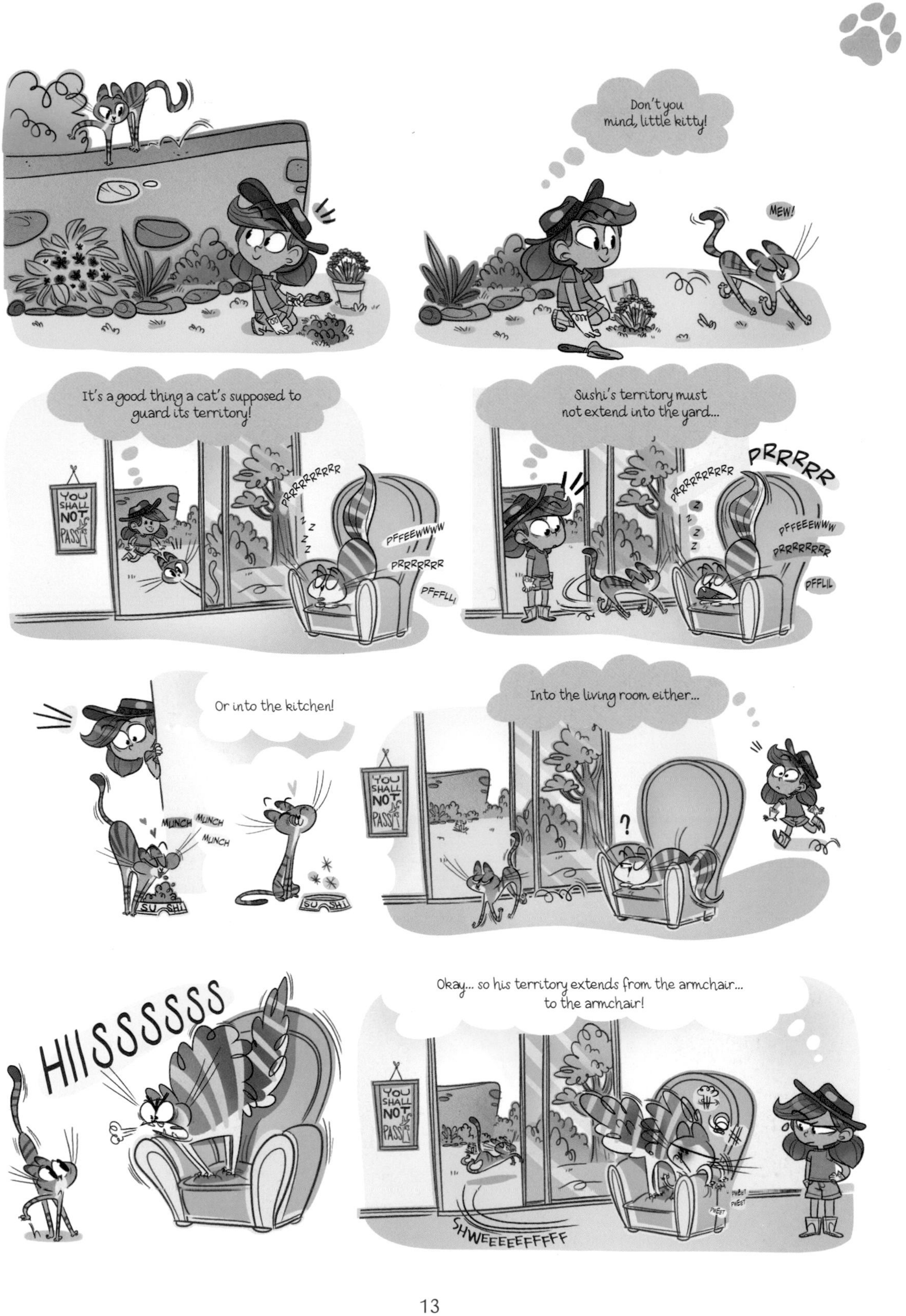

Don't you mind, little kitty!
MEW!
It's a good thing a cat's supposed to guard its territory!
YOU SHALL NOT PASS!
PRRRRRRRRR
Z Z Z Z
PFFEEWWWW
PRRRRRRR
PFFFLL!
Sushi's territory must not extend into the yard...
PRRRRR
PRRRRRRRRR
PFFEEEWWW
PRRRRRRRR
PFFLIL
Or into the kitchen!
MUNCH MUNCH MUNCH
SU SHI
SU SHI
Into the living room either...
YOU SHALL NOT PASS!
?
HIISSSSSS
Okay... so his territory extends from the armchair... to the armchair!
YOU SHALL NOT PASS!
PWEET PWEET PWEET
SHWEEEEEFFFFF

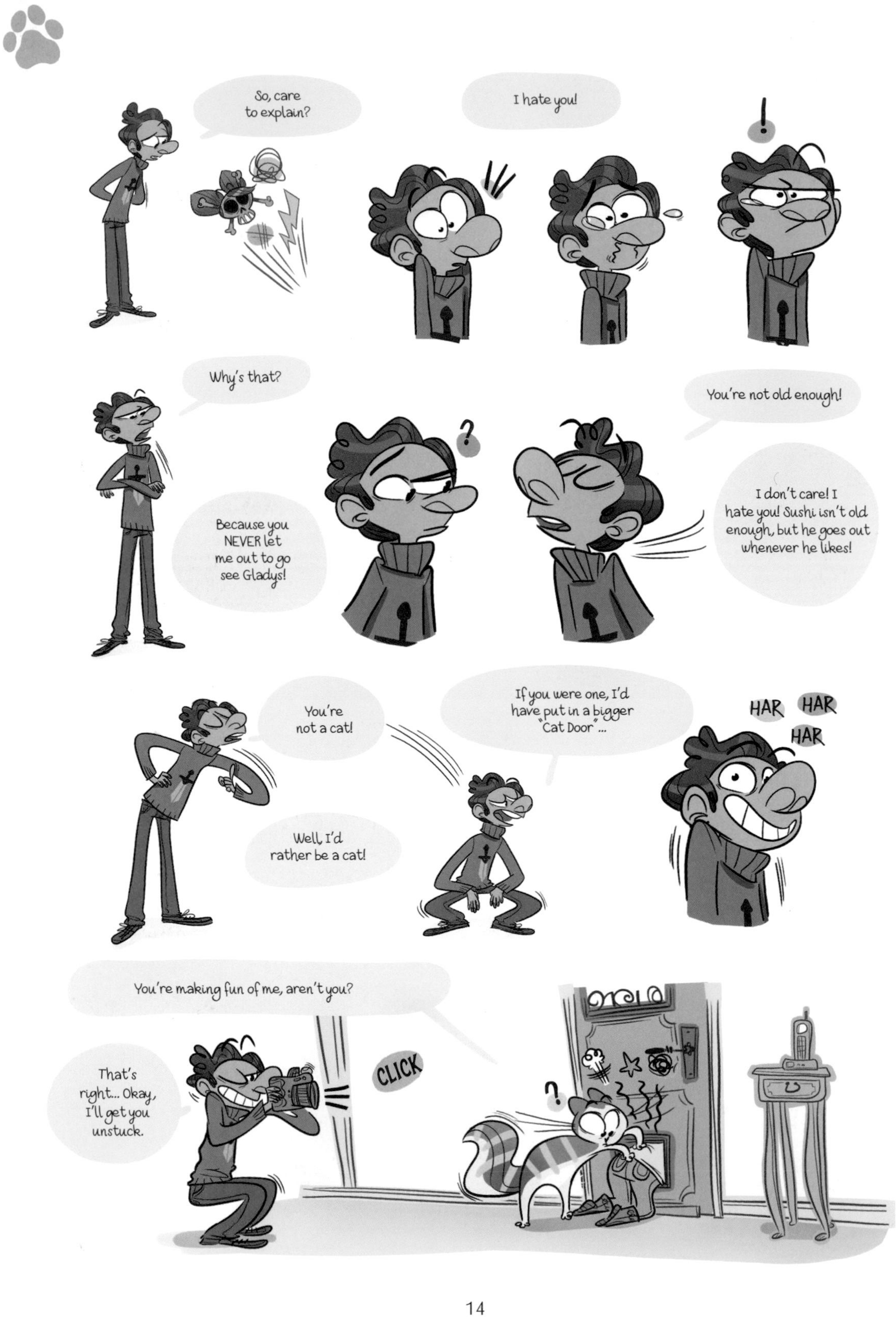
So, care to explain?
I hate you!
!
Why's that?
Because you NEVER let me out to go see Gladys!
?
You're not old enough!
I don't care! I hate you! Sushi isn't old enough, but he goes out whenever he likes!
You're not a cat!
Well, I'd rather be a cat!
If you were one, I'd have put in a bigger "Cat Door"...
HAR HAR HAR
You're making fun of me, aren't you?
That's right... Okay, I'll get you unstuck.
CLICK
?

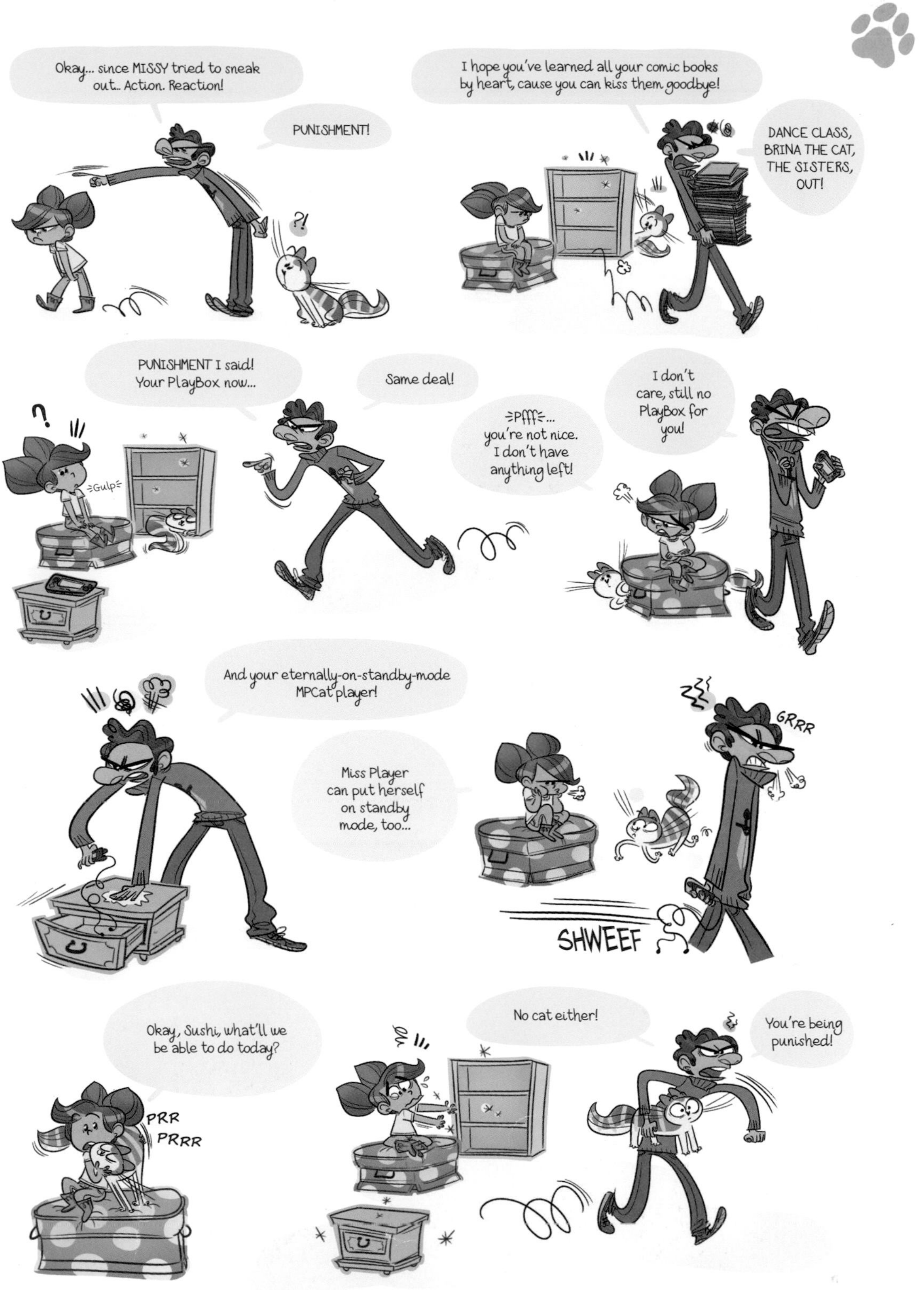

Okay... since MISSY tried to sneak out.. Action. Reaction!
PUNISHMENT!
?!
I hope you've learned all your comic books by heart, cause you can kiss them goodbye!
DANCE CLASS, BRINA THE CAT, THE SISTERS, OUT!
PUNISHMENT I said! Your PlayBox now...
?
Gulp
Same deal!
Pfff... you're not nice. I don't have anything left!
I don't care, still no PlayBox for you!
And your eternally-on-standby-mode MPCat player!
Miss Player can put herself on standby mode, too...
GRRR
SHWEEF
Okay, Sushi, what'll we be able to do today?
PRR
PRRR
No cat either!
You're being punished!

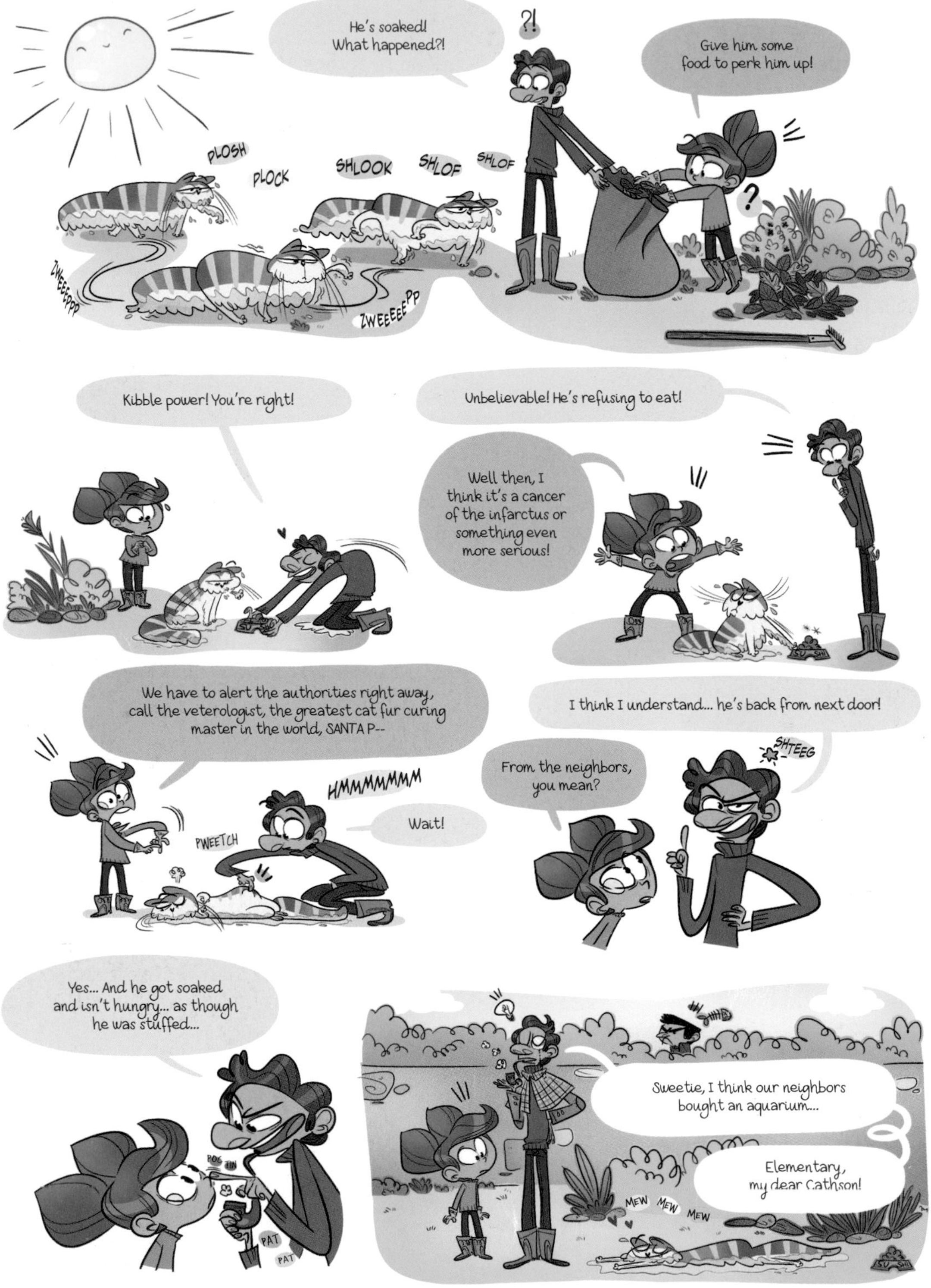

He's soaked! What happened?!
?!
Give him some food to perk him up!
PLOSH
PLOCK
SHLOOK
SHLOF
SHLOF
?
Kibble power! You're right!
Unbelievable! He's refusing to eat!
Well then, I think it's a cancer of the infarctus or something even more serious!
We have to alert the authorities right away, call the veterologist, the greatest cat fur curing master in the world, SANTA P--
HMMMMMMM
PWEETCH
Wait!
I think I understand... he's back from next door!
SHTEEG
From the neighbors, you mean?
Yes... And he got soaked and isn't hungry... as though he was stuffed...
PAT
PAT
Sweetie, I think our neighbors bought an aquarium...
Elementary, my dear Cathson!
MEW
MEW
MEW

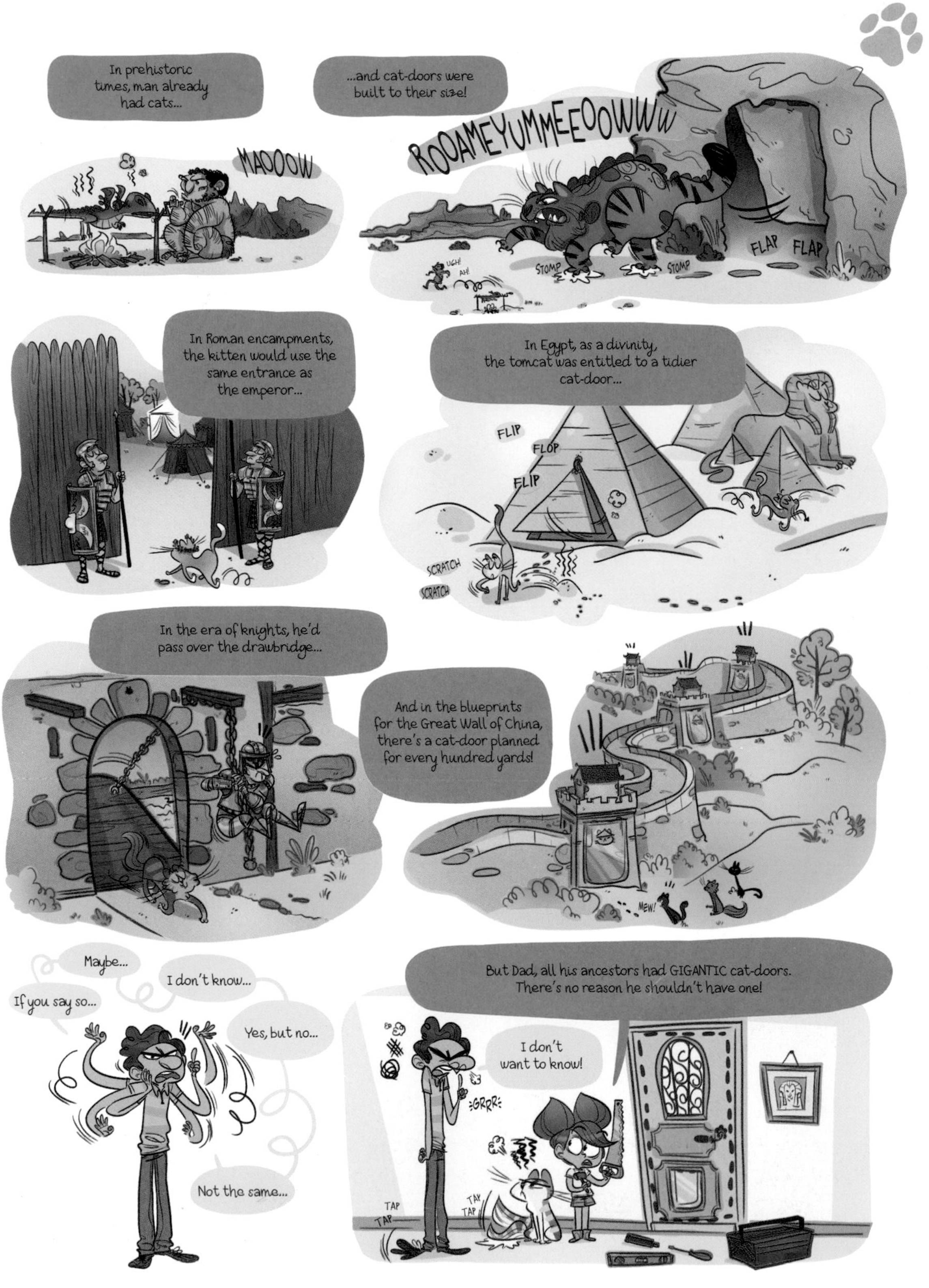
In prehistoric times, man already had cats...
MAOOOW
...and cat-doors were built to their size!
ROOAMEYUMMEEOOWWW
UGH!
AH!
STOMP
STOMP
FLAP
FLAP
In Roman encampments, the kitten would use the same entrance as the emperor...
In Egypt, as a divinity, the tomcat was entitled to a tidier cat-door...
FLIP
FLOP
FLIP
SCRATCH
SCRATCH
In the era of knights, he'd pass over the drawbridge...
And in the blueprints for the Great Wall of China, there's a cat-door planned for every hundred yards!
MEW!
Maybe...
I don't know...
If you say so...
Yes, but no...
Not the same...
But Dad, all his ancestors had GIGANTIC cat-doors. There's no reason he shouldn't have one!
I don't want to know!
GRRR
TAP
TAP
TAP
TAP

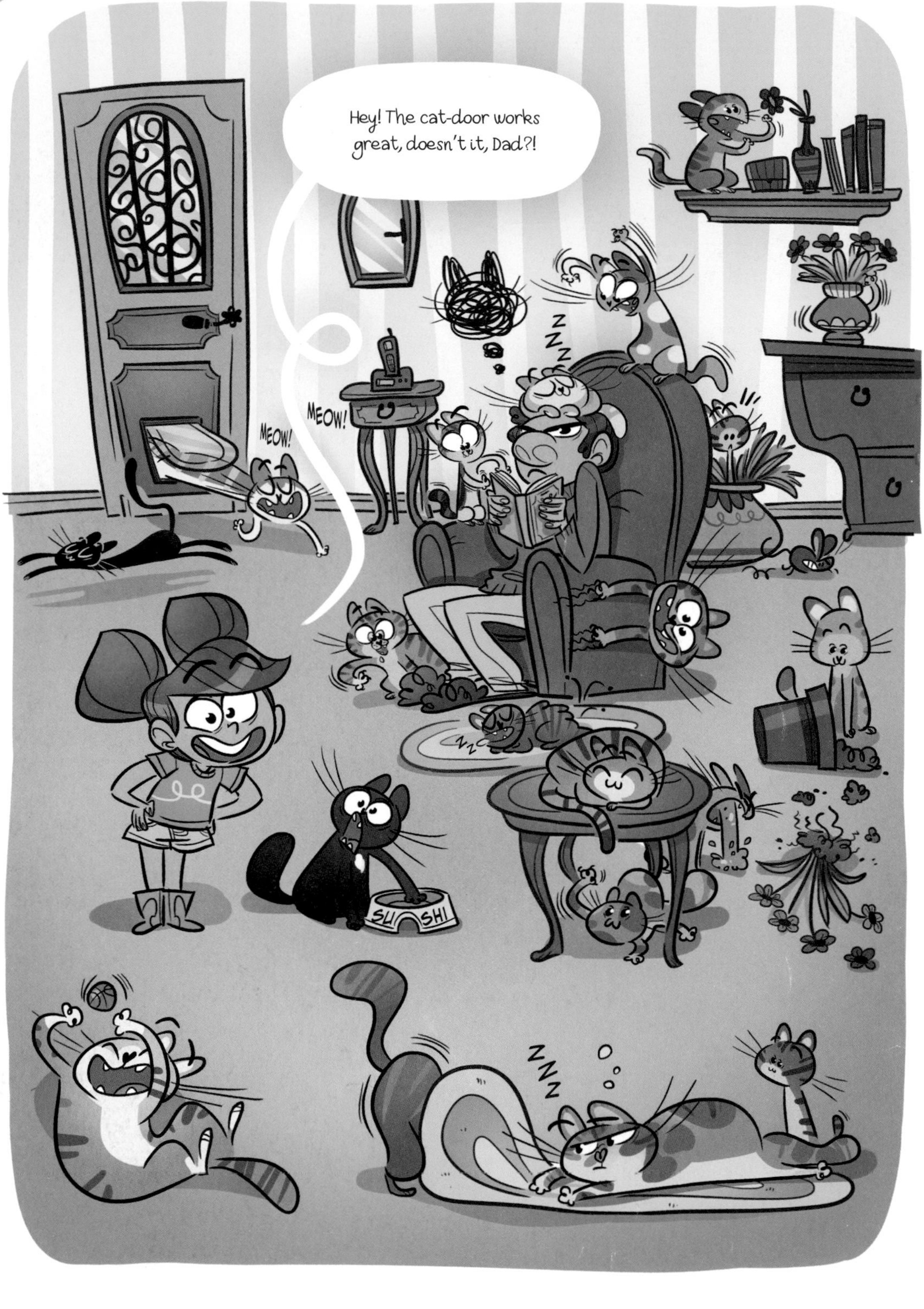
Hey! The cat-door works great, doesn't it, Dad?!
MEOW!
MEOW!
SU SHI

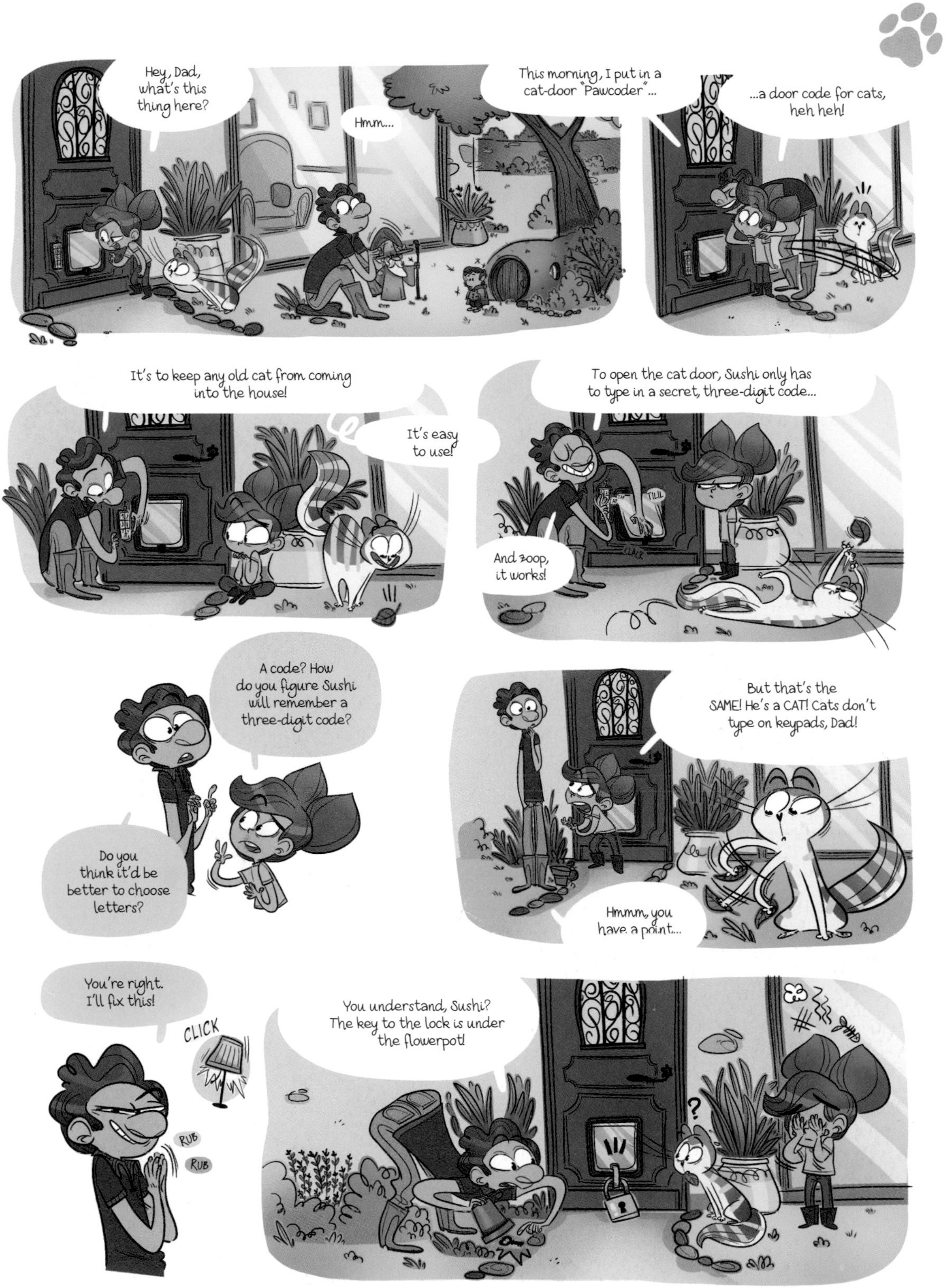
Hey, Dad, what's this thing here?
Hmm...
This morning, I put in a cat-door "Pawcoder"...
...a door code for cats, heh heh!
It's to keep any old cat from coming into the house!
It's easy to use!
To open the cat door, Sushi only has to type in a secret, three-digit code...
TILIL
CLACK
And zoop, it works!
A code? How do you figure Sushi will remember a three-digit code?
Do you think it'd be better to choose letters?
But that's the SAME! He's a CAT! Cats don't type on keypads, Dad!
Hmmm, you have a point...
You're right. I'll fix this!
CLICK
RUB
RUB
You understand, Sushi? The key to the lock is under the flowerpot!
?

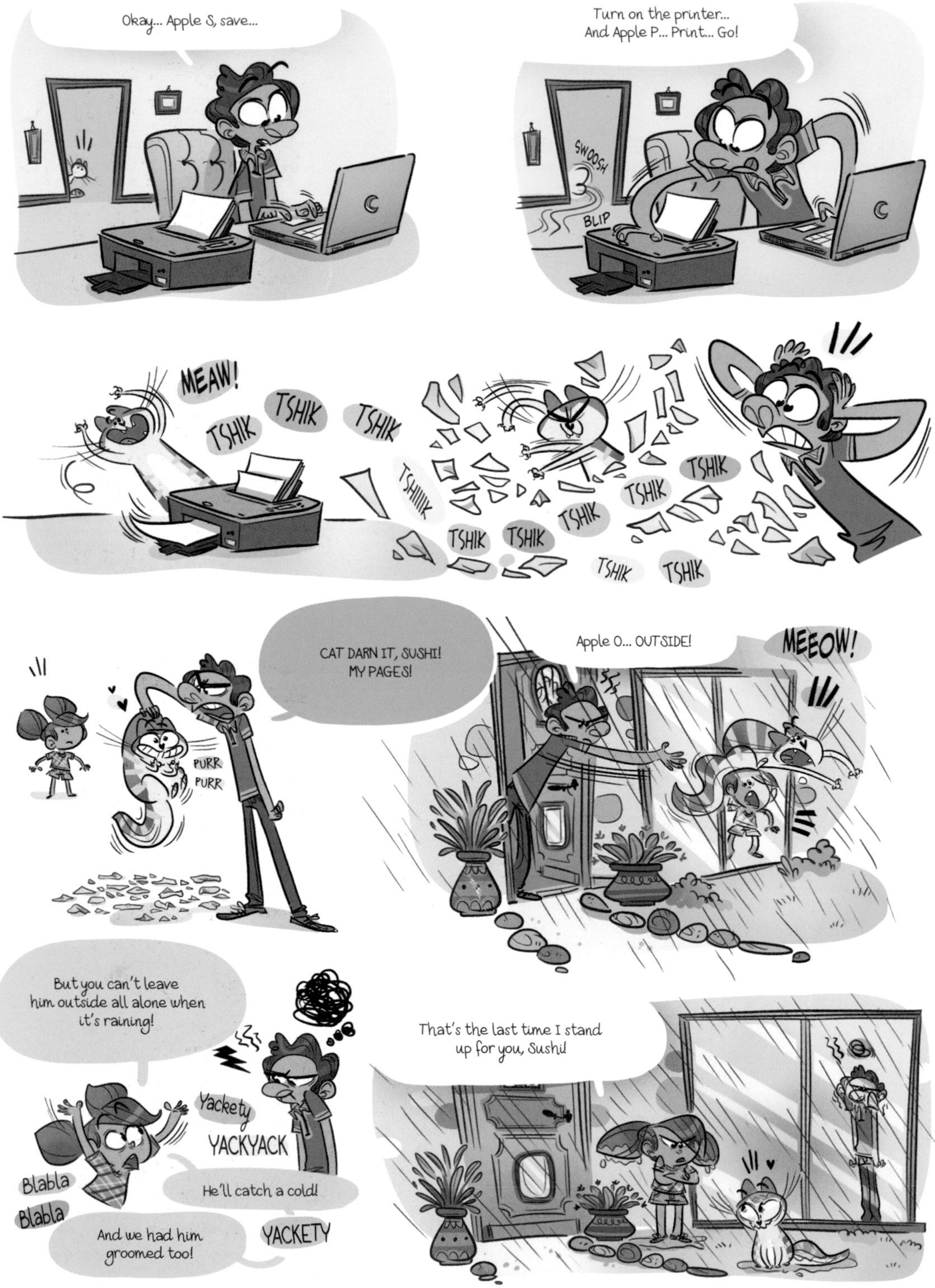

Okay... Apple S, save...
Turn on the printer... And Apple P... Print... Go!
SWOOSH
BLIP
MEAW!
TSHIK
TSHIK
TSHIK
TSHIIIIK
TSHIK
TSHIK
TSHIK
TSHIK
TSHIK
TSHIK
TSHIK
CAT DARN IT, SUSHI! MY PAGES!
PURR
PURR
Apple O... OUTSIDE!
MEEOW!
But you can't leave him outside all alone when it's raining!
Yackety
YACKYACK
Blabla
Blabla
He'll catch a cold!
And we had him groomed too!
YACKETY
That's the last time I stand up for you, Sushi!

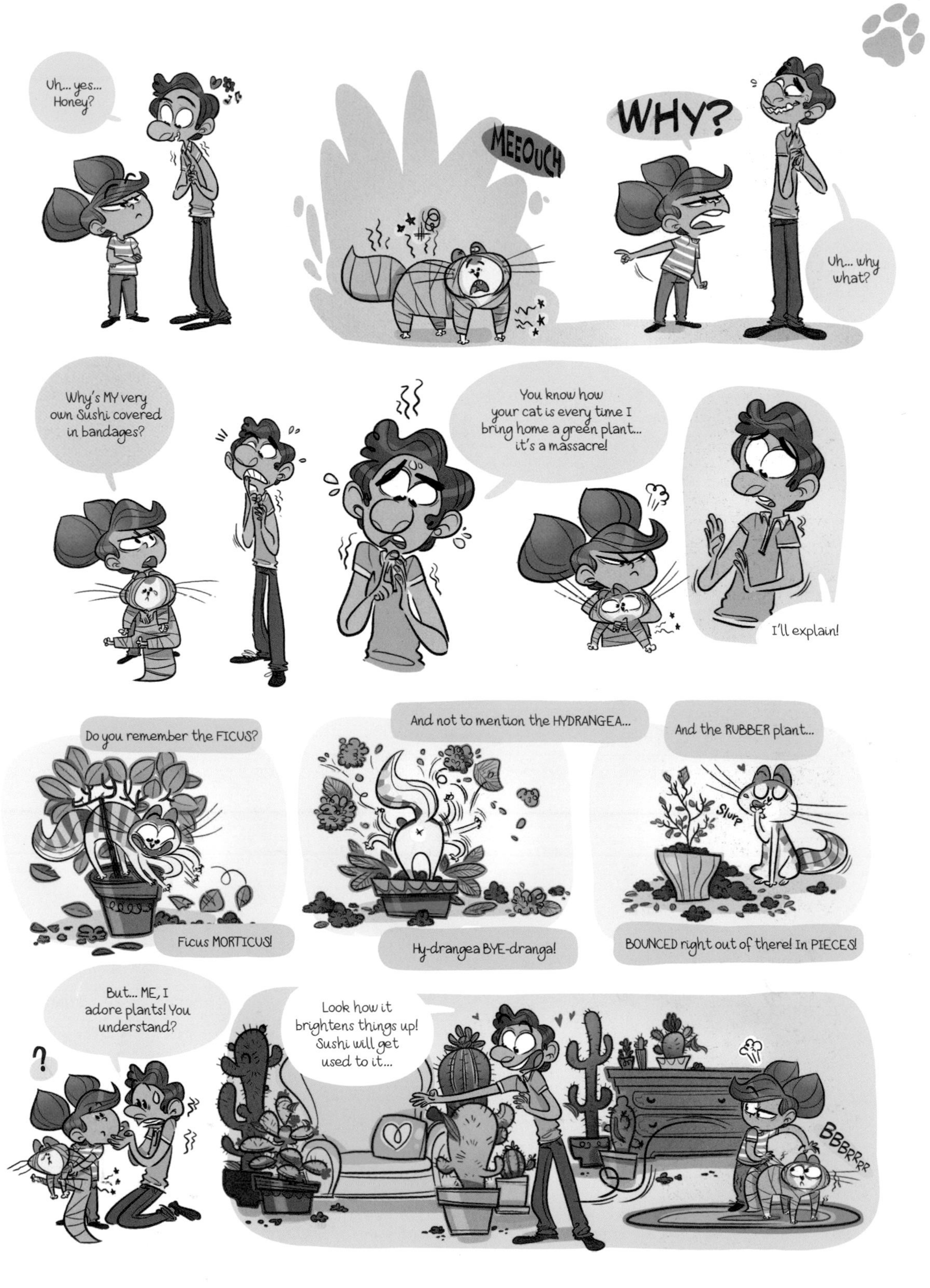
Uh... yes... Honey?
MEEOUCH
WHY?
Uh... why what?
Why's MY very own Sushi covered in bandages?
You know how your cat is every time I bring home a green plant... it's a massacre!
I'll explain!
Do you remember the FICUS?
Ficus MORTICUS!
And not to mention the HYDRANGEA...
Hy-drangea BYE-dranga!
And the RUBBER plant...
Slurp
BOUNCED right out of there! In PIECES!
But... ME, I adore plants! You understand?
?
Look how it brightens things up! Sushi will get used to it...
BBBRRRR

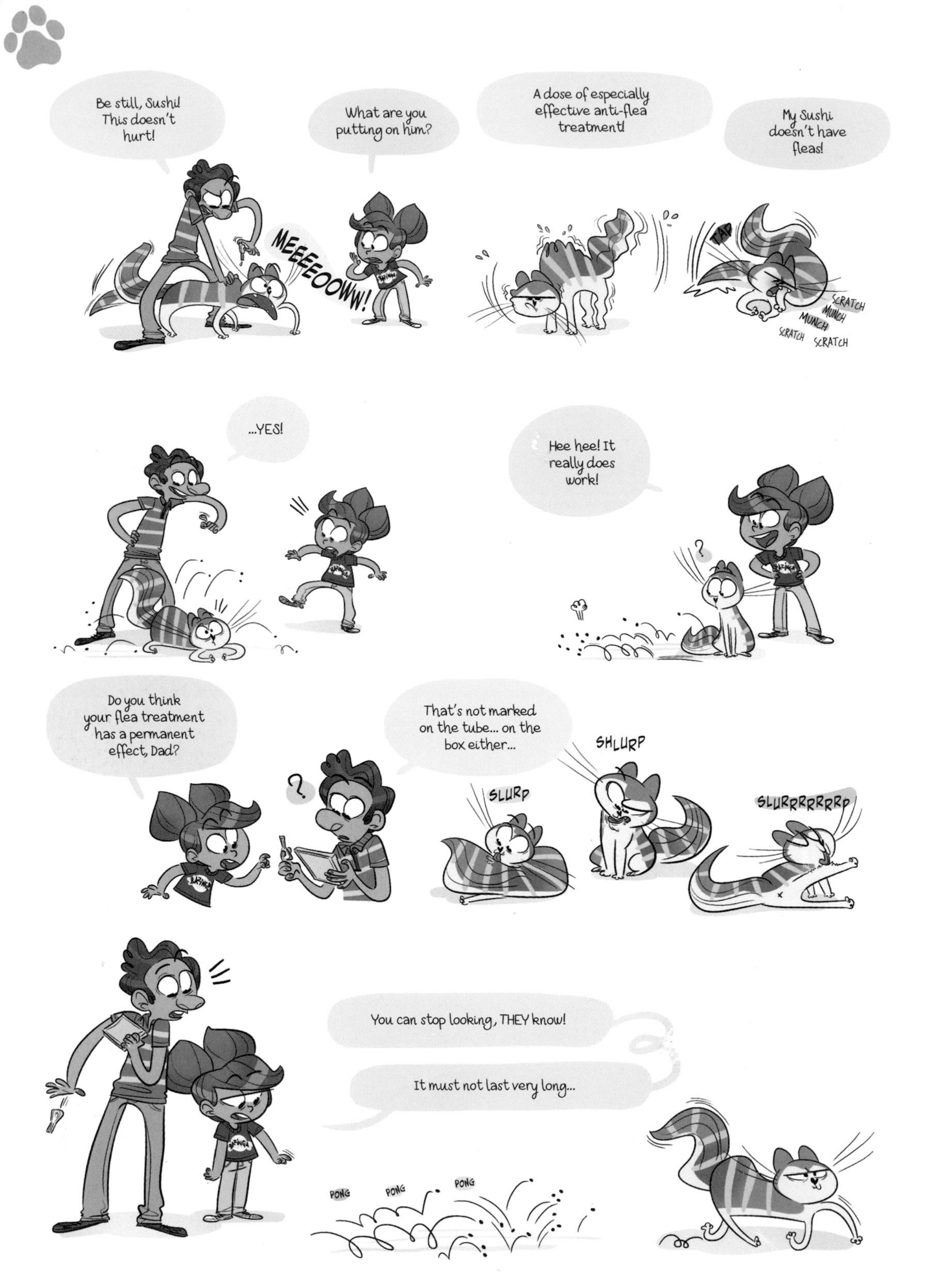
Be still, Sushi! This doesn't hurt!
MEEEEOOWW!
What are you putting on him?
A dose of especially effective anti-flea treatment!
My Sushi doesn't have fleas!
SCRATCH
MUNCH
MUNCH
SCRATCH
SCRATCH
...YES!
Hee hee! It really does work!
Do you think your flea treatment has a permanent effect, Dad?
That's not marked on the tube... on the box either...
SLURP
SHLURP
SLURRRRRRP
You can stop looking, THEY know!
It must not last very long...
PONG
PONG
PONG

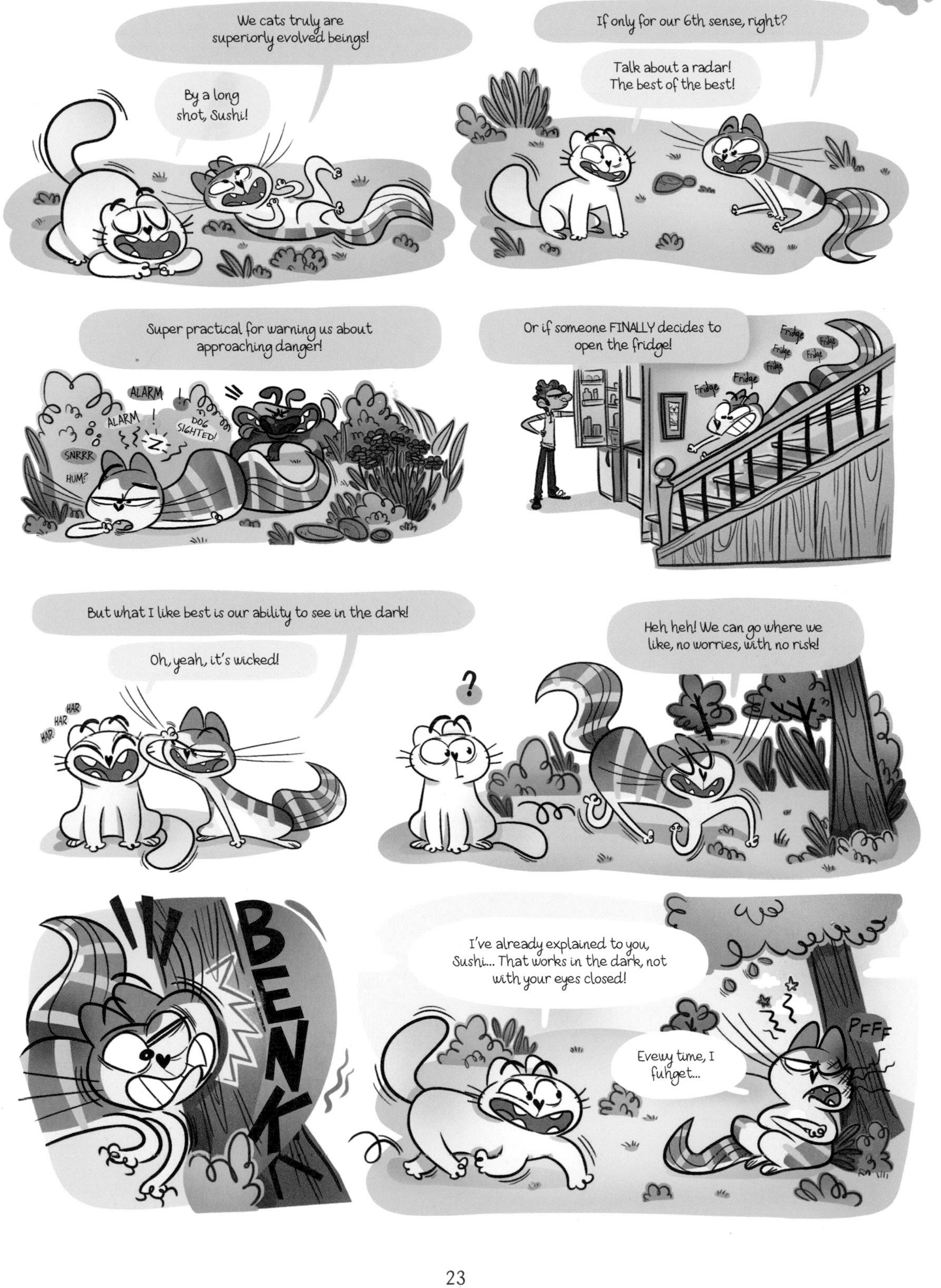
We cats truly are superiorly evolved beings!
By a long shot, Sushi!
If only for our 6th sense, right?
Talk about a radar! The best of the best!
Super practical for warning us about approaching danger!
ALARM
ALARM
DOG SIGHTED!
SNRRR
HUM?
Or if someone FINALLY decides to open the fridge!
Fridge
Fridge
Fridge
Fridge
But what I like best is our ability to see in the dark!
Oh, yeah, it's wicked!
HAR
HAR
HAR
?
Heh heh! We can go where we like, no worries, with no risk!
BENK!
I've already explained to you, Sushi... That works in the dark, not with your eyes closed!
Evewy time, I fuhget...
PFFF

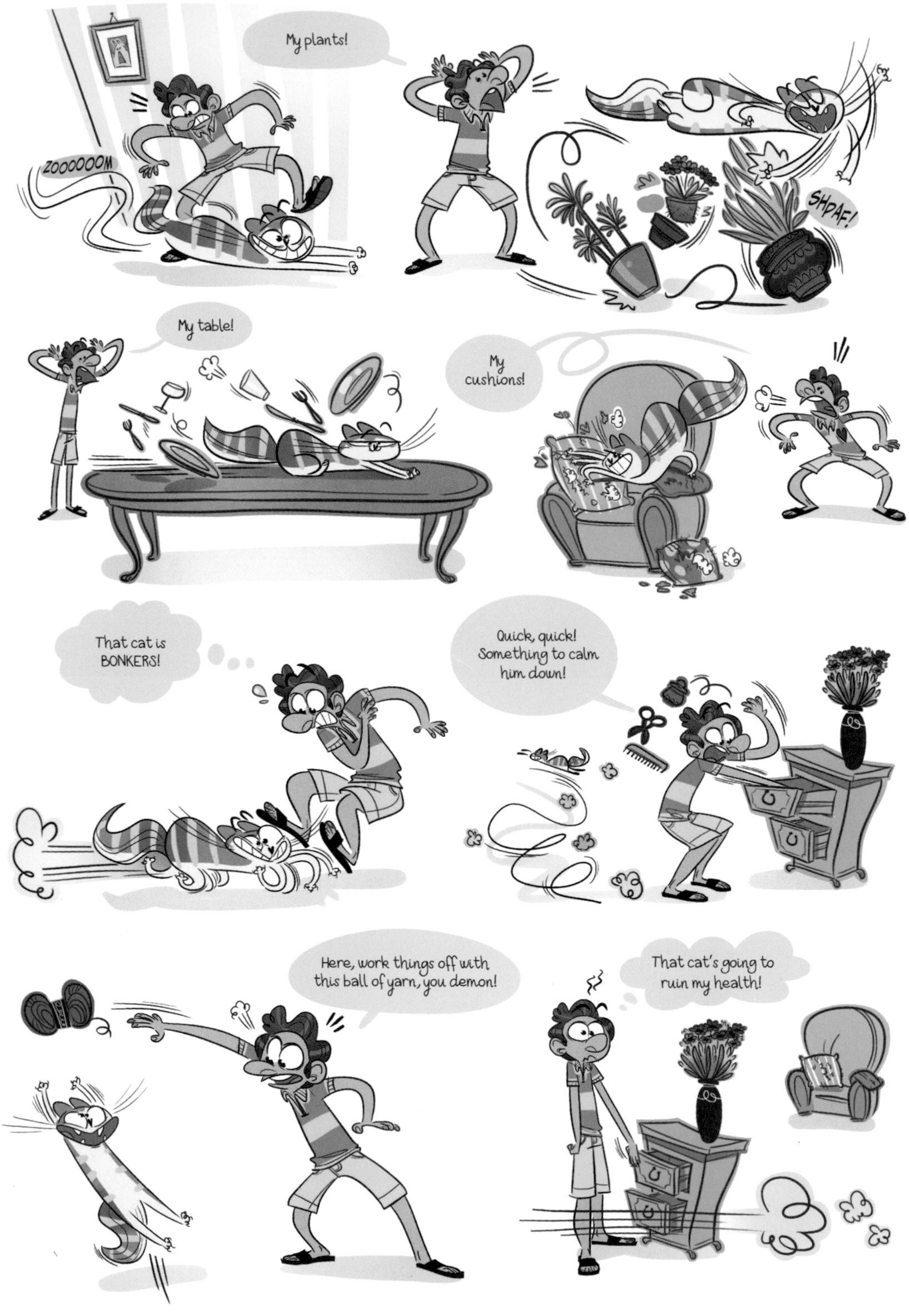
ZOOOOOOM
My plants!
SHPAF!
My table!
My cushions!
That cat is BONKERS!
Quick, quick! Something to calm him down!
Here, work things off with this ball of yarn, you demon!
That cat's going to ruin my health!

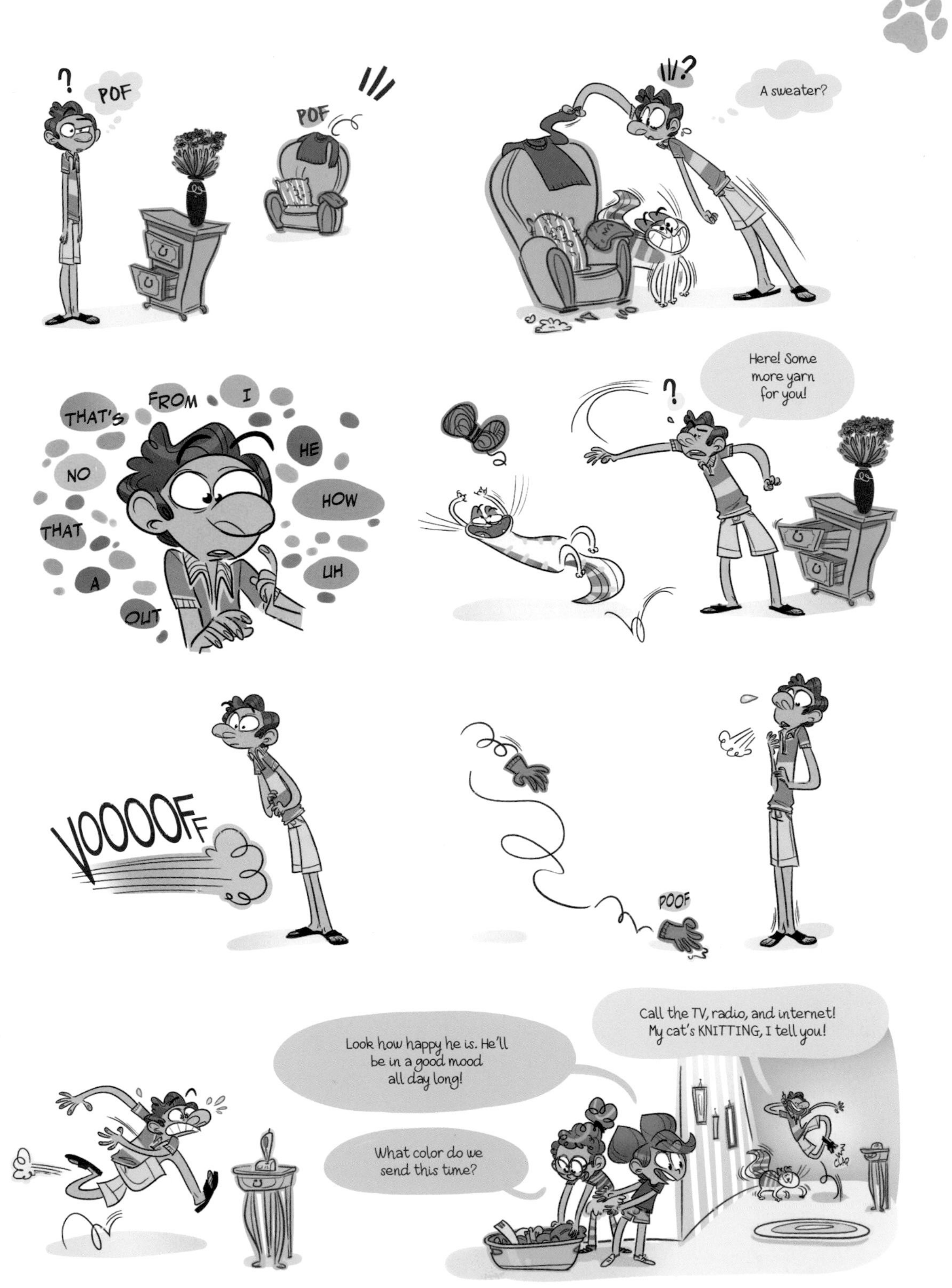
?
POF
POF
///
///?
A sweater?
THAT'S
FROM
I
HE
NO
HOW
THAT
UH
A
OUT
?
Here! Some more yarn for you!
VOOOOFFF
POOF
Call the TV, radio, and internet! My cat's KNITTING, I tell you!
Look how happy he is. He'll be in a good mood all day long!
What color do we send this time?

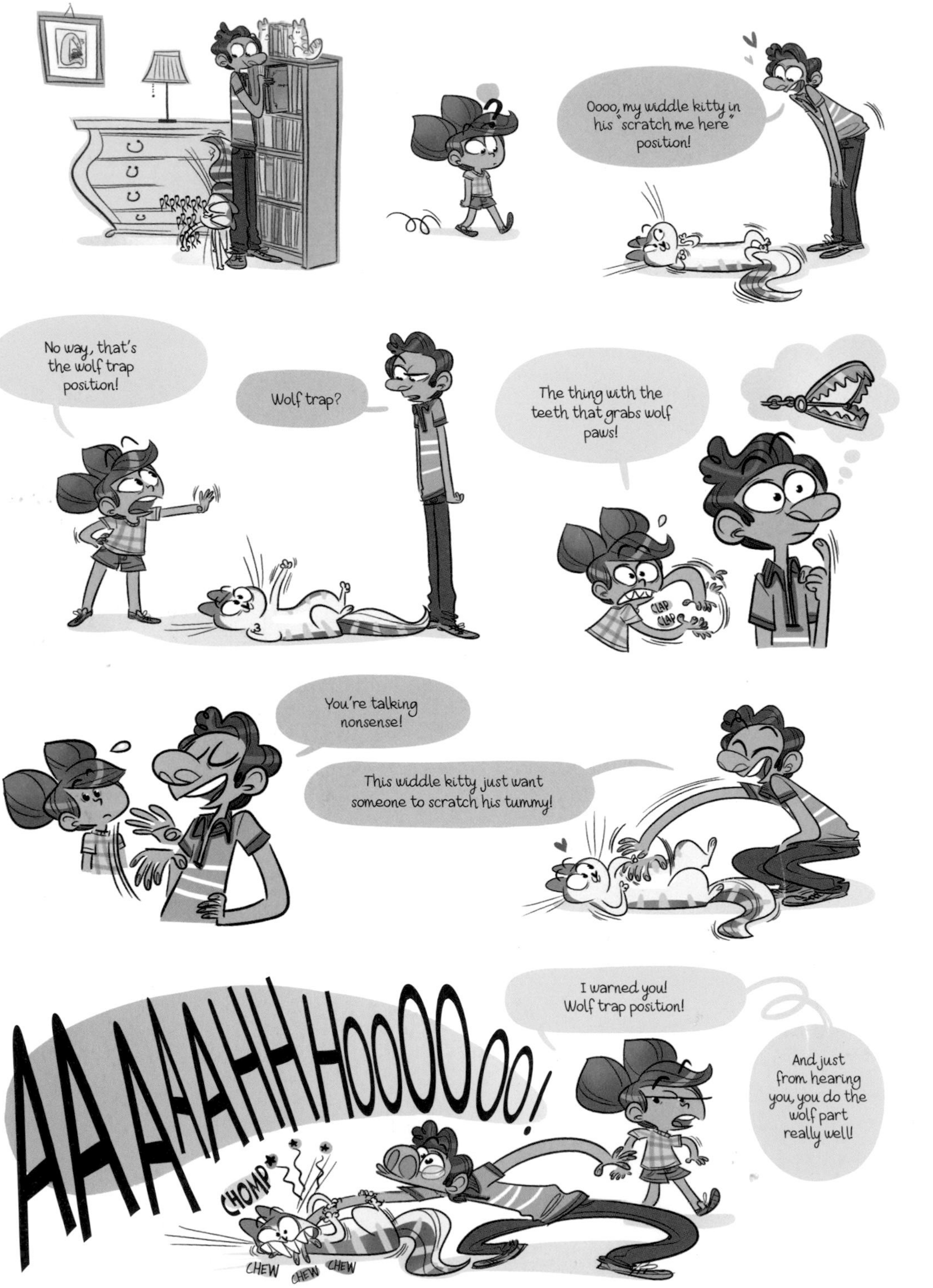
Oooo, my widdle kitty in his "scratch me here" position!
No way, that's the wolf trap position!
Wolf trap?
The thing with the teeth that grabs wolf paws!
CLAP CLAP
You're talking nonsense!
This widdle kitty just want someone to scratch his tummy!
AAAAHHHOOOOOO!
CHOMP
CHEW CHEW CHEW
I warned you! Wolf trap position!
And just from hearing you, you do the wolf part really well!

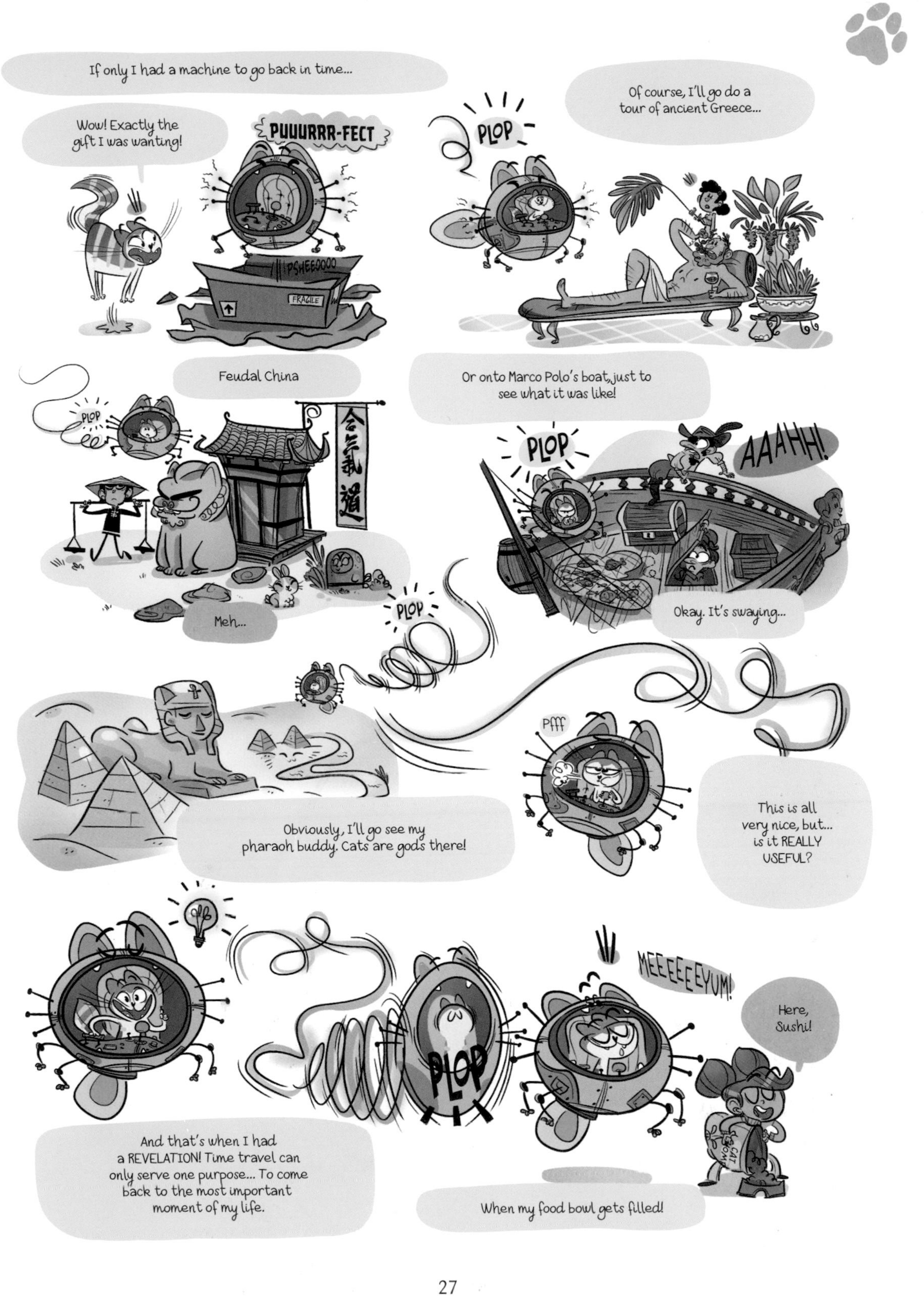

If only I had a machine to go back in time...
Wow! Exactly the gift I was wanting!
PUUURRR-FECT
PSHEEOOOO
FRAGILE
Of course, I'll go do a tour of ancient Greece...
PLOP
Feudal China
PLOP
Meh...
Or onto Marco Polo's boat, just to see what it was like!
PLOP
AAAHH!
Okay. It's swaying...
PLOP
Obviously, I'll go see my pharaoh buddy. Cats are gods there!
Pfff
This is all very nice, but... is it REALLY USEFUL?
And that's when I had a REVELATION! Time travel can only serve one purpose... To come back to the most important moment of my life.
PLOP
MEEEEEEYUM!
Here, Sushi!
When my food bowl gets filled!

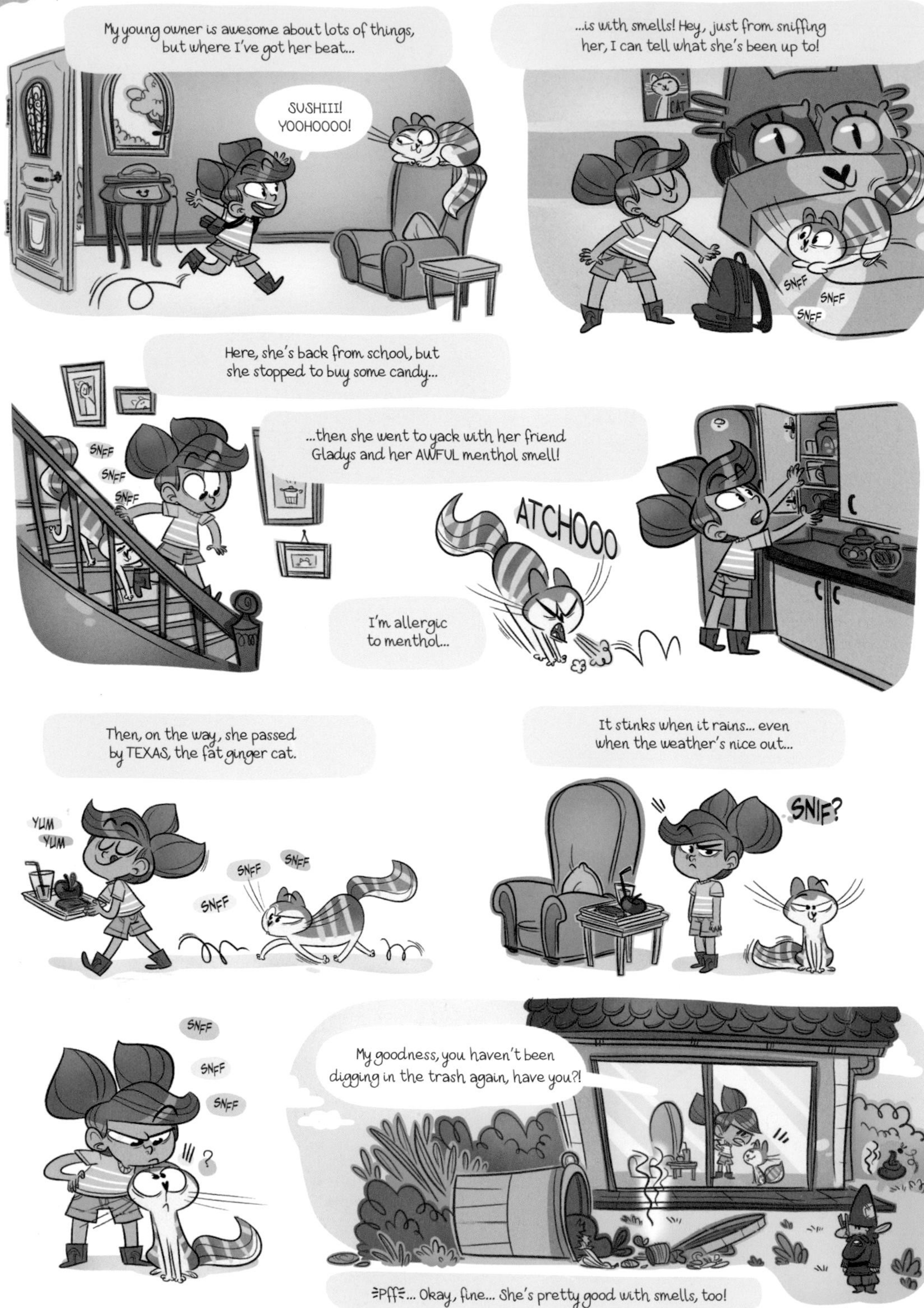
My young owner is awesome about lots of things, but where I've got her beat...
SUSHIII! YOOHOOOO!
...is with smells! Hey, just from sniffing her, I can tell what she's been up to!
SNFF
SNFF
SNFF
Here, she's back from school, but she stopped to buy some candy...
SNFF
SNFF
SNFF
...then she went to yack with her friend Gladys and her AWFUL menthol smell!
ATCHOOO
I'm allergic to menthol...
Then, on the way, she passed by TEXAS, the fat ginger cat.
YUM
YUM
SNFF
SNFF
SNFF
It stinks when it rains... even when the weather's nice out...
SNIF?
SNFF
SNFF
SNFF
?
My goodness, you haven't been digging in the trash again, have you?!
Pff... Okay, fine... She's pretty good with smells, too!

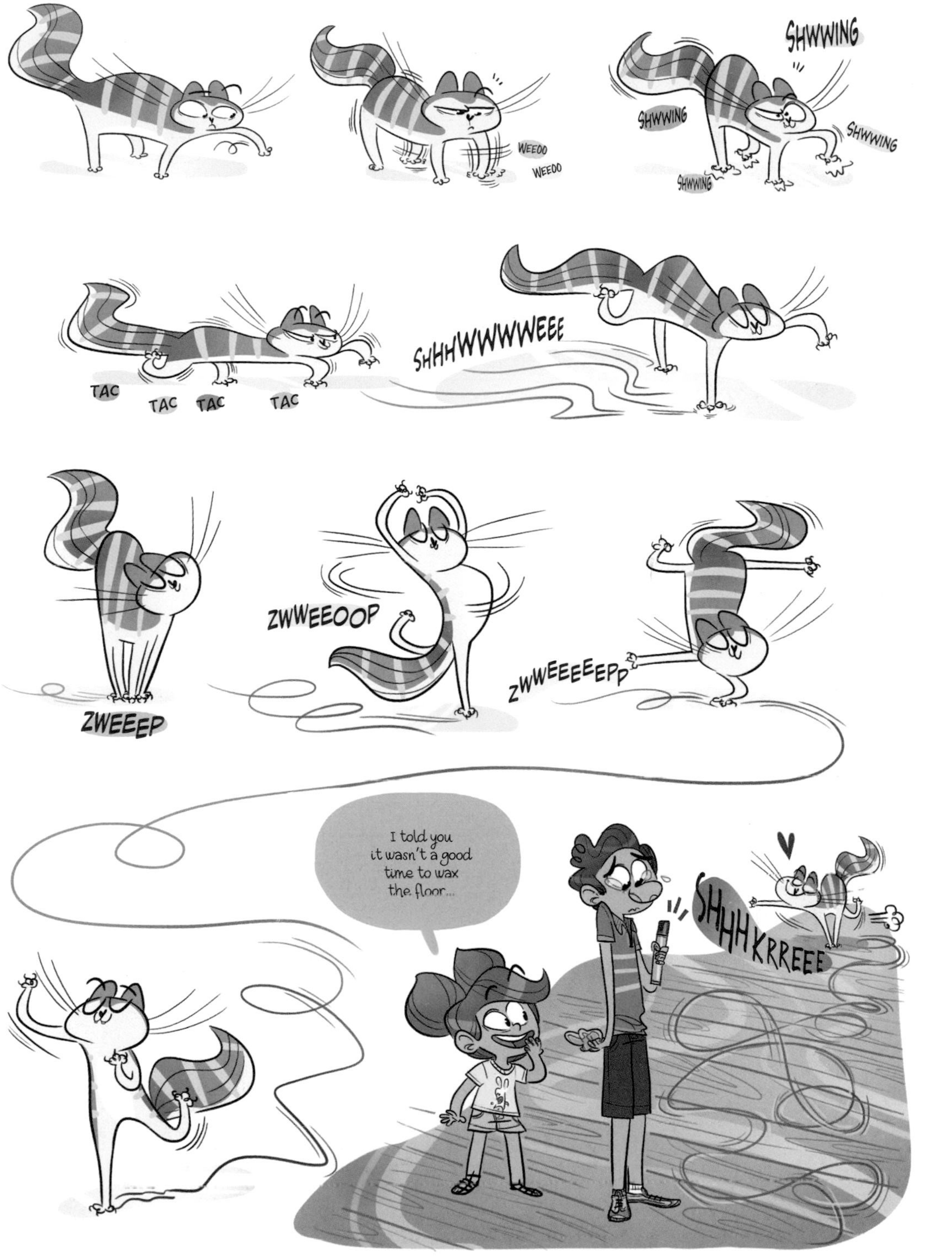
WEEDOO
WEEDOO
SHWWING
SHWWING
SHWWING
SHWWING
TAC
TAC
TAC
TAC
SHHWWWWEEE
ZWEEEP
ZWWEEOOP
ZWWEEEEEPP
I told you it wasn't a good time to wax the floor...
SHHHKRREEE

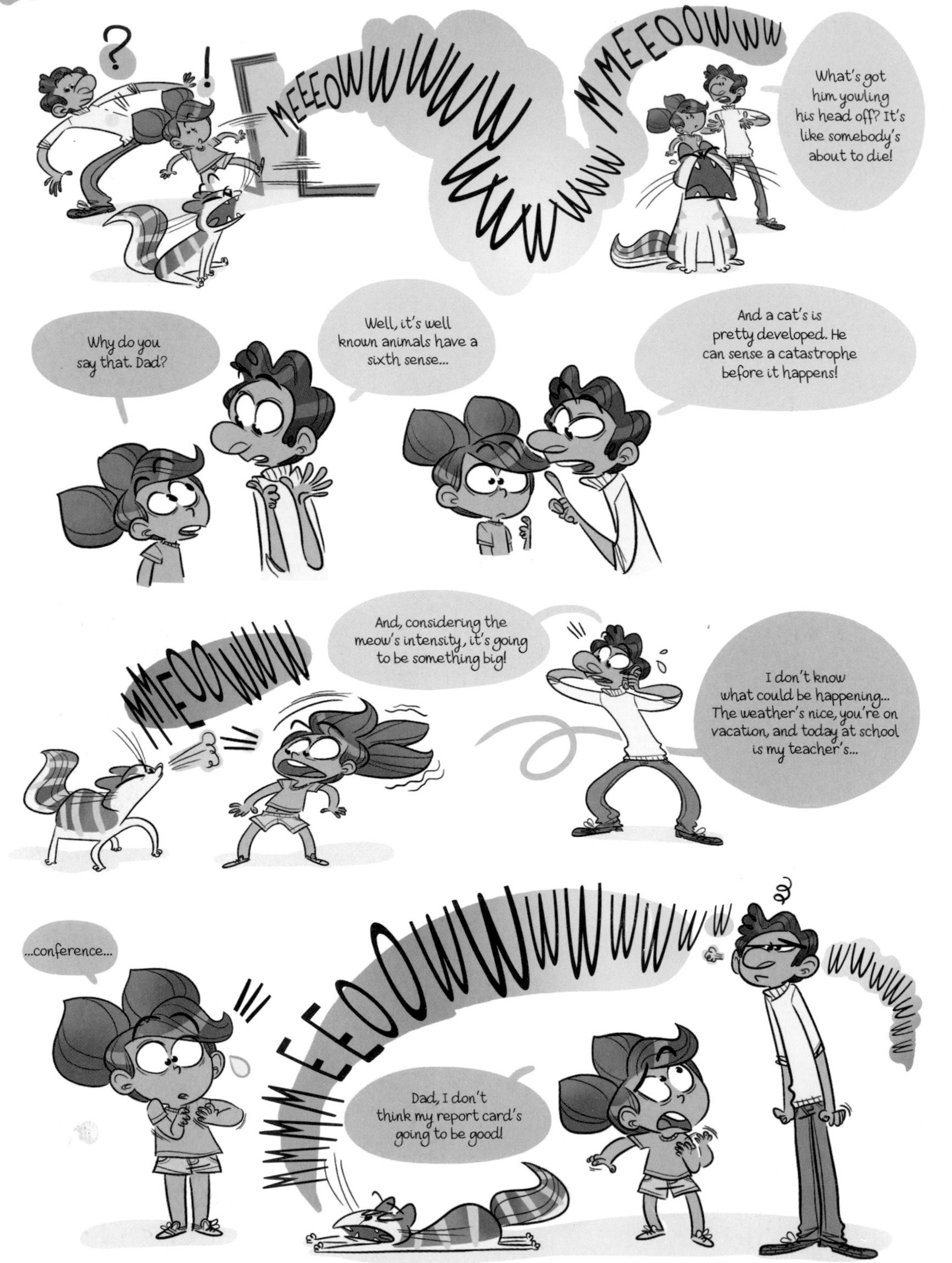
?
!
MEEEOWWWWWWWWWWWWWW
MMEEOOWWW
What's got him yowling his head off? It's like somebody's about to die!
Why do you say that. Dad?
Well, it's well known animals have a sixth sense...
And a cat's is pretty developed. He can sense a catastrophe before it happens!
MMEOOWWW
And, considering the meow's intensity, it's going to be something big!
I don't know what could be happening... The weather's nice, you're on vacation, and today at school is my teacher's...
...conference...
MMMMEEOOWWWWWWWWWWWWWWWWWW
Dad, I don't think my report card's going to be good!

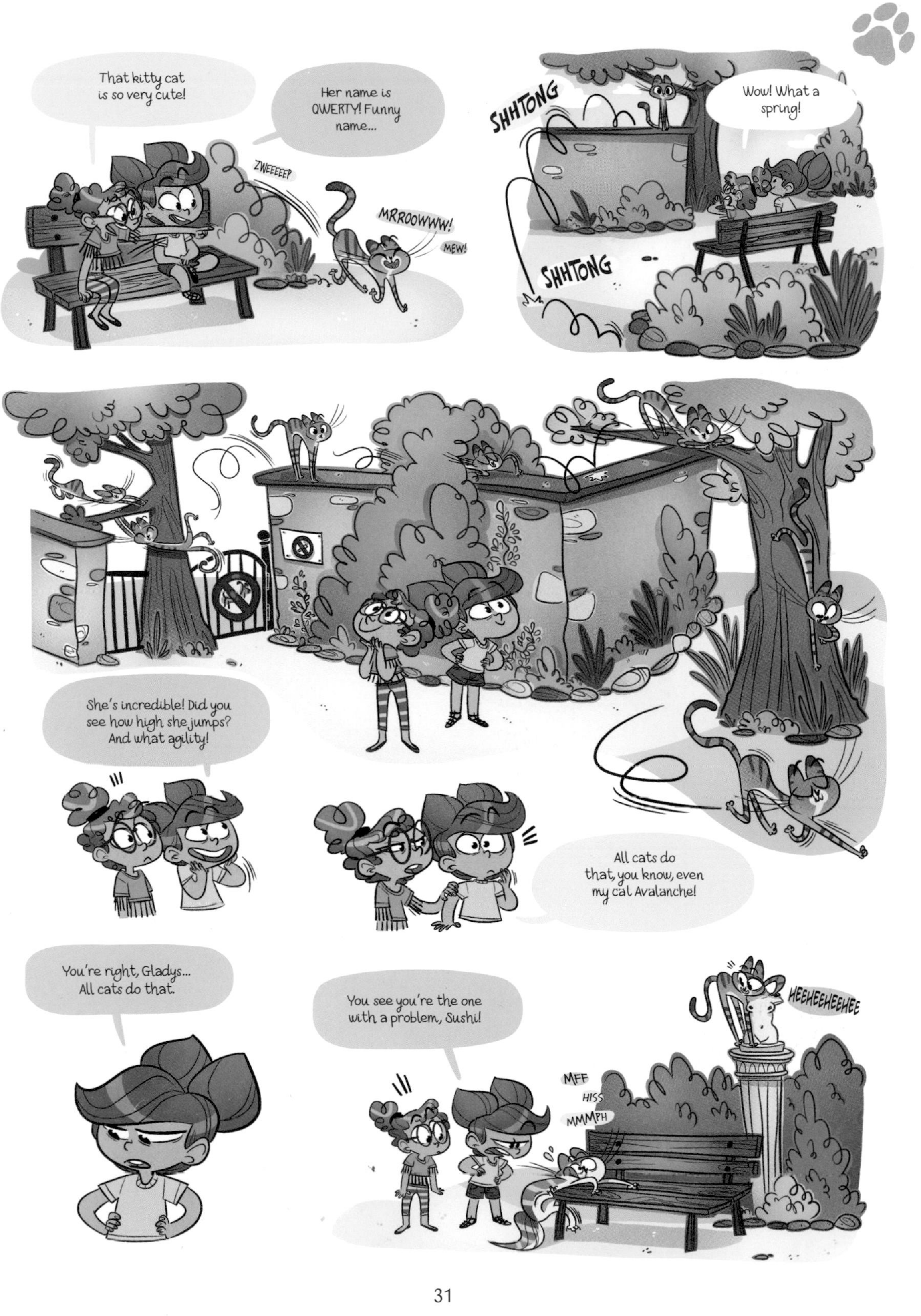

That kitty cat is so very cute!
Her name is QWERTY! Funny name...
ZWEEEEEP
MRROOWWW!
MEW!
SHHTONG
SHHTONG
Wow! What a spring!
She's incredible! Did you see how high she jumps? And what agility!
All cats do that, you know, even my cat Avalanche!
You're right, Gladys... All cats do that.
You see you're the one with a problem, Sushi!
HEEHEEHEEHEE
MFF
HISS
MMMPH

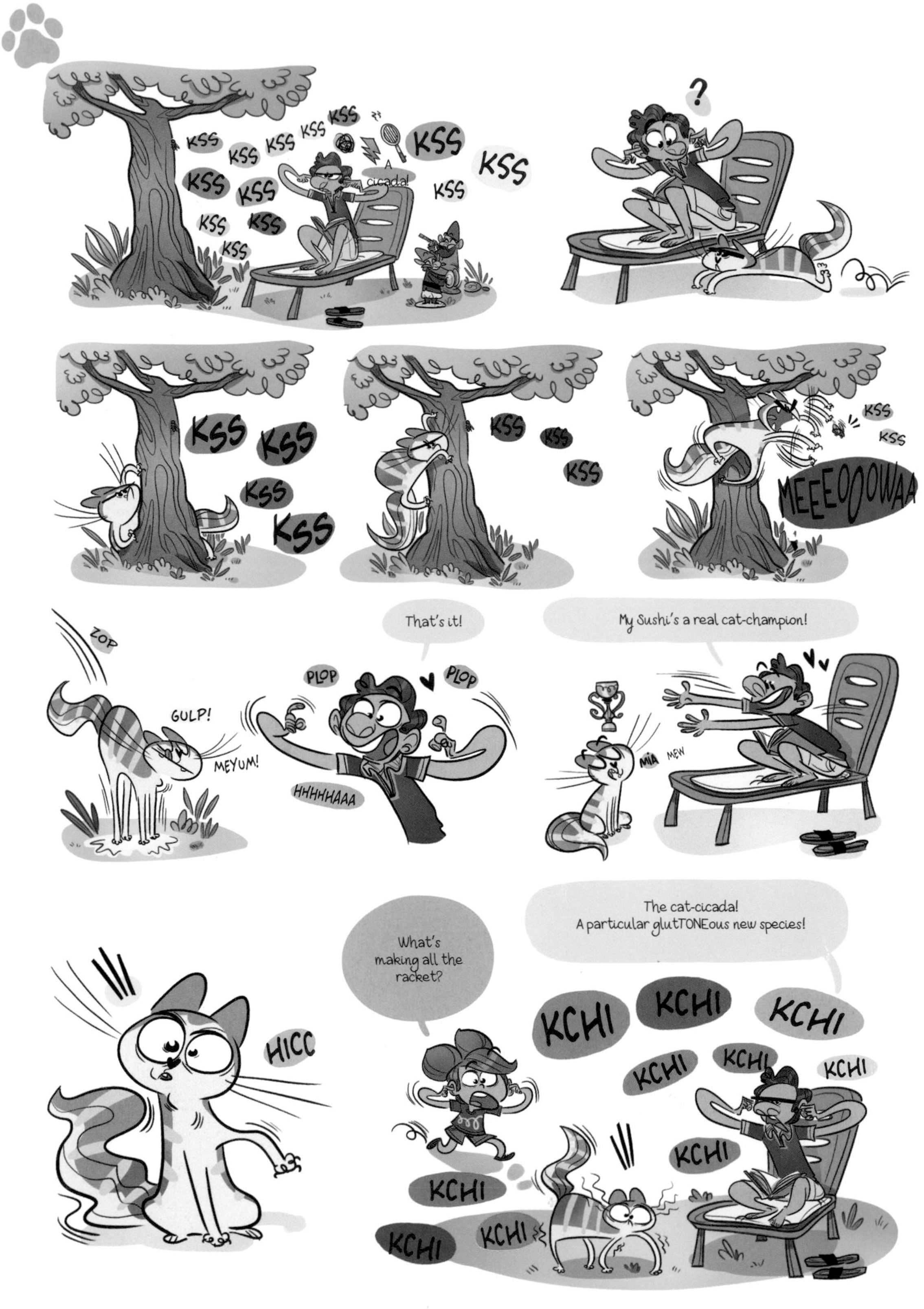

KSS KSS KSS KSS KSS
A cicada!
KSS KSS KSS KSS KSS KSS KSS KSS
?
KSS KSS KSS KSS
KSS KSS KSS
KSS KSS
MEEEOOOWAA
ZOP
GULP!
MEYUM!
That's it!
PLOP PLOP
HHHHHAAA
My Sushi's a real cat-champion!
MIA MEW
HICC
What's making all the racket?
The cat-cicada!
A particular glutTONEous new species!
KCHI KCHI KCHI KCHI KCHI KCHI KCHI KCHI KCHI KCHI

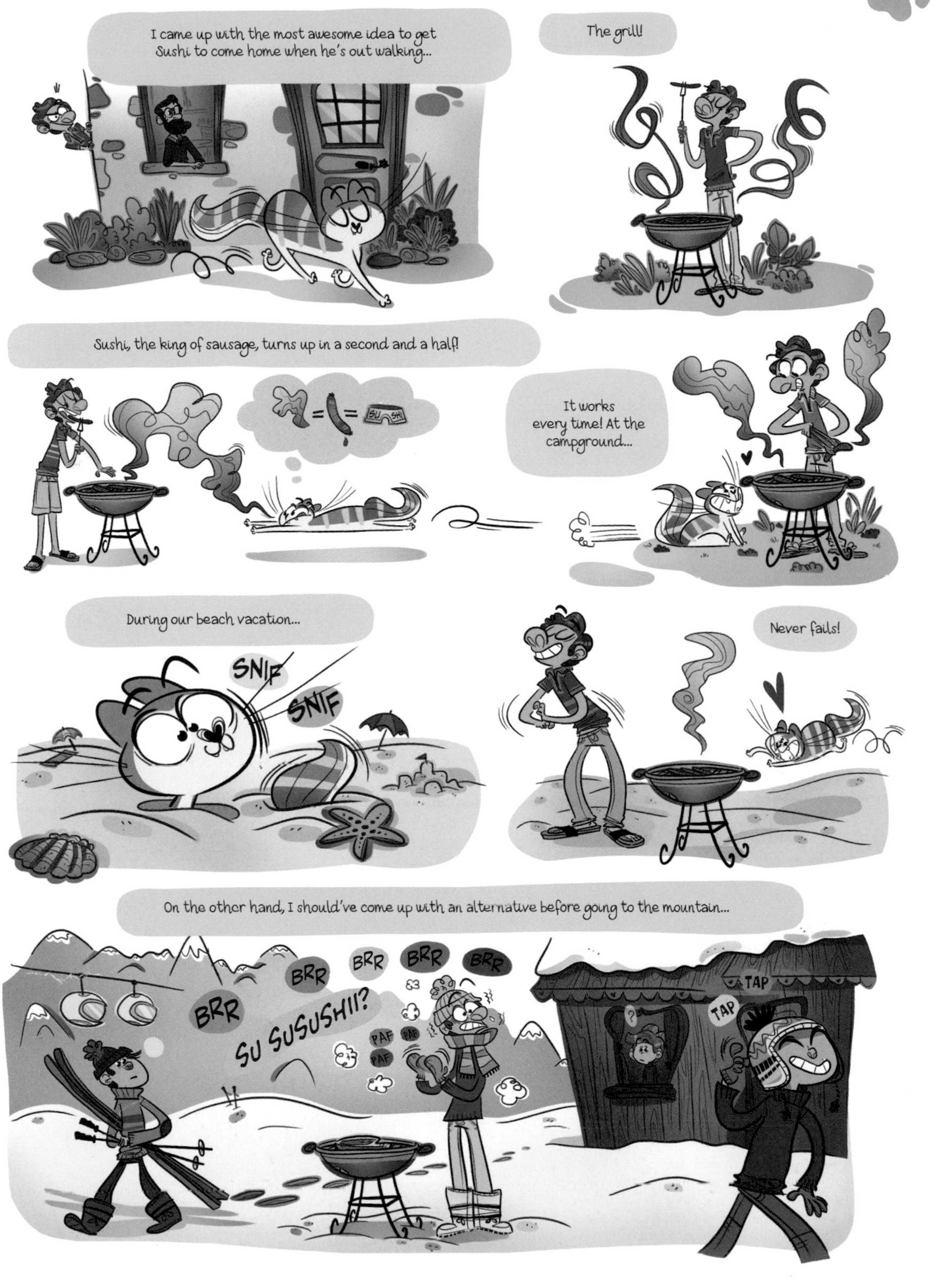
I came up with the most awesome idea to get Sushi to come home when he's out walking...
The grill!
Sushi, the king of sausage, turns up in a second and a half!
SU SHI
It works every time! At the campground...
During our beach vacation...
SNIF
SNIF
Never fails!
On the other hand, I should've come up with an alternative before going to the mountain...
BRR
BRR
BRR
BRR
BRR
SU SUSUSHI!?
PAF
PAF
PAF
TAP
TAP

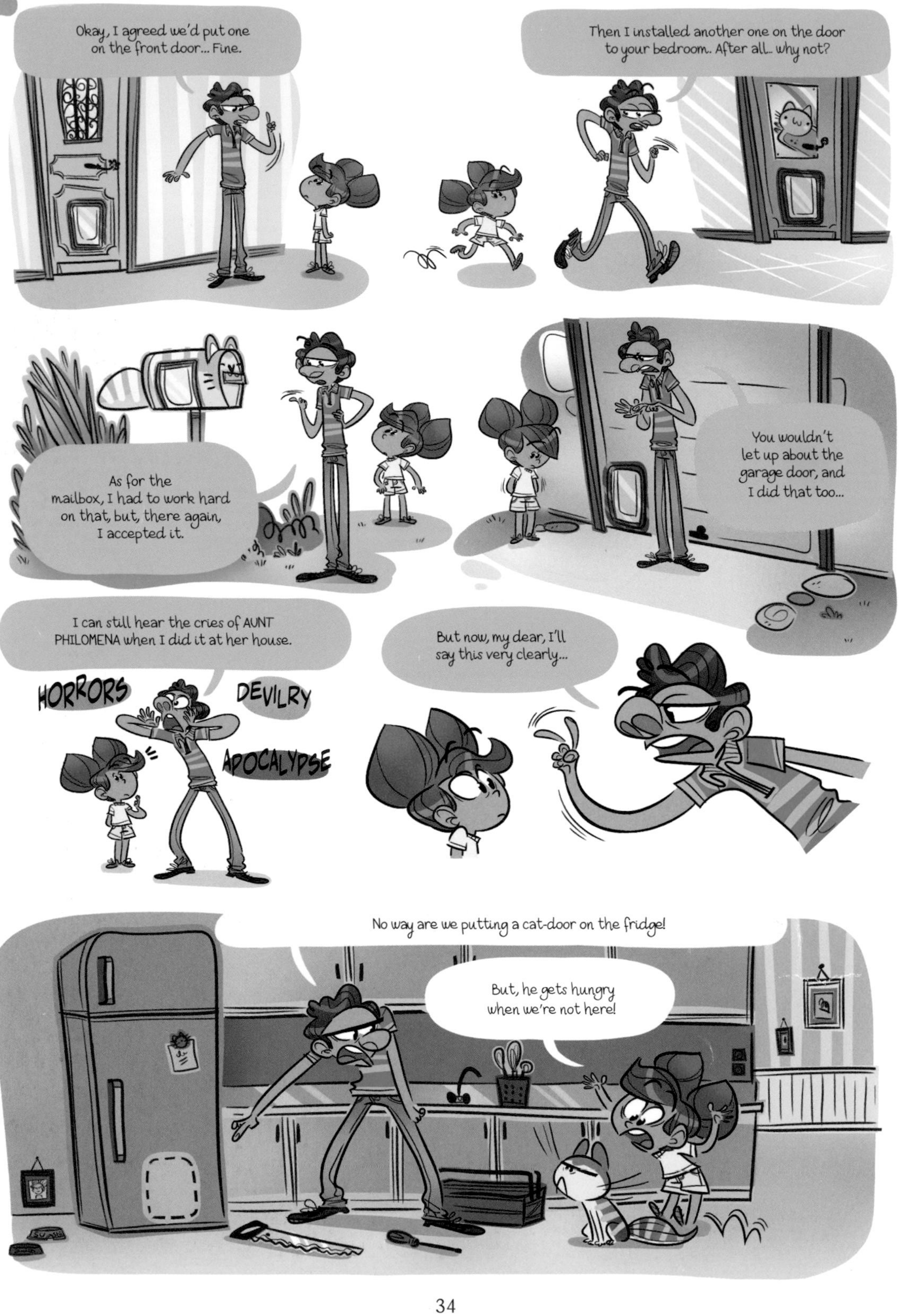
Okay, I agreed we'd put one on the front door... Fine.
Then I installed another one on the door to your bedroom. After all... why not?
As for the mailbox, I had to work hard on that, but, there again, I accepted it.
You wouldn't let up about the garage door, and I did that too...
I can still hear the cries of AUNT PHILOMENA when I did it at her house.
HORRORS
DEVILRY
APOCALYPSE
But now, my dear, I'll say this very clearly...
No way are we putting a cat-door on the fridge!
But, he gets hungry when we're not here!

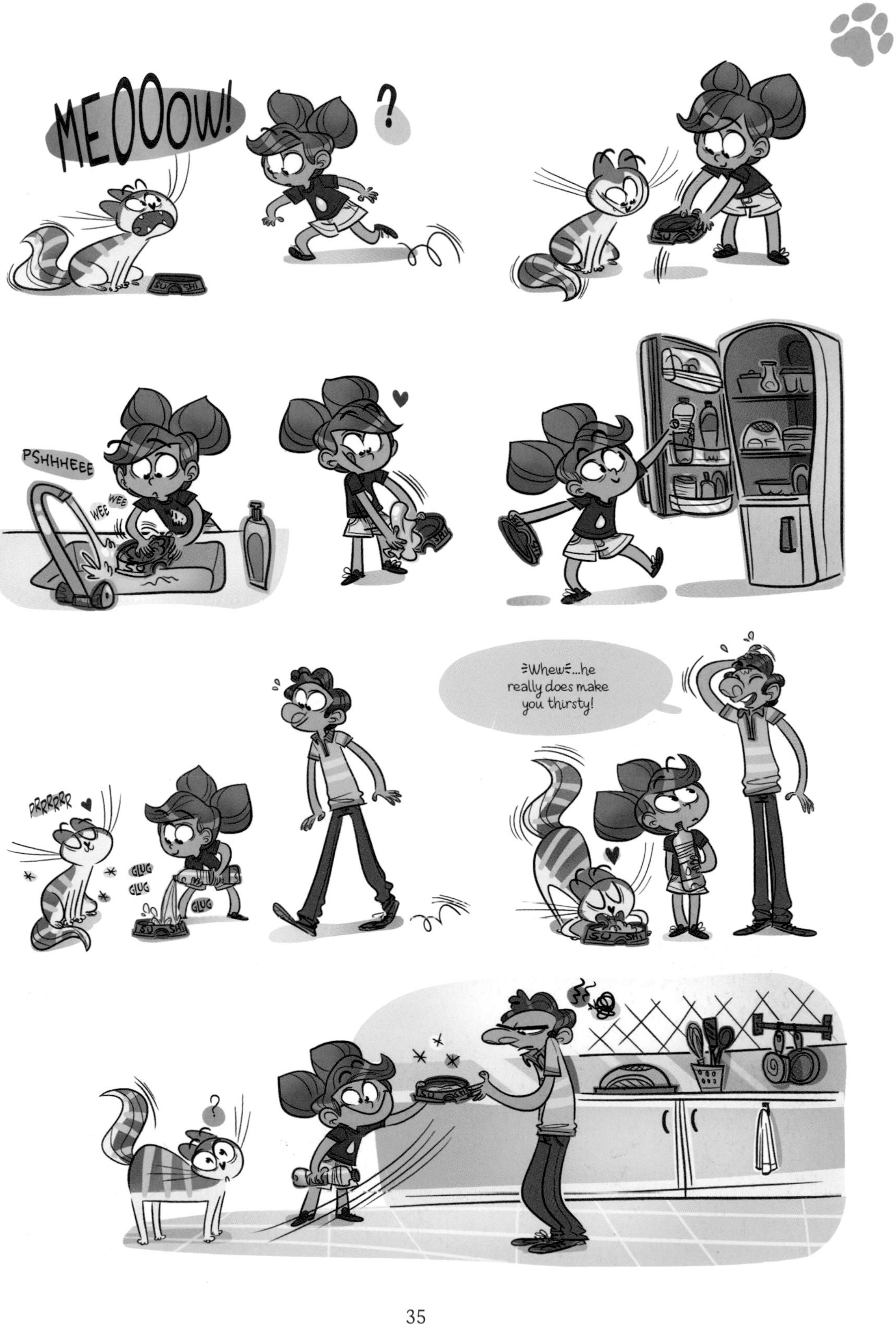
MEOOOW!
?
PSHHHEEE
WEE WEE
PRRRRR
GLUG
GLUG
GLUG
Whew...he really does make you thirsty!
?

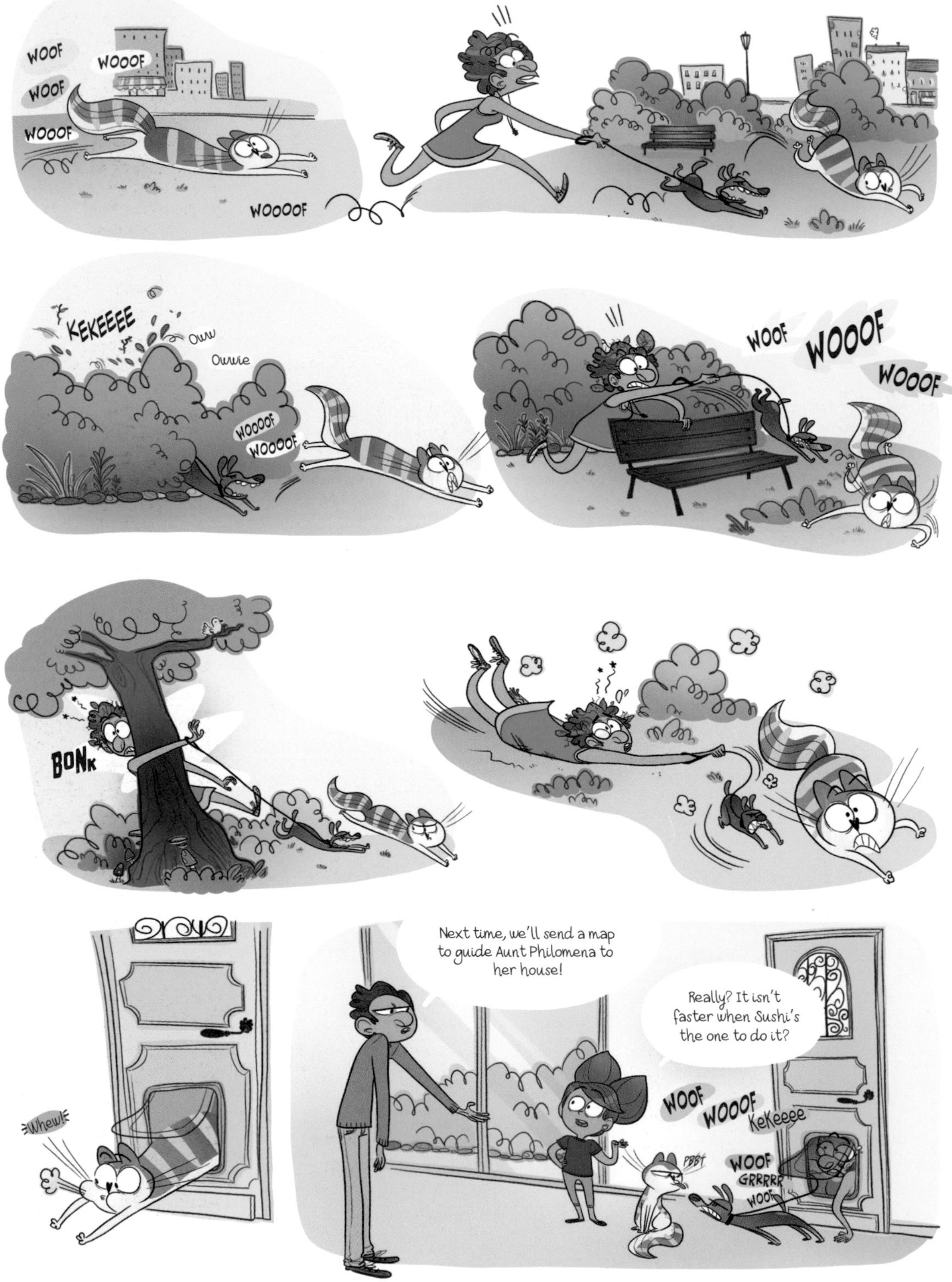
WOOF
WOOOF
WOOF
WOOOF
WOOOOF
KEKEEEE
Oww
Owwie
WOOOOF
WOOOOF
WOOF
WOOOF
WOOOF
BONK
Whew!
Next time, we'll send a map to guide Aunt Philomena to her house!
Really? It isn't faster when Sushi's the one to do it?
WOOF
WOOOF
KeKeeee
PBBT
WOOF
GRRRRR
WOOF

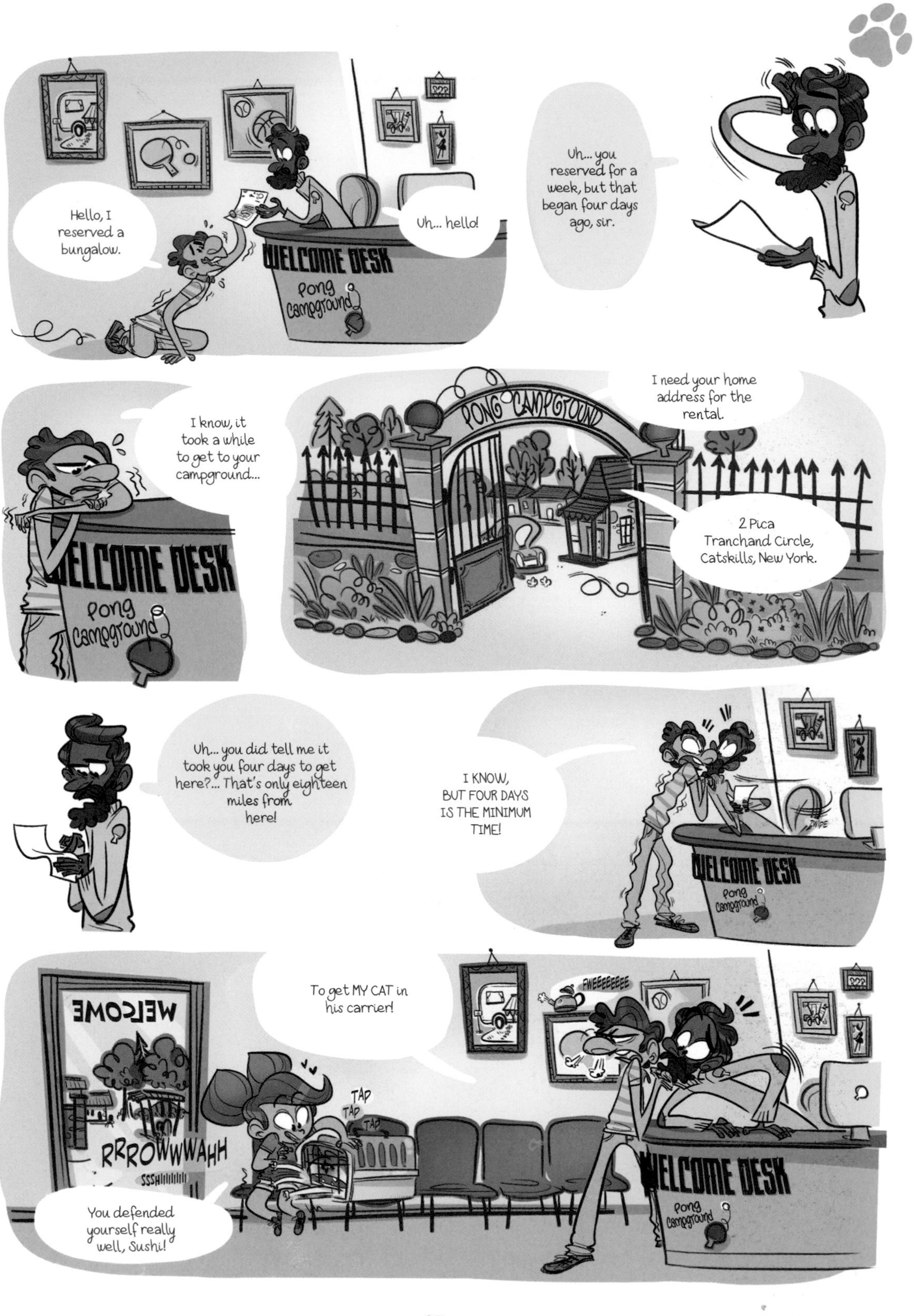
Hello, I reserved a bungalow.
Uh... hello!
WELCOME DESK
Pong Campground
Uh... you reserved for a week, but that began four days ago, sir.
I know, it took a while to get to your campground...
PONG CAMPGROUND
I need your home address for the rental.
2 Pica Tranchand Circle, Catskills, New York.
Uh... you did tell me it took you four days to get here?... That's only eighteen miles from here!
I KNOW, BUT FOUR DAYS IS THE MINIMUM TIME!
To get MY CAT in his carrier!
WELCOME
FWEEEEEEEE
TAP
TAP
TAP
RRROWWWAHH
SSSHIIIIIII
You defended yourself really well, Sushi!

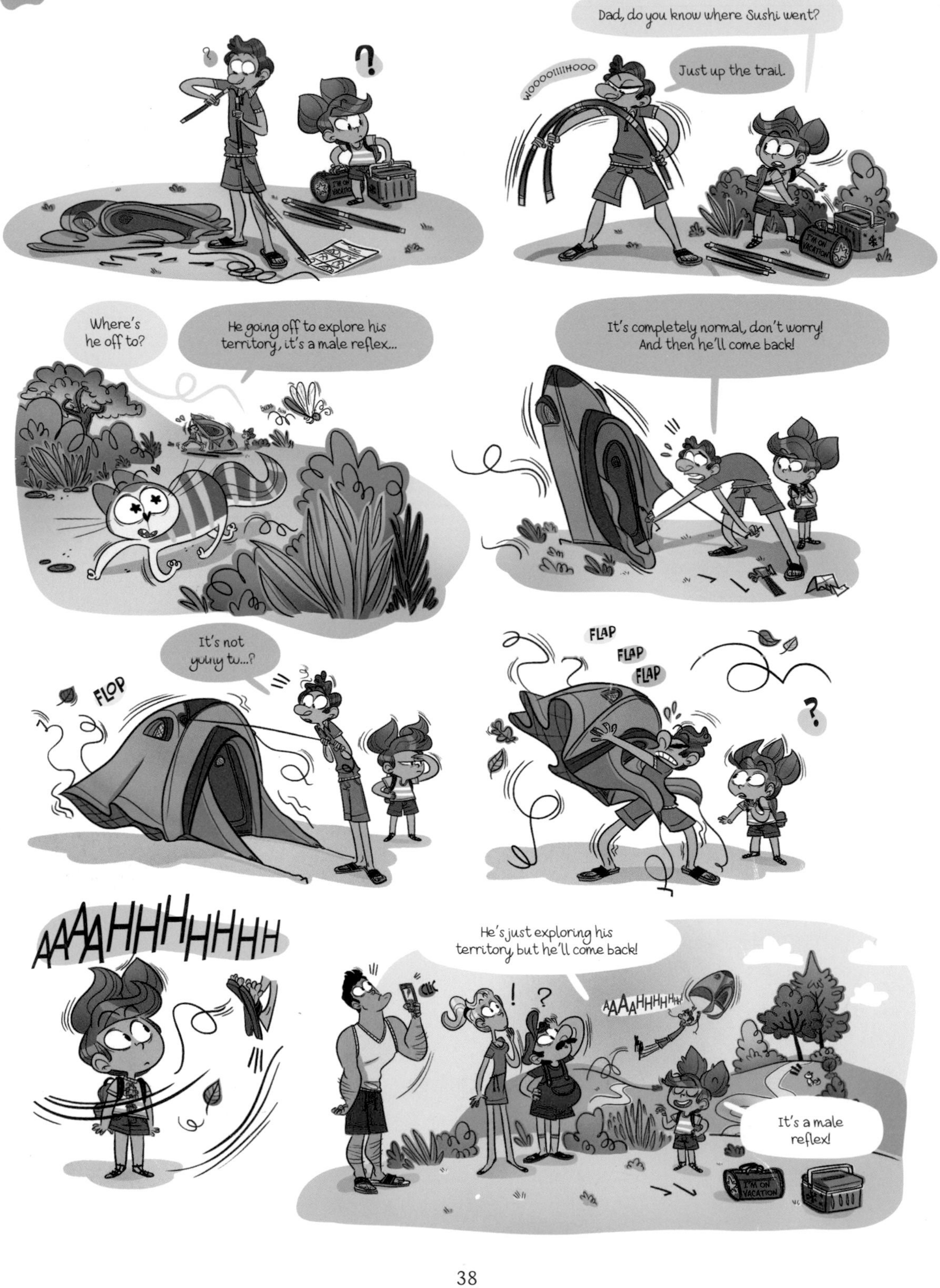

Dad, do you know where Sushi went?
WOOOOIIIIHOOO
Just up the trail.
Where's he off to?
He going off to explore his territory, it's a male reflex...
It's completely normal, don't worry! And then he'll come back!
FLOP
It's not going to...?
FLAP
FLAP
FLAP
AAAAHHHHHHHH
He's just exploring his territory, but he'll come back!
CLIC
AAAAHHHHHHH
It's a male reflex!
I'M ON VACATION

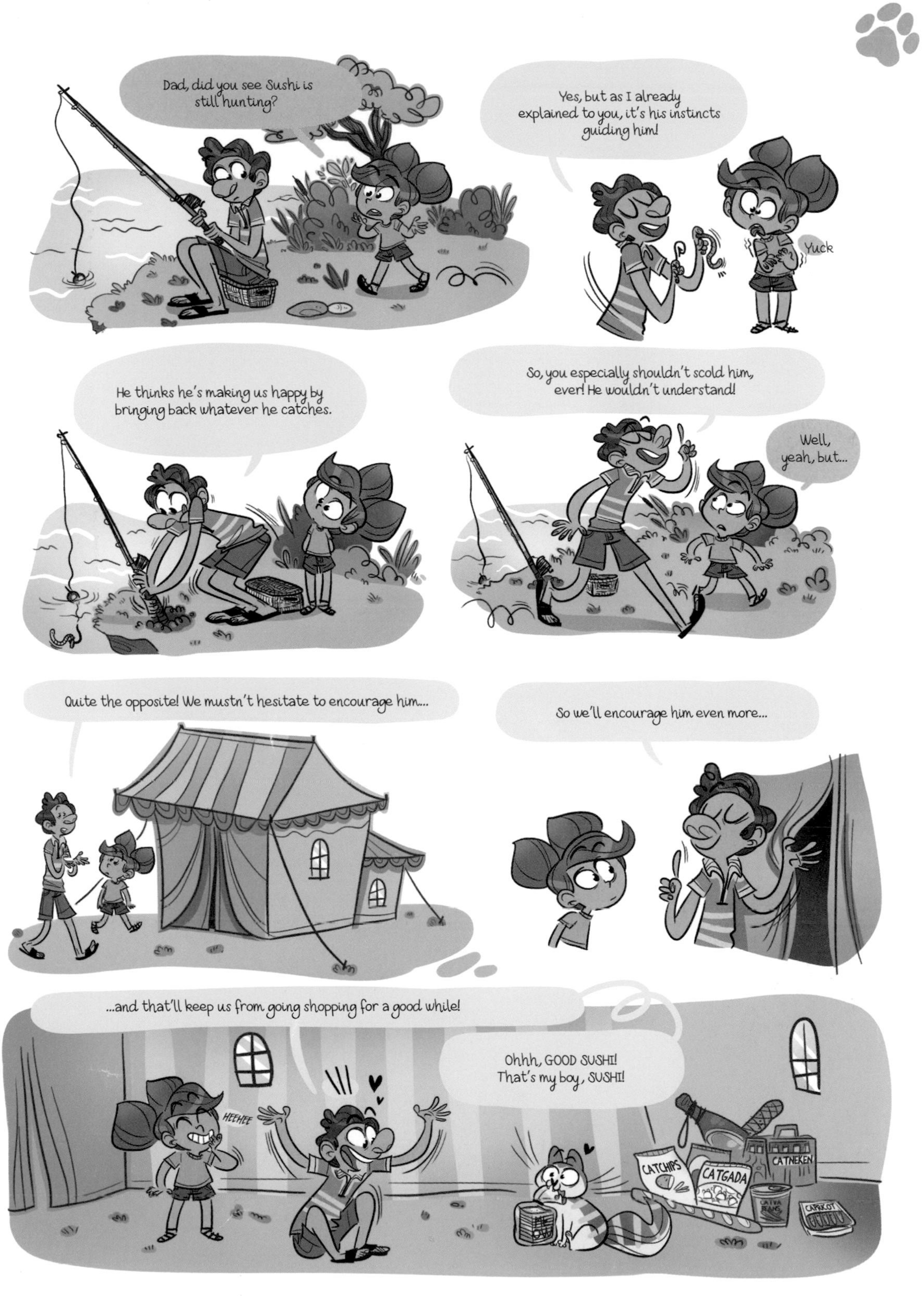
Dad, did you see Sushi is still hunting?
Yes, but as I already explained to you, it's his instincts guiding him!
Yuck
He thinks he's making us happy by bringing back whatever he catches.
So, you especially shouldn't scold him, ever! He wouldn't understand!
Well, yeah, but...
Quite the opposite! We mustn't hesitate to encourage him...
So we'll encourage him even more...
...and that'll keep us from going shopping for a good while!
HEEHEE
Ohhh, GOOD SUSHI! That's my boy, SUSHI!
CATCHIPS
CATGADA
CATNEKEN
CAPRICOT

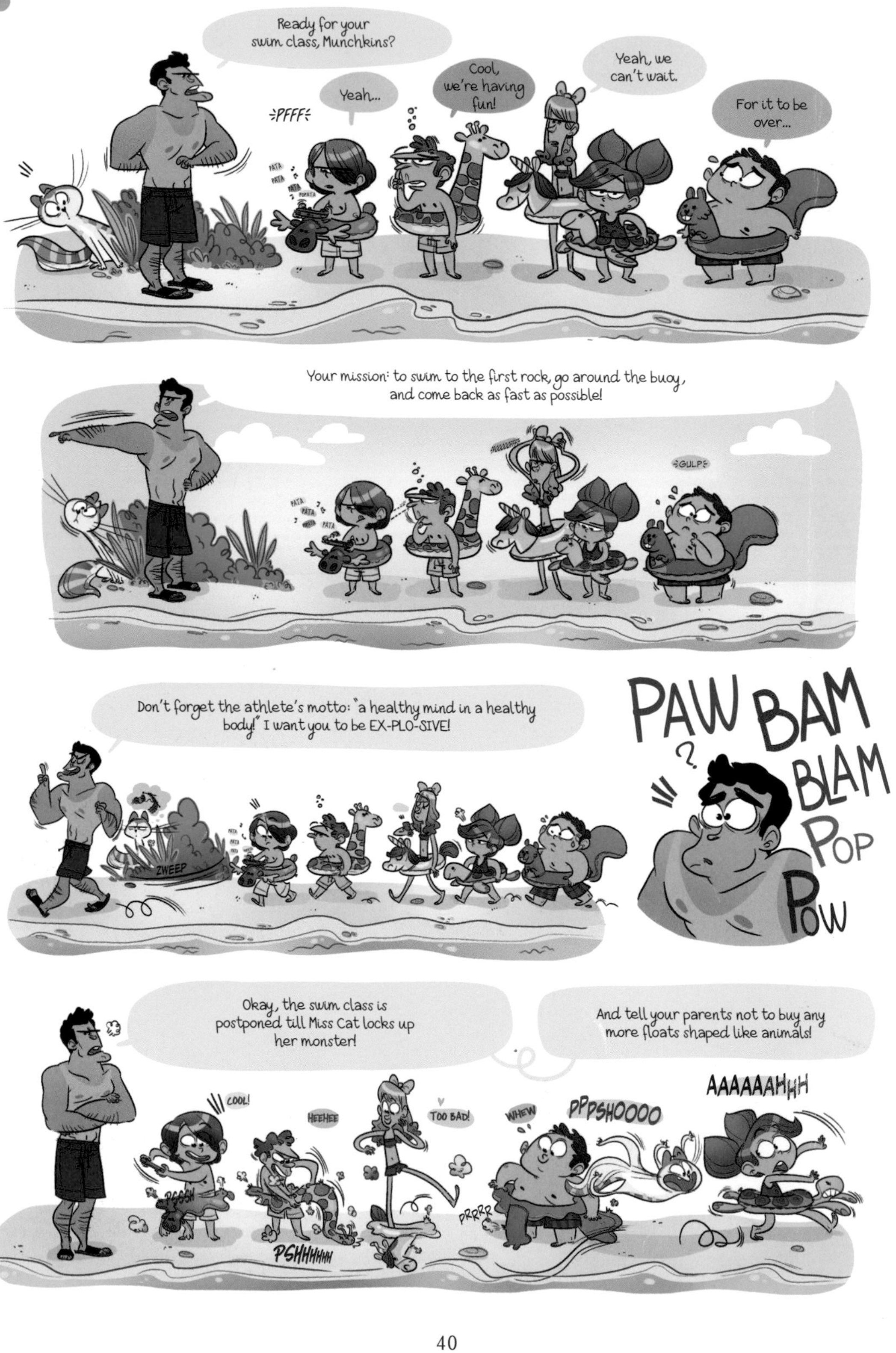

Ready for your swim class, Munchkins?
PFFF
Yeah...
Cool, we're having fun!
Yeah, we can't wait.
For it to be over...
Your mission: to swim to the first rock, go around the buoy, and come back as fast as possible!
GULP
Don't forget the athlete's motto: "a healthy mind in a healthy body!" I want you to be EX-PLO-SIVE!
ZWEEP
PAW
BAM
BLAM
POP
POW
Okay, the swim class is postponed till Miss Cat locks up her monster!
And tell your parents not to buy any more floats shaped like animals!
COOL!
HEEHEE
TOO BAD!
WHEW
PPPSHOOOO
AAAAAAHHH
PSHHHHHH
PRRRR

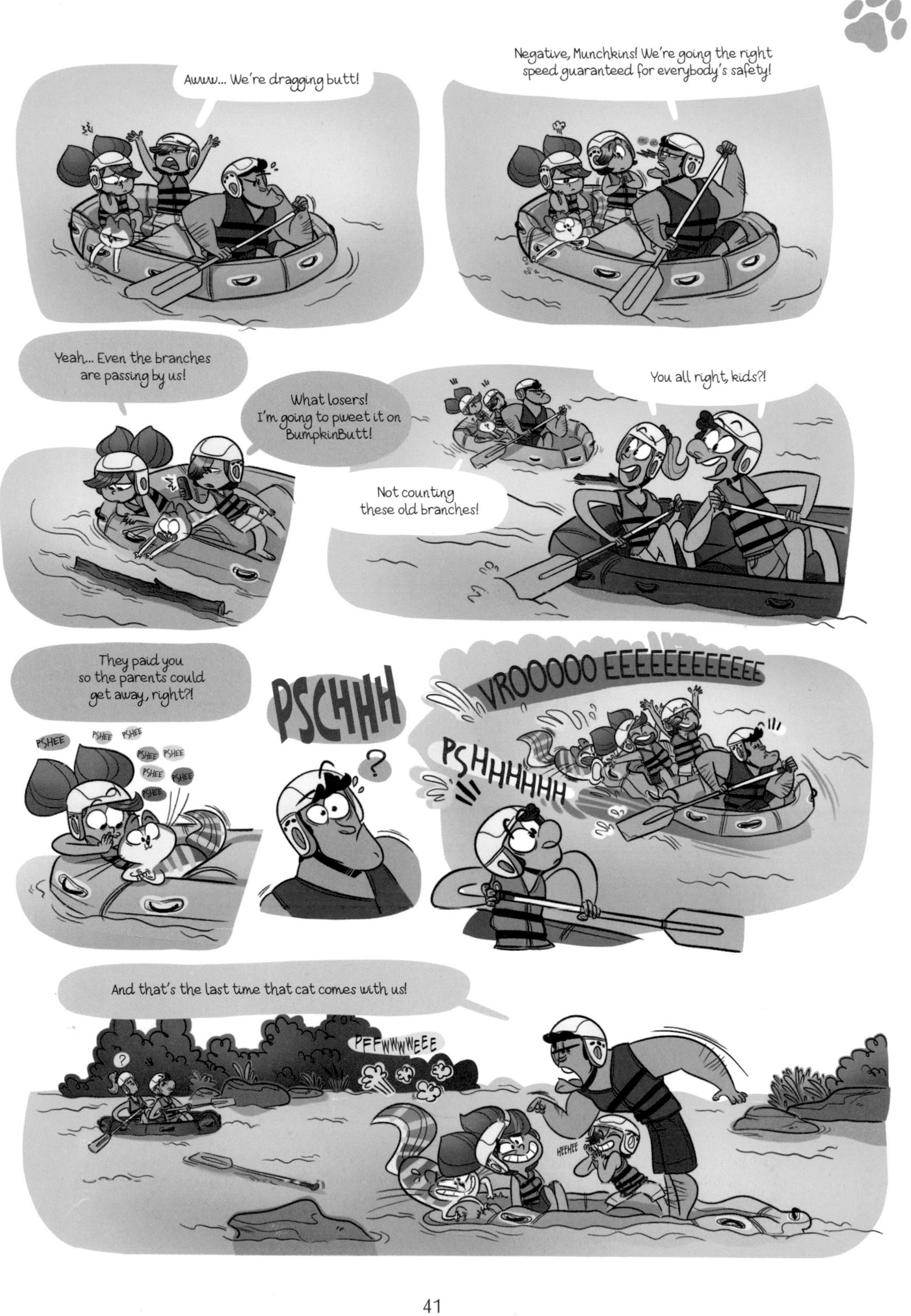
Awww... We're dragging butt!
Negative, Munchkins! We're going the right speed guaranteed for everybody's safety!
Yeah... Even the branches are passing by us!
What losers! I'm going to pweet it on BumpkinButt!
You all right, kids?!
Not counting these old branches!
They paid you so the parents could get away, right?!
PSHEE
PSHEE
PSHEE
PSHEE
PSHEE
PSHEE
PSHEE
PSHEE
PSCHHH
?
VROOOOO EEEEEEEEEEE
PSHHHHHH
And that's the last time that cat comes with us!
PFFWWWWEEE
?
HEEHEE

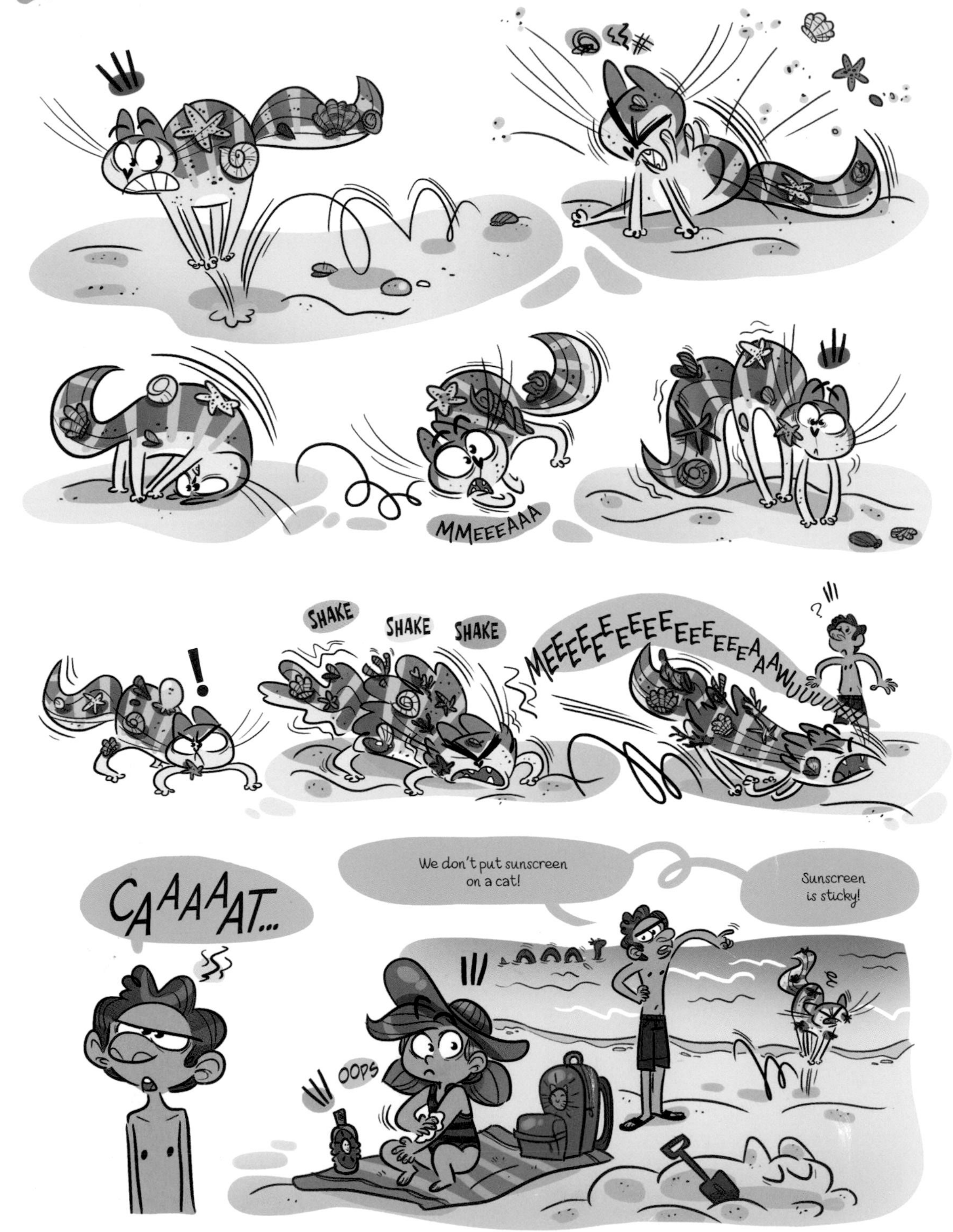
MMEEEAAA
SHAKE
SHAKE
SHAKE
MEEEEEEEEEEEEEEEEAAAWUUUU
CAAAAAT...
We don't put sunscreen on a cat!
Sunscreen is sticky!
OOPS

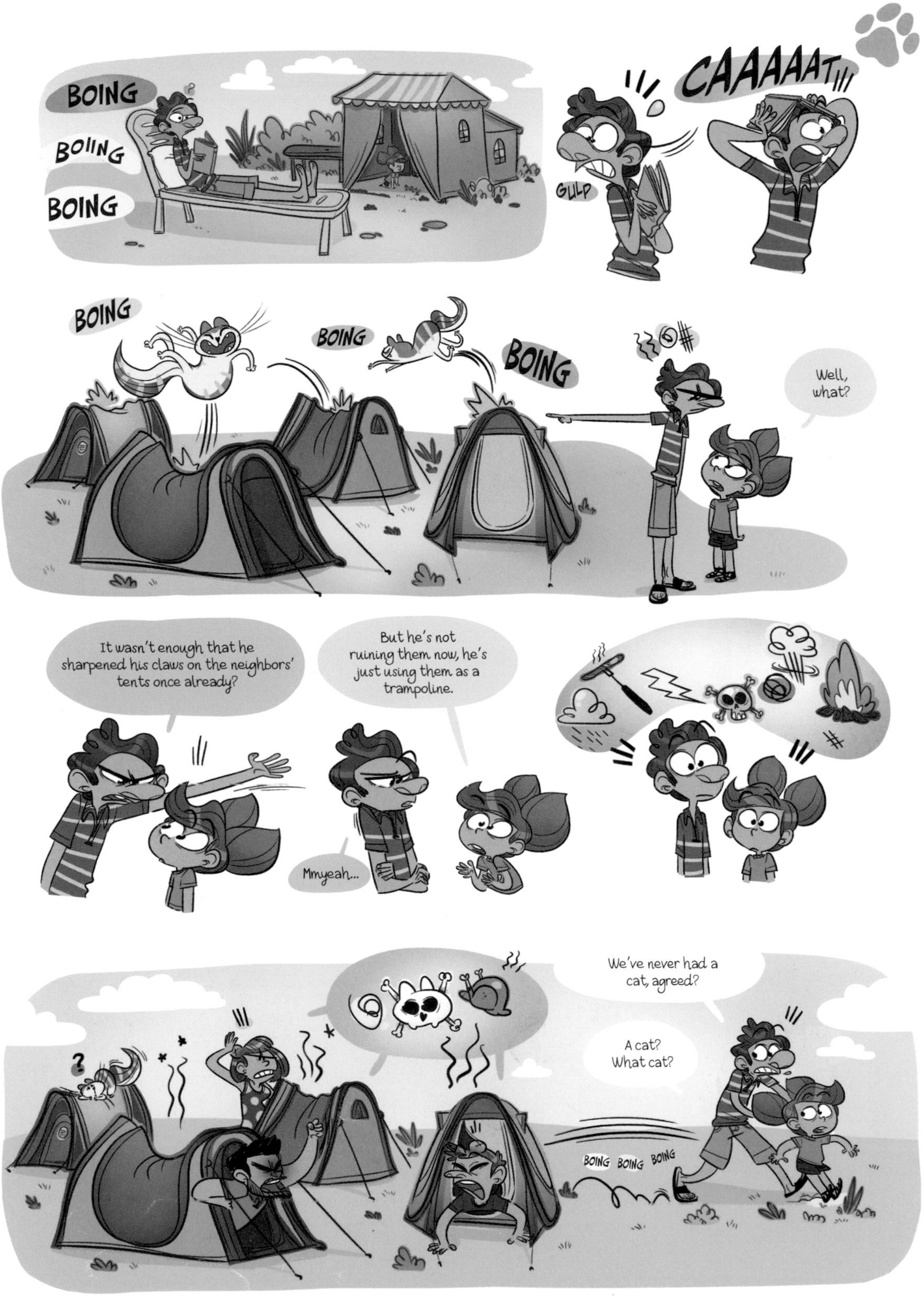
BOING
BOIING
BOING
GULP
CAAAAAT
BOING
BOING
BOING
Well, what?
It wasn't enough that he sharpened his claws on the neighbors' tents once already?
But he's not ruining them now, he's just using them as a trampoline.
Mmyeah...
We've never had a cat, agreed?
A cat? What cat?
BOING BOING BOING

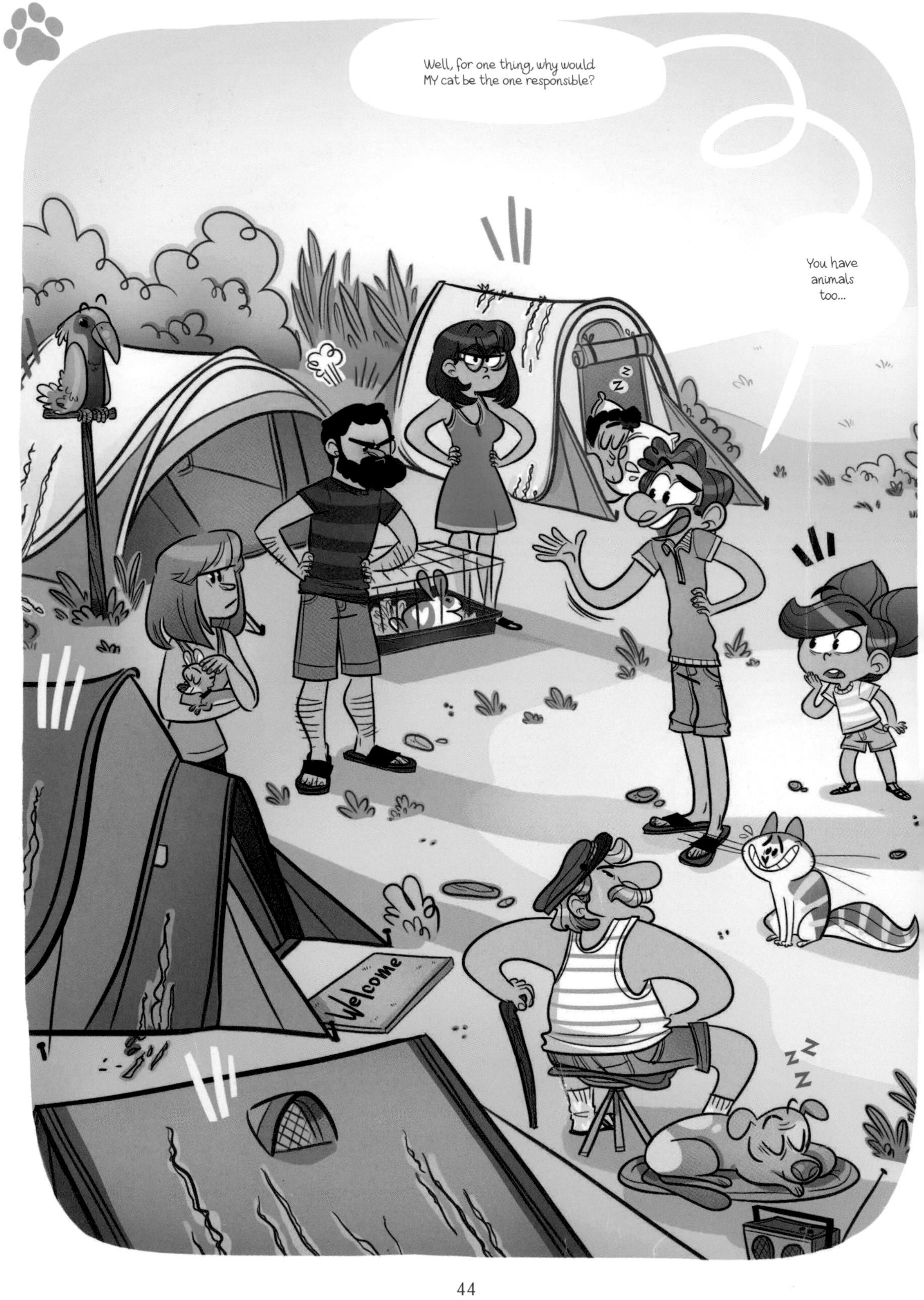
Well, for one thing, why would
MY cat be the one responsible?
You have
animals
too...
Welcome

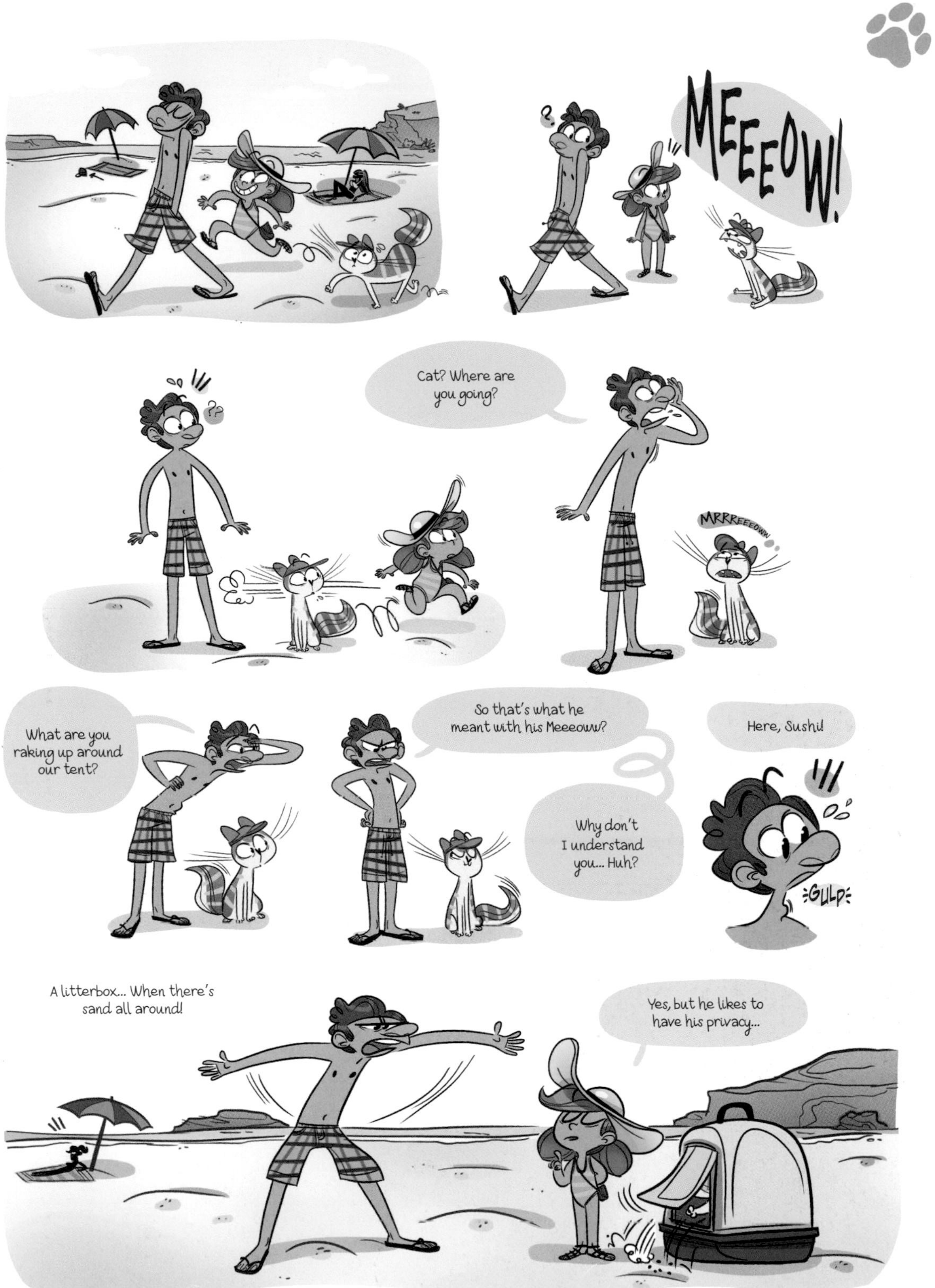
MEEEOW!
Cat? Where are you going?
MRRREEEOWW
What are you raking up around our tent?
So that's what he meant with his Meeeoww?
Why don't I understand you... Huh?
Here, Sushi!
GULP
A litterbox... When there's sand all around!
Yes, but he likes to have his privacy...

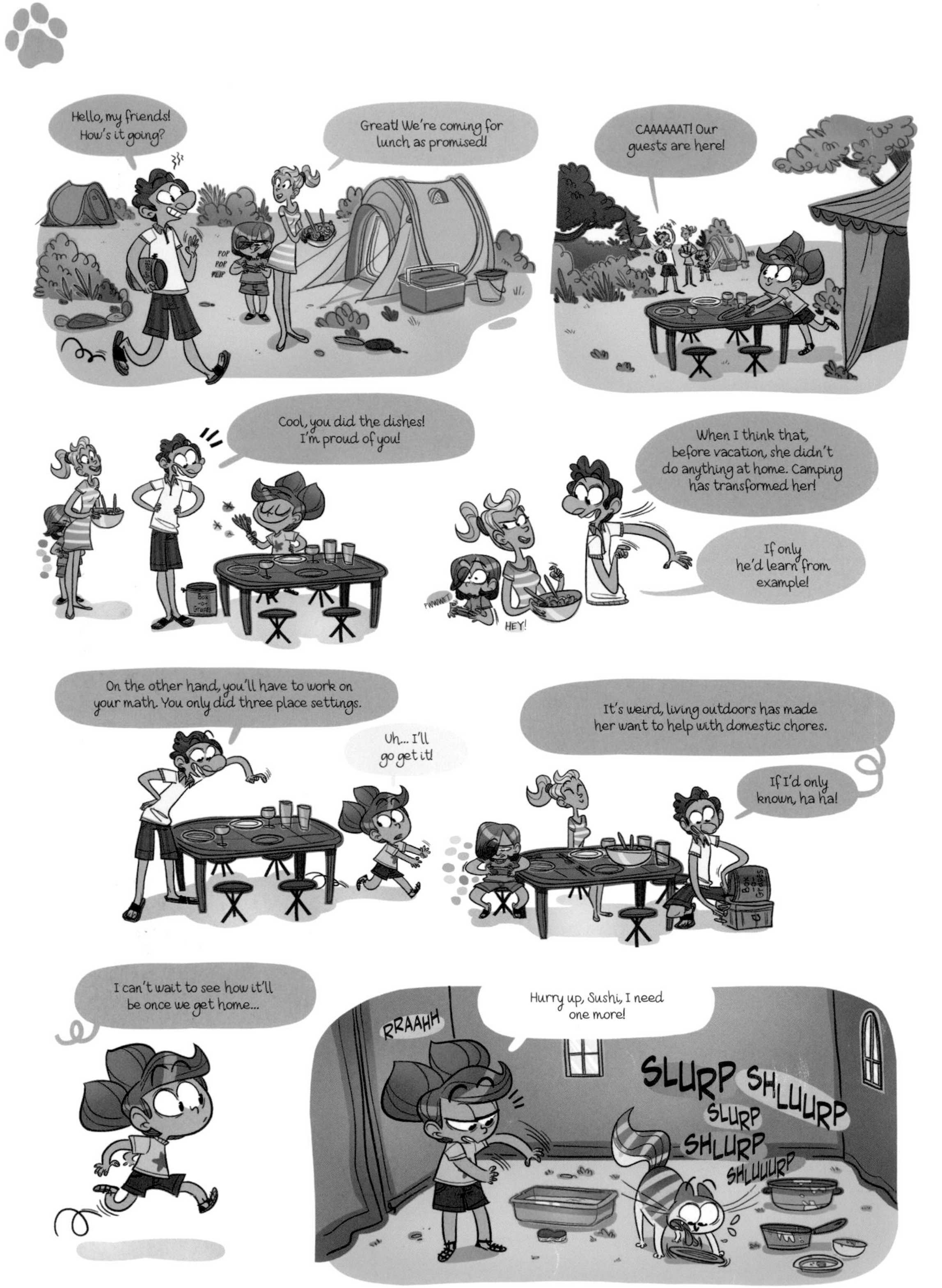

Hello, my friends! How's it going?
POP POP PLIP
Great! We're coming for lunch as promised!
CAAAAAAT! Our guests are here!
Cool, you did the dishes! I'm proud of you!
When I think that, before vacation, she didn't do anything at home. Camping has transformed her!
If only he'd learn from example!
HEY!
On the other hand, you'll have to work on your math. You only did three place settings.
Uh... I'll go get it!
It's weird, living outdoors has made her want to help with domestic chores.
If I'd only known, ha ha!
I can't wait to see how it'll be once we get home...
RRAAHH
Hurry up, Sushi, I need one more!
SLURP
SHLUURP
SLURP
SHLURP
SHLUUURP

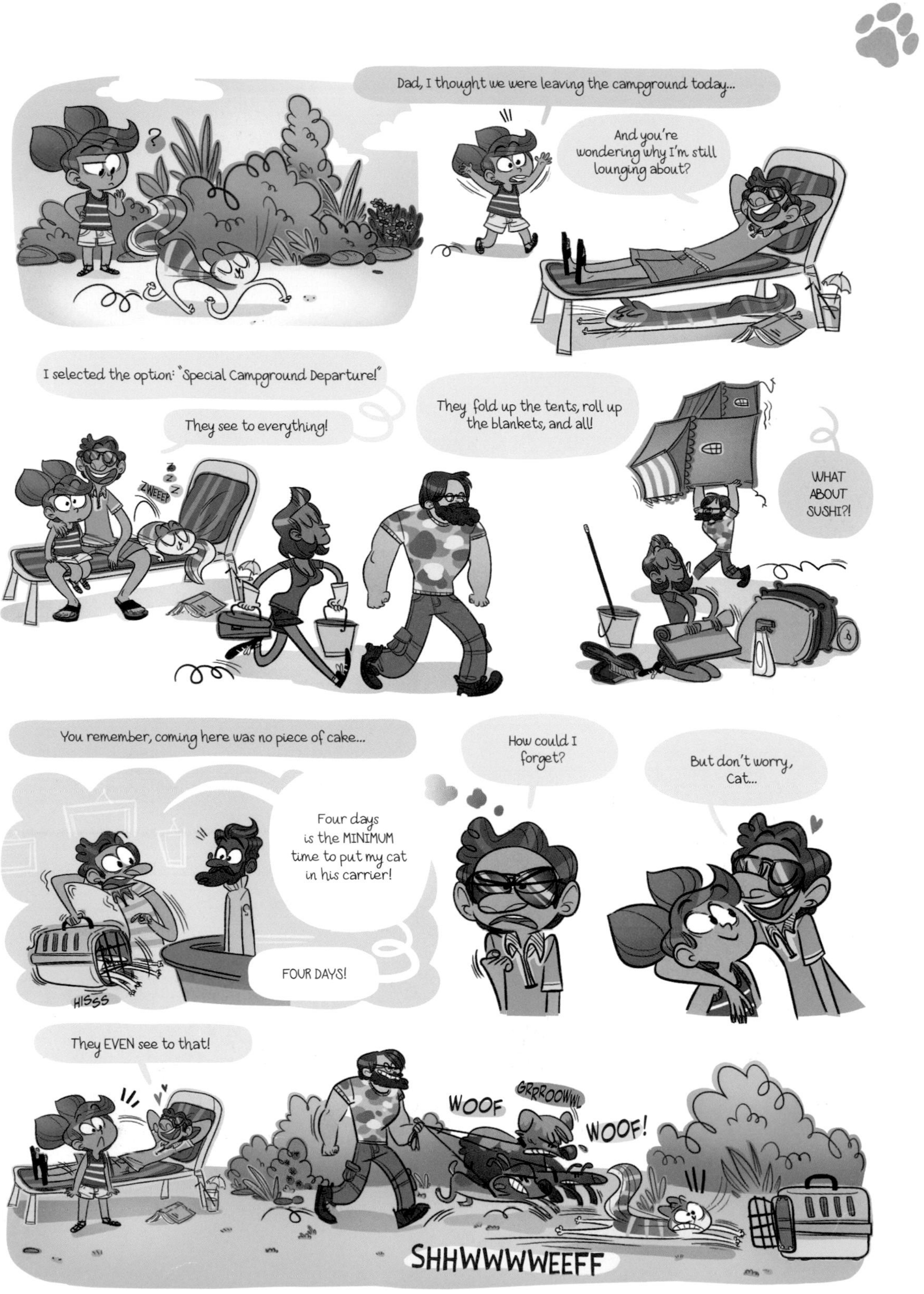

?
Dad, I thought we were leaving the campground today...
And you're wondering why I'm still lounging about?
I selected the option: "Special Campground Departure!"
They see to everything!
ZWEEEP
They fold up the tents, roll up the blankets, and all!
WHAT ABOUT SUSHI?!
You remember, coming here was no piece of cake...
Four days is the MINIMUM time to put my cat in his carrier!
FOUR DAYS!
HISSS
How could I forget?
But don't worry, Cat...
They EVEN see to that!
WOOF
GRRROOWWL
WOOF!
SHHWWWWEEFF

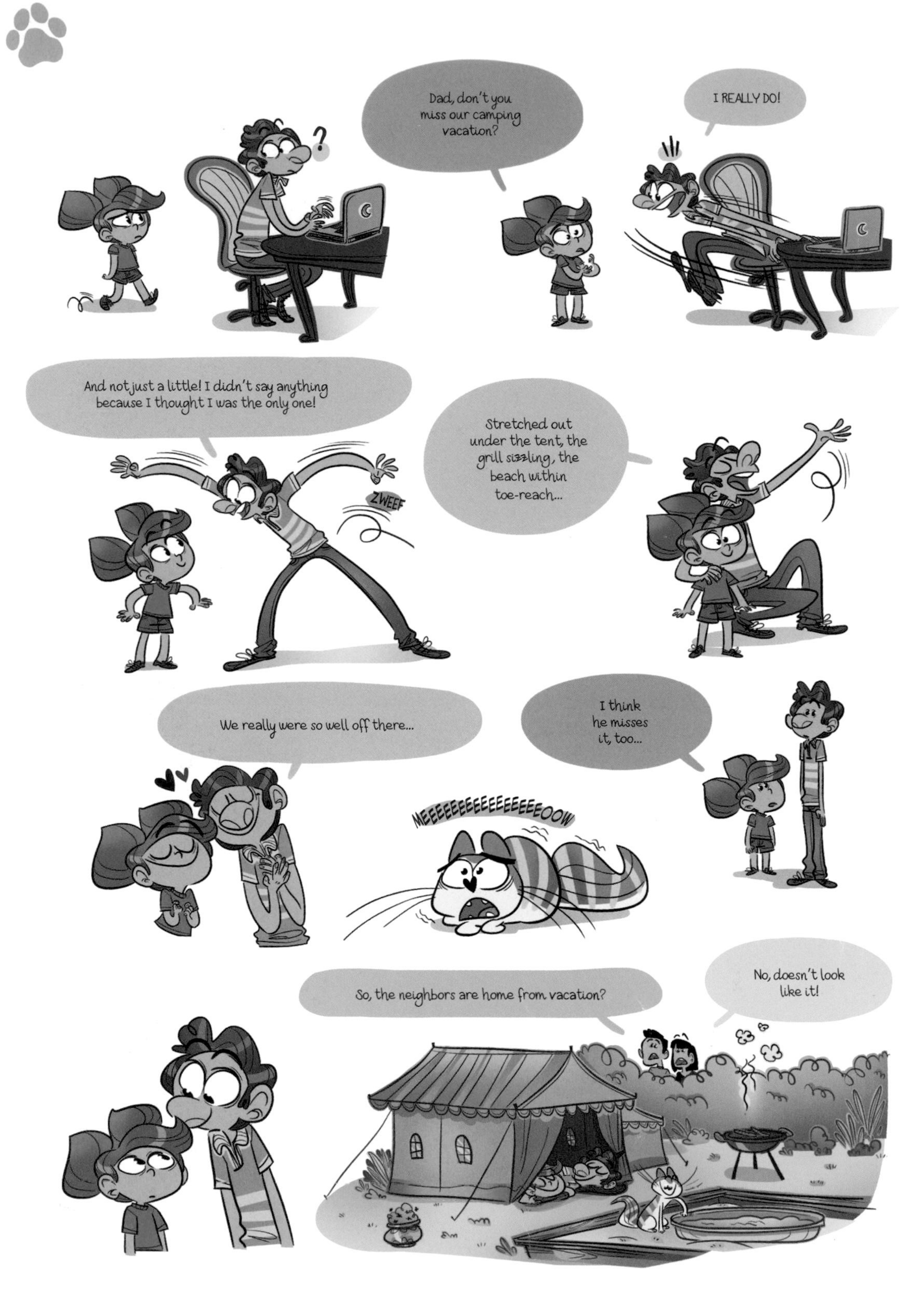
Dad, don't you miss our camping vacation?
I REALLY DO!
And not just a little! I didn't say anything because I thought I was the only one!
ZWEEF
Stretched out under the tent, the grill sizzling, the beach within toe-reach...
We really were so well off there...
I think he misses it, too...
MEEEEEEEEEEEEEEEEEOOW
So, the neighbors are home from vacation?
No, doesn't look like it!

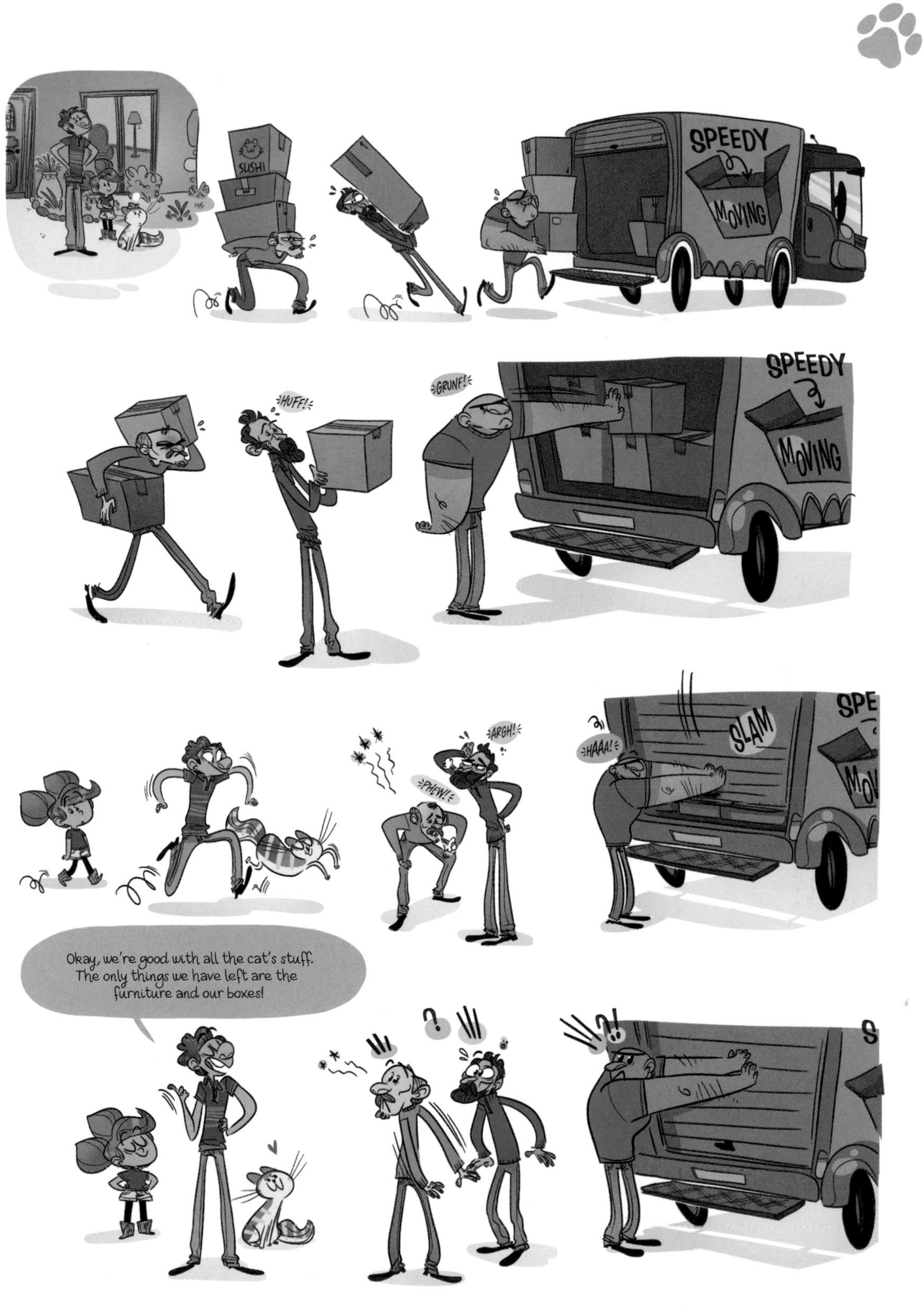
SUSHI
SPEEDY
MOVING
HUFF!
GRUNF!
SPEEDY
MOVING
ARGH!
PHEW!
HAAA!
SLAM
Okay, we're good with all the cat's stuff. The only things we have left are the furniture and our boxes!
?!

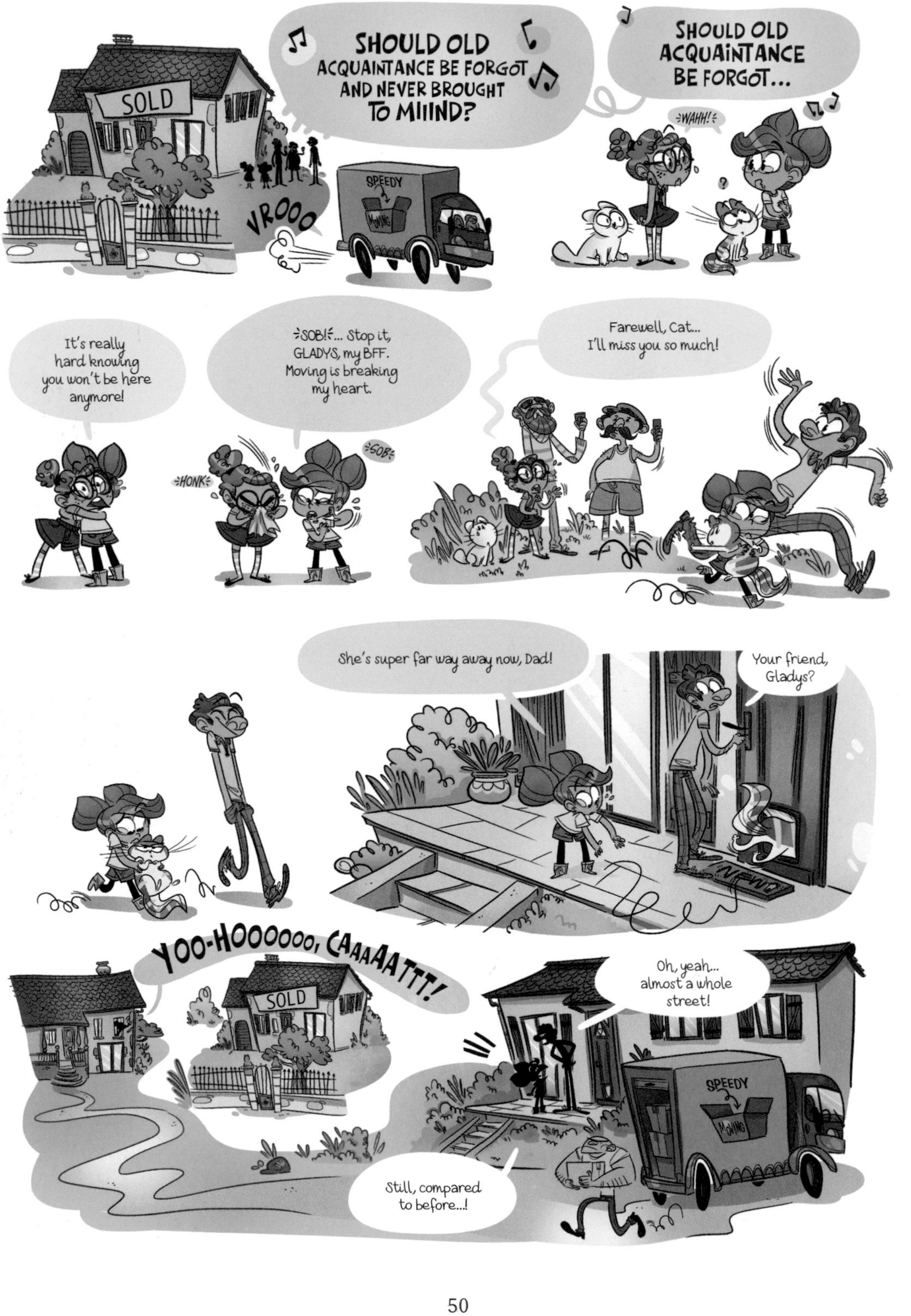
SOLD
SHOULD OLD ACQUAINTANCE BE FORGOT AND NEVER BROUGHT TO MIIIND?
SPEEDY
MOVING
VROOO
SHOULD OLD ACQUAINTANCE BE FORGOT...
WAHH!
It's really hard knowing you won't be here anymore!
SOB!... Stop it, GLADYS, my BFF. Moving is breaking my heart.
HONK
SOB
Farewell, Cat... I'll miss you so much!
She's super far way away now, Dad!
Your friend, Gladys?
NEW!
YOO-HOOOOOO, CAAAAATTT!
SOLD
Oh, yeah... almost a whole street!
SPEEDY
MOVING
Still, compared to before...!

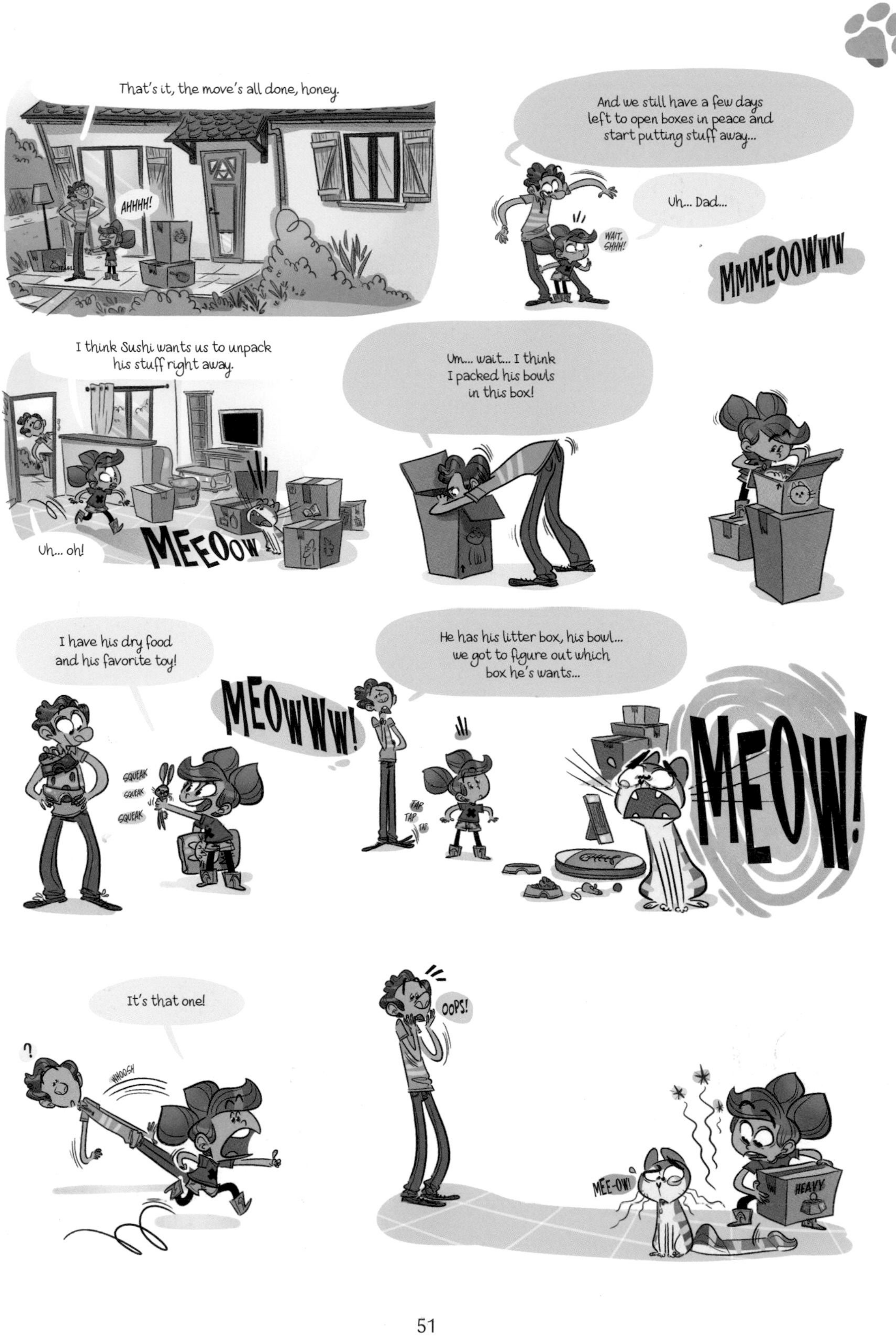
That's it, the move's all done, honey.
AHHHH!
And we still have a few days left to open boxes in peace and start putting stuff away...
WAIT, SHHH!
Uh... Dad...
MMMEOOWWW
I think Sushi wants us to unpack his stuff right away.
Uh... oh!
MEEOOW
Um... wait... I think I packed his bowls in this box!
I have his dry food and his favorite toy!
SQUEAK
SQUEAK
SQUEAK
MEOWWW!
He has his litter box, his bowl... we got to figure out which box he's wants...
TAP
TAP
TAP
MEOW!
It's that one!
?
WHOOSH
OOPS!
MEE-OW!
HEAVY

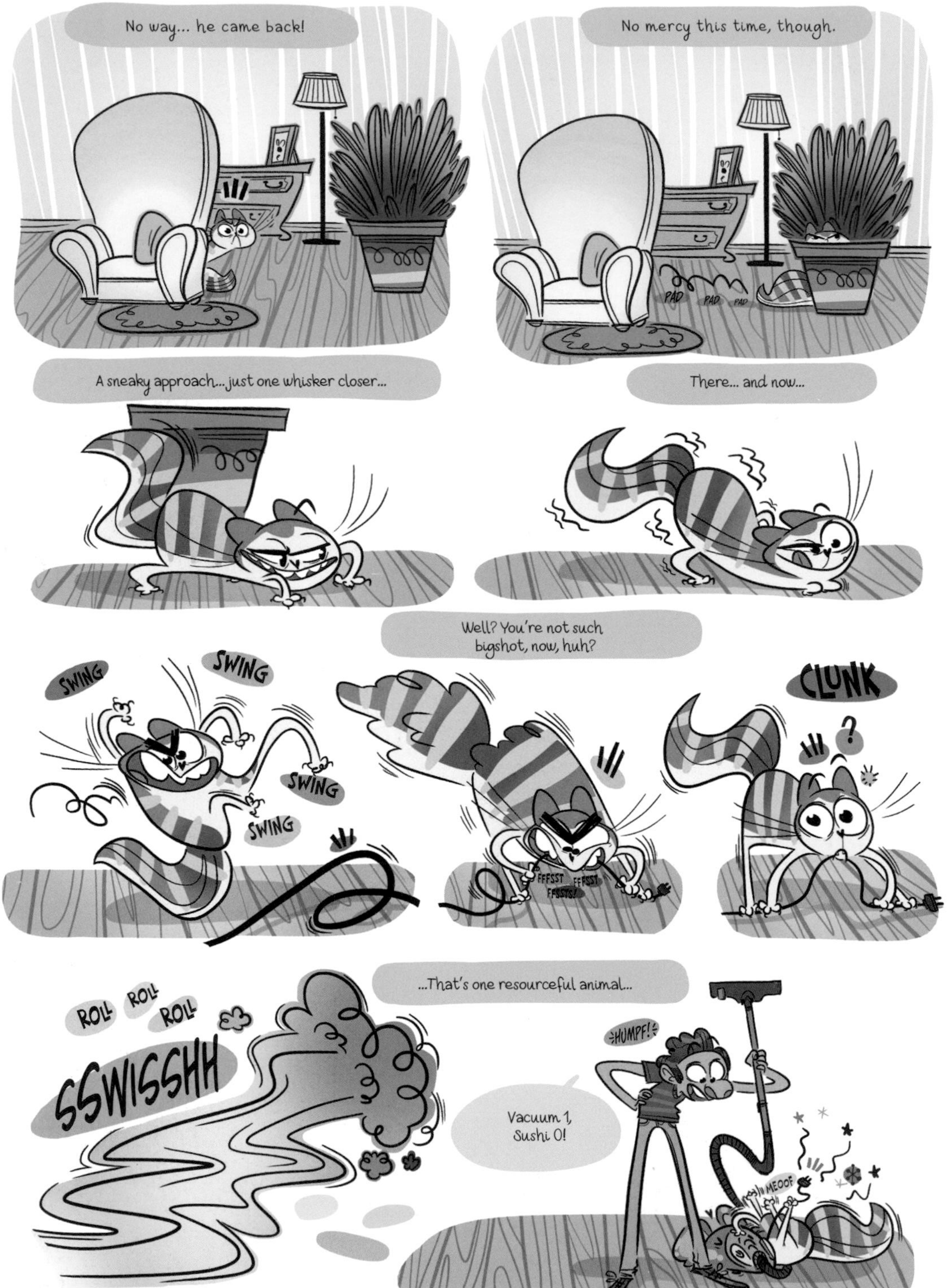
No way... he came back!
No mercy this time, though.
PAD PAD PAD
A sneaky approach... just one whisker closer...
There... and now...
Well? You're not such bigshot, now, huh?
SWING
SWING
SWING
SWING
FFFSST FFFSST
CLUNK
...That's one resourceful animal...
ROLL ROLL ROLL
SSWISSHH
HUMPF!
Vacuum 1, Sushi 0!
MEOOF

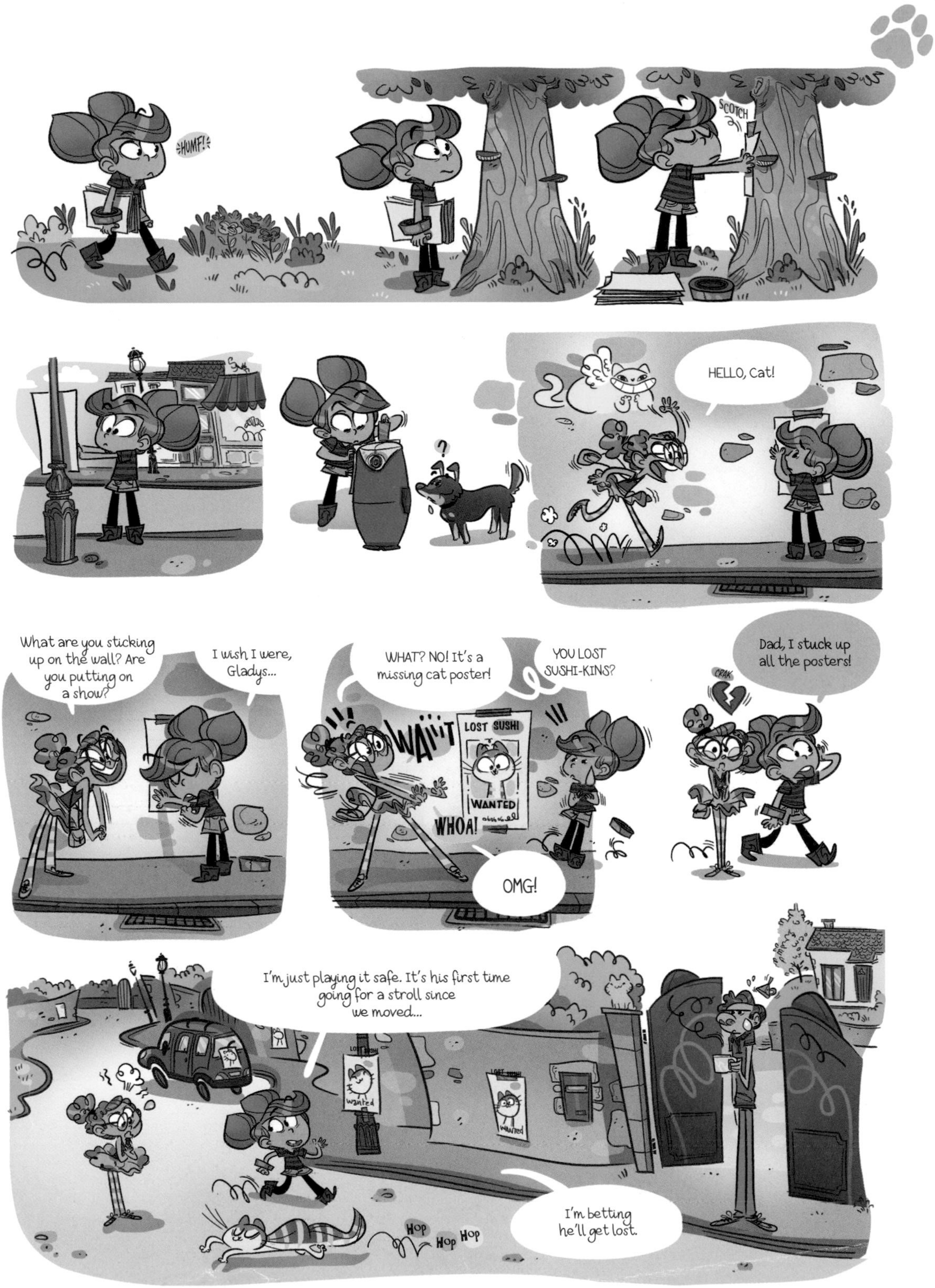
HUMF!
SCOTCH
HELLO, Cat!
What are you sticking up on the wall? Are you putting on a show?
I wish I were, Gladys...
WHAT? NO! It's a missing cat poster!
YOU LOST SUSHI-KINS?
WAIT
LOST SUSHI
WANTED
WHOA!
OMG!
CRAK
Dad, I stuck up all the posters!
I'm just playing it safe. It's his first time going for a stroll since we moved...
I'm betting he'll get lost.
HOP
HOP
HOP

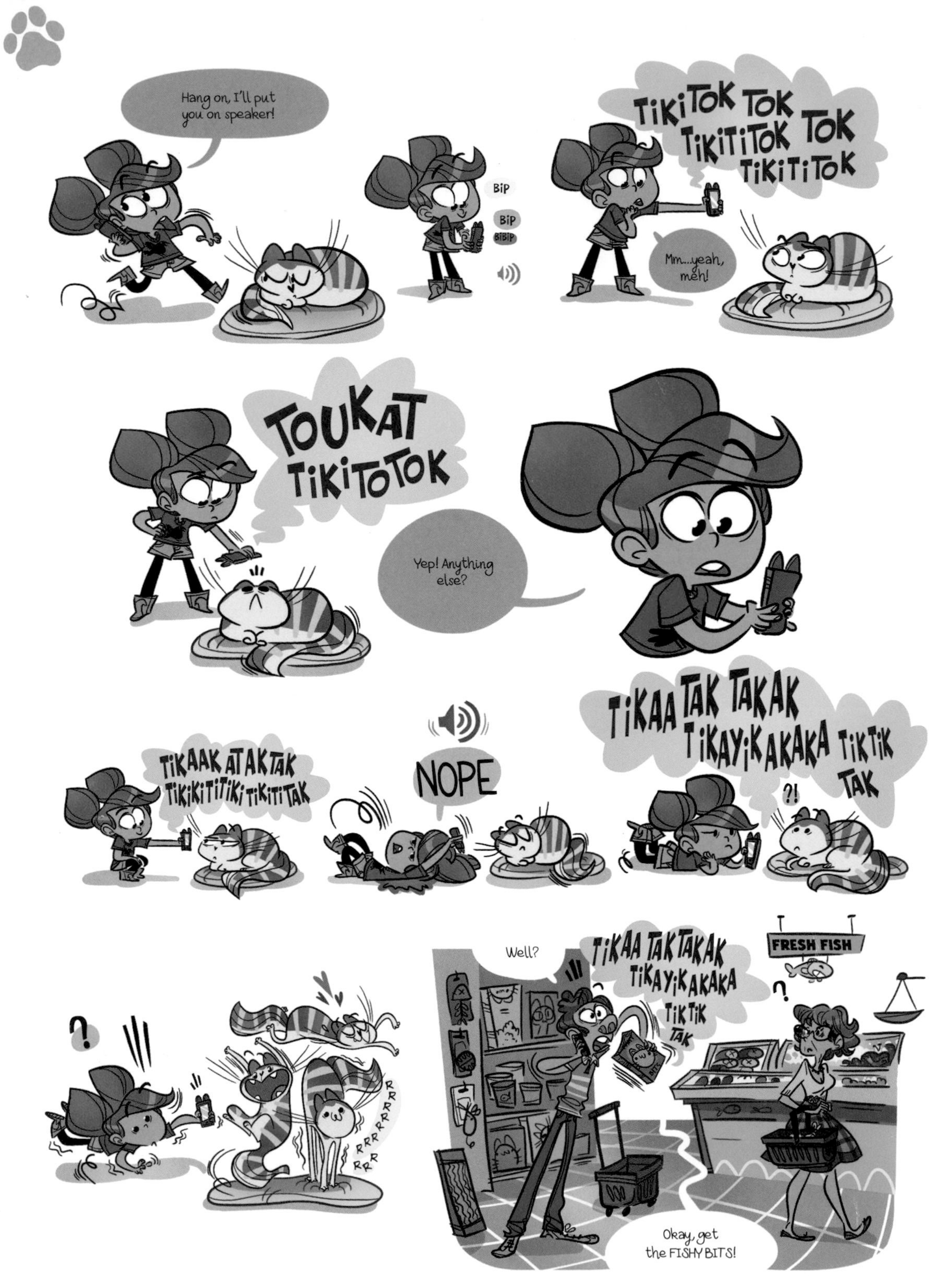
Hang on, I'll put you on speaker!
BiP
BiP
BiBiP
TiKiTOK TOK TiKiTiTOK TOK TiKiTiTOK
Mm...yeah, meh!
TOUKAT TiKiTOTOK
Yep! Anything else?
TiKAAK ATAKTAK TiKiKiTiTiKi TiKiTiTAK
NOPE
TiKAA TAK TAKAK TiKAYiKAKAKA TiKTiK TAK
?!
?
RRRRR
RRRR
RRR
Well?
TiKAA TAKTAKAK TiKAYiKAKAKA TiKTiK TAK
FRESH FISH
?
Okay, get the FISHY BITS!

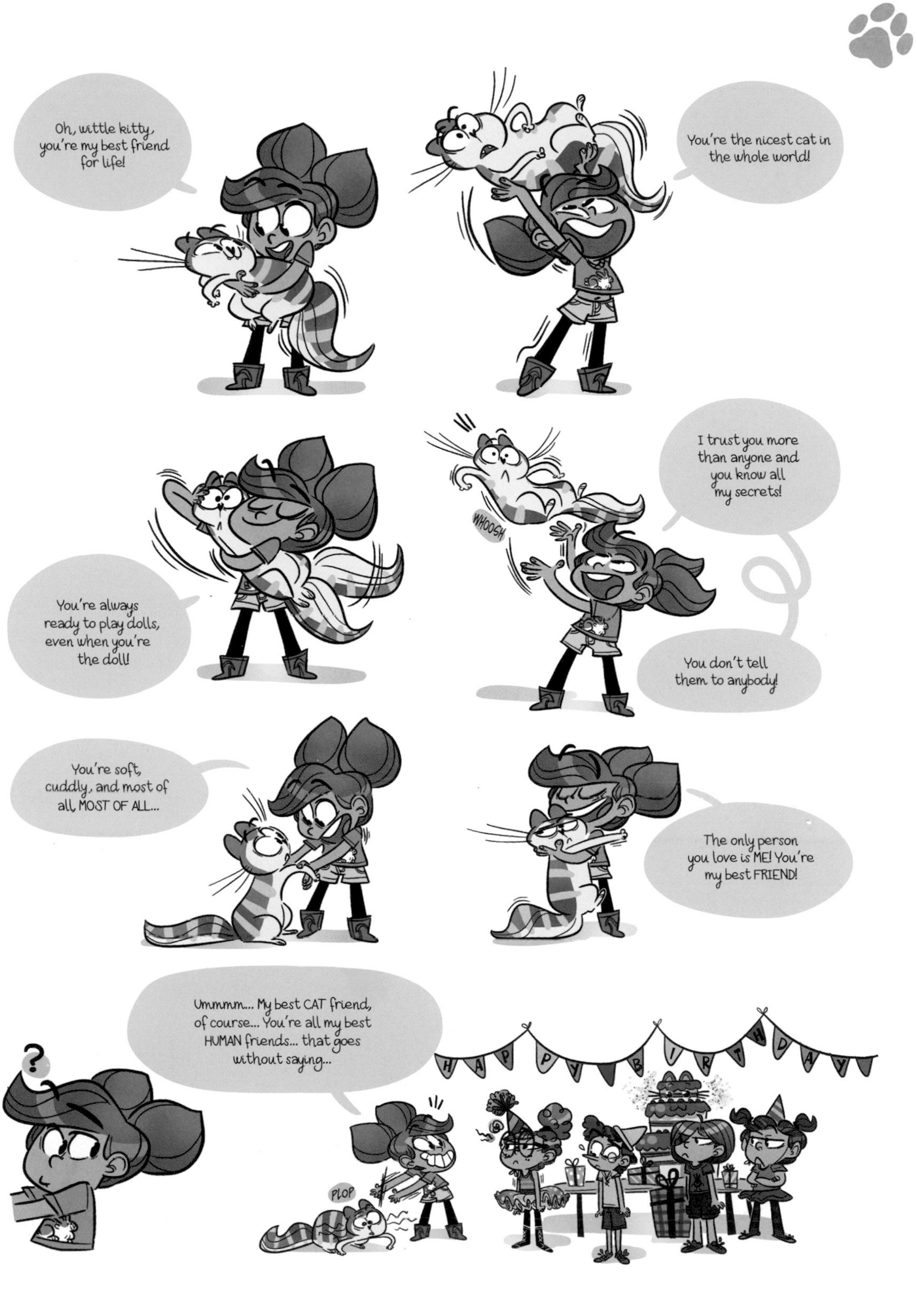
Oh, wittle kitty, you're my best friend for life!
You're the nicest cat in the whole world!
You're always ready to play dolls, even when you're the doll!
I trust you more than anyone and you know all my secrets!
WHOOSH
You don't tell them to anybody!
You're soft, cuddly, and most of all, MOST OF ALL...
The only person you love is ME! You're my best FRIEND!
?
Ummmm... My best CAT friend, of course... You're all my best HUMAN friends... that goes without saying...
HAPPY BIRTHDAY
PLOP

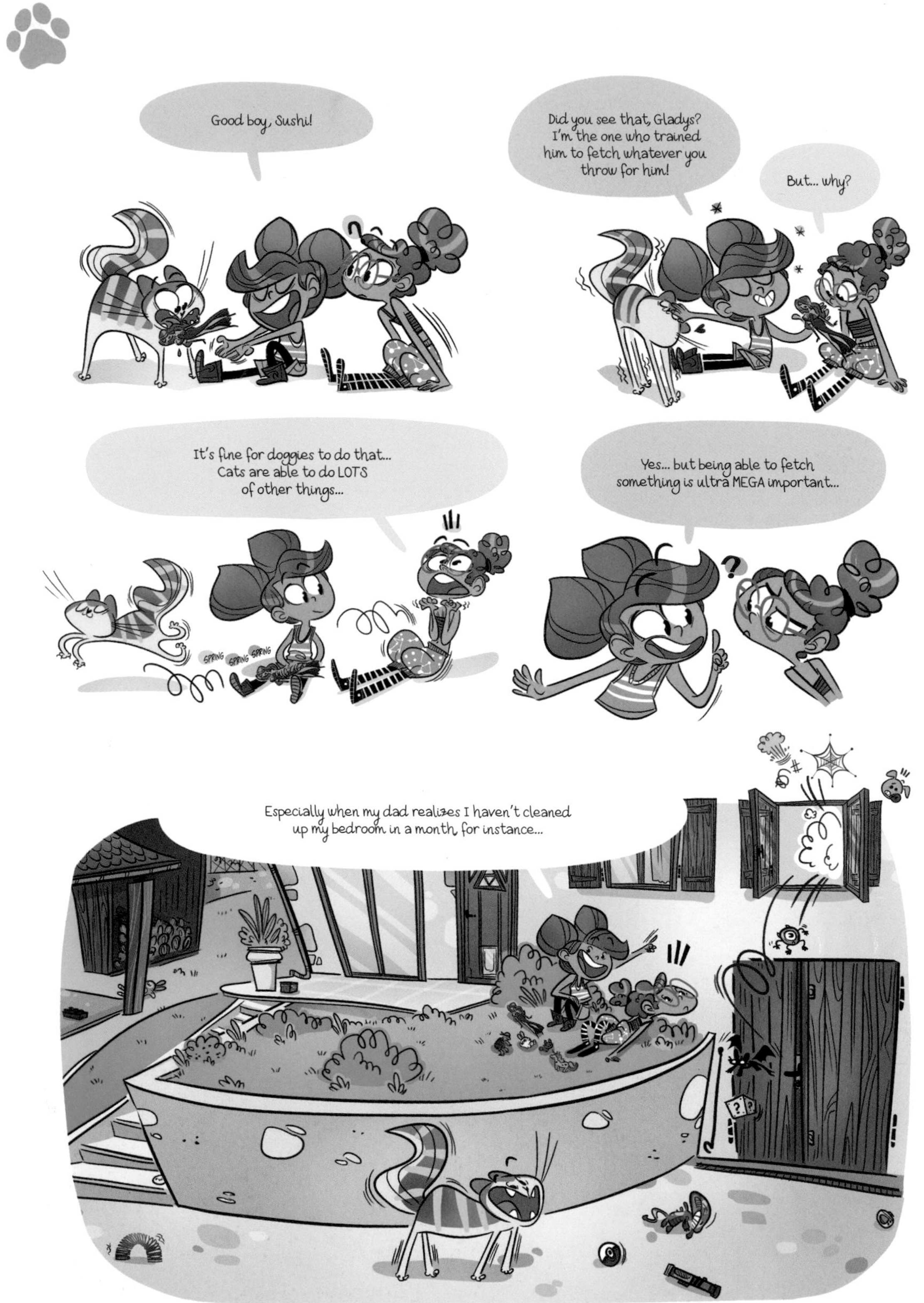
Good boy, Sushi!
Did you see that, Gladys? I'm the one who trained him to fetch whatever you throw for him!
But... why?
It's fine for doggies to do that... Cats are able to do LOTS of other things...
SPRING SPRING SPRING
Yes... but being able to fetch something is ultra MEGA important...
Especially when my dad realizes I haven't cleaned up my bedroom in a month, for instance...

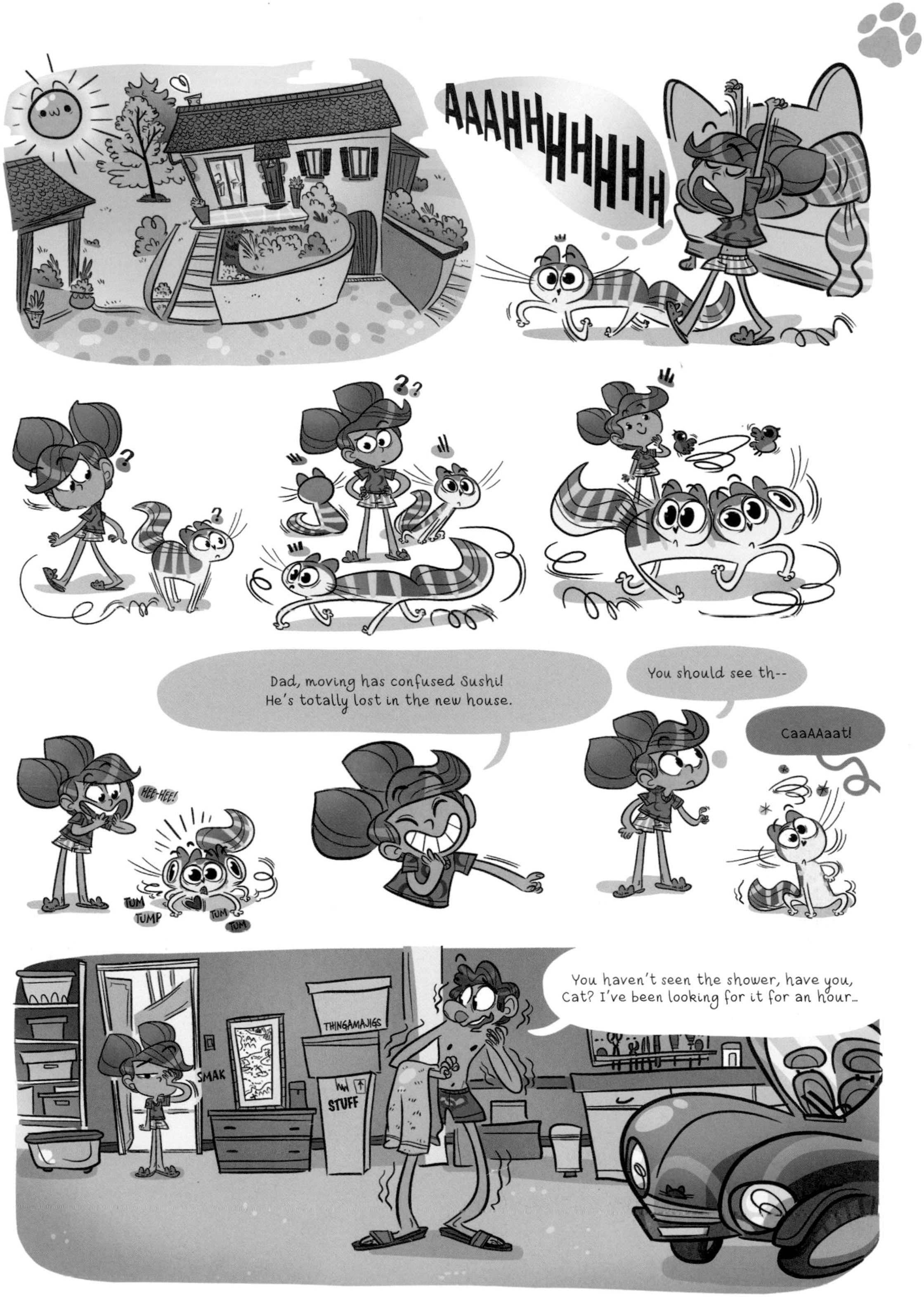
AAAHHHHHHH
HEE-HEE!
TUM
TUMP
TUM
TUM
Dad, moving has confused Sushi! He's totally lost in the new house.
You should see th--
CaaAAaat!
THINGAMAJIGS
SMAK
STUFF
You haven't seen the shower, have you, Cat? I've been looking for it for an hour...

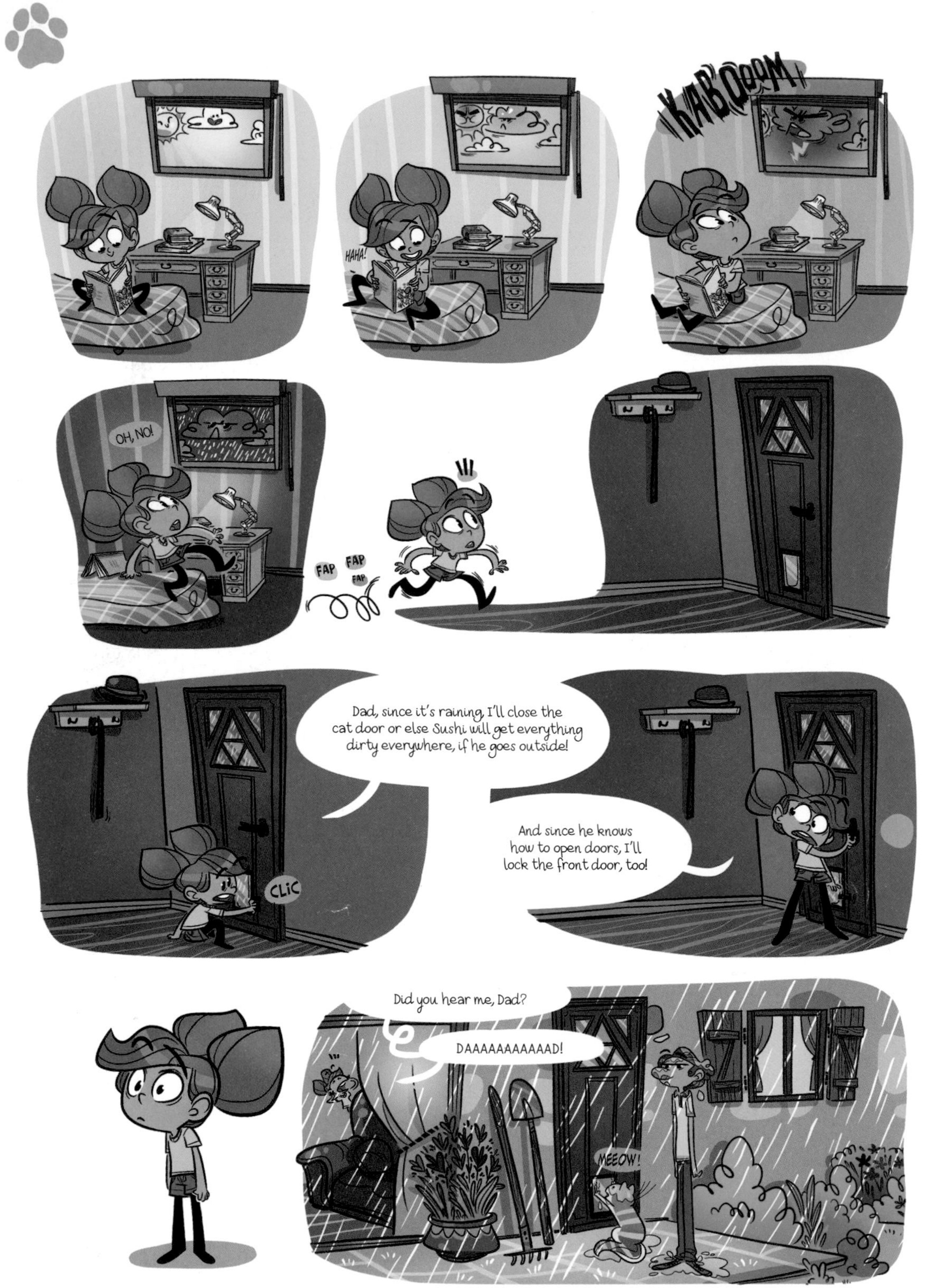
KABOOOM
HAHA!
OH, NO!
FAP FAP FAP
Dad, since it's raining, I'll close the cat door or else Sushi will get everything dirty everywhere, if he goes outside!
CLIC
And since he knows how to open doors, I'll lock the front door, too!
Did you hear me, Dad?
DAAAAAAAAAAAD!
MEEOW!

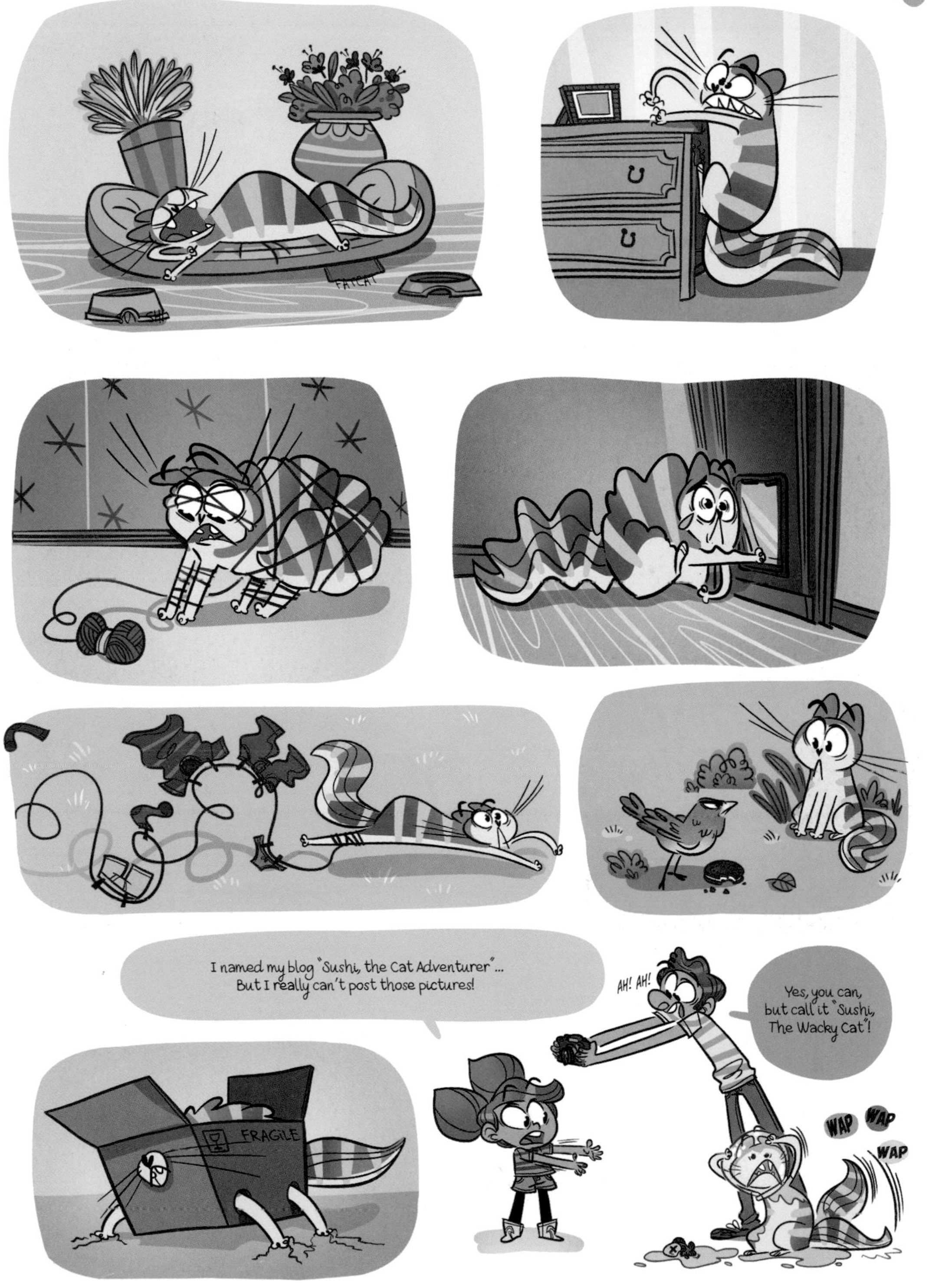
FRAGILE
I named my blog "Sushi, the Cat Adventurer"...
But I really can't post those pictures!
AH! AH!
Yes, you can, but call it "Sushi, The Wacky Cat"!
WAP
WAP
WAP

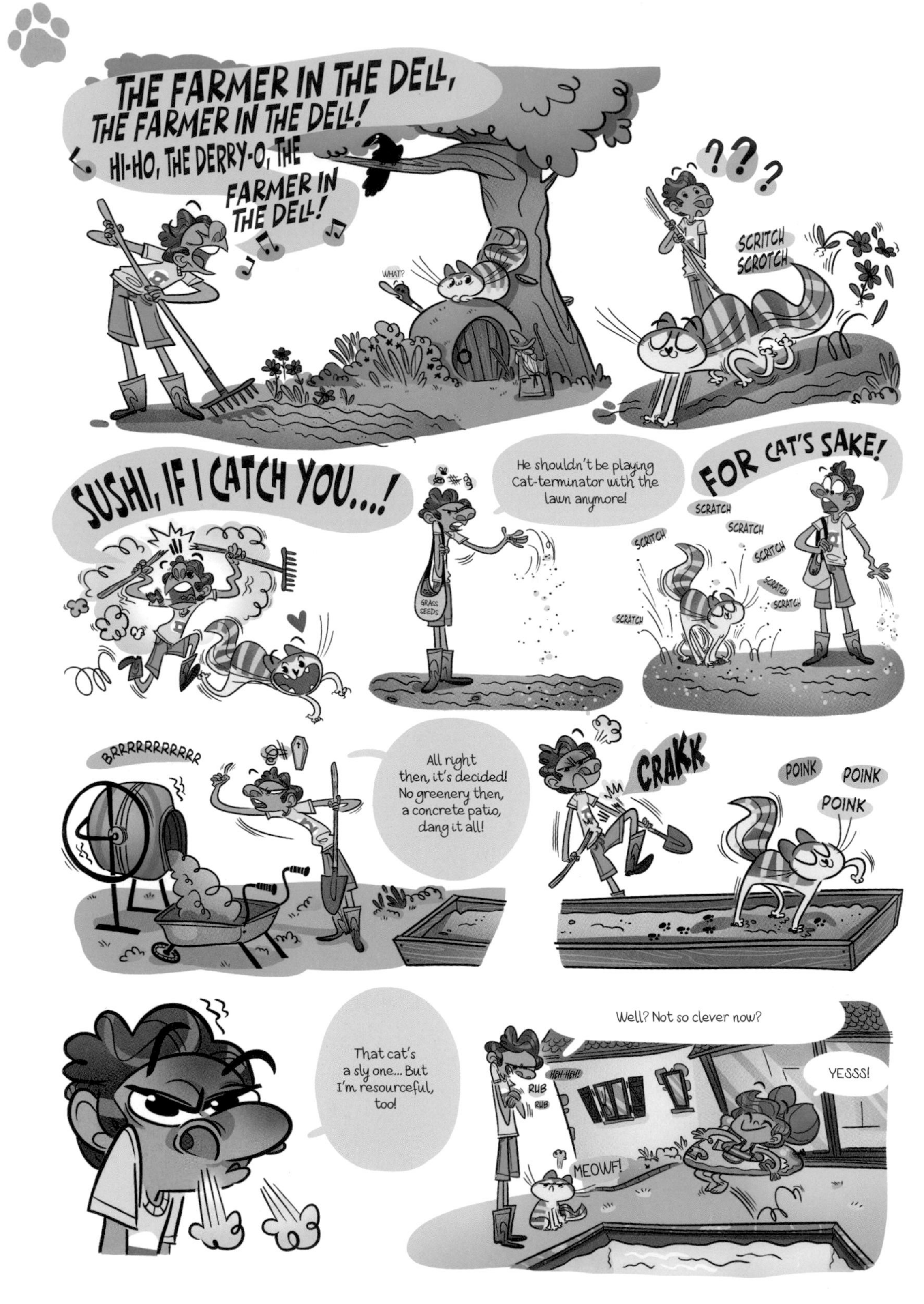
THE FARMER IN THE DELL, THE FARMER IN THE DELL! HI-HO, THE DERRY-O, THE FARMER IN THE DELL!
WHAT?
???
SCRITCH SCROTCH
SUSHI, IF I CATCH YOU...!
He shouldn't be playing Cat-terminator with the lawn anymore!
GRASS SEEDS
FOR CAT'S SAKE!
SCRATCH
SCRATCH
SCRATCH
SCRITCH
SCRATCH
SCRATCH
SCRATCH
BRRRRRRRRRRR
All right then, it's decided! No greenery then, a concrete patio, dang it all!
CRAKK
POINK
POINK
POINK
That cat's a sly one... But I'm resourceful, too!
Well? Not so clever now?
HEH-HEH!
RUB
RUB
YESSS!
MEOWF!

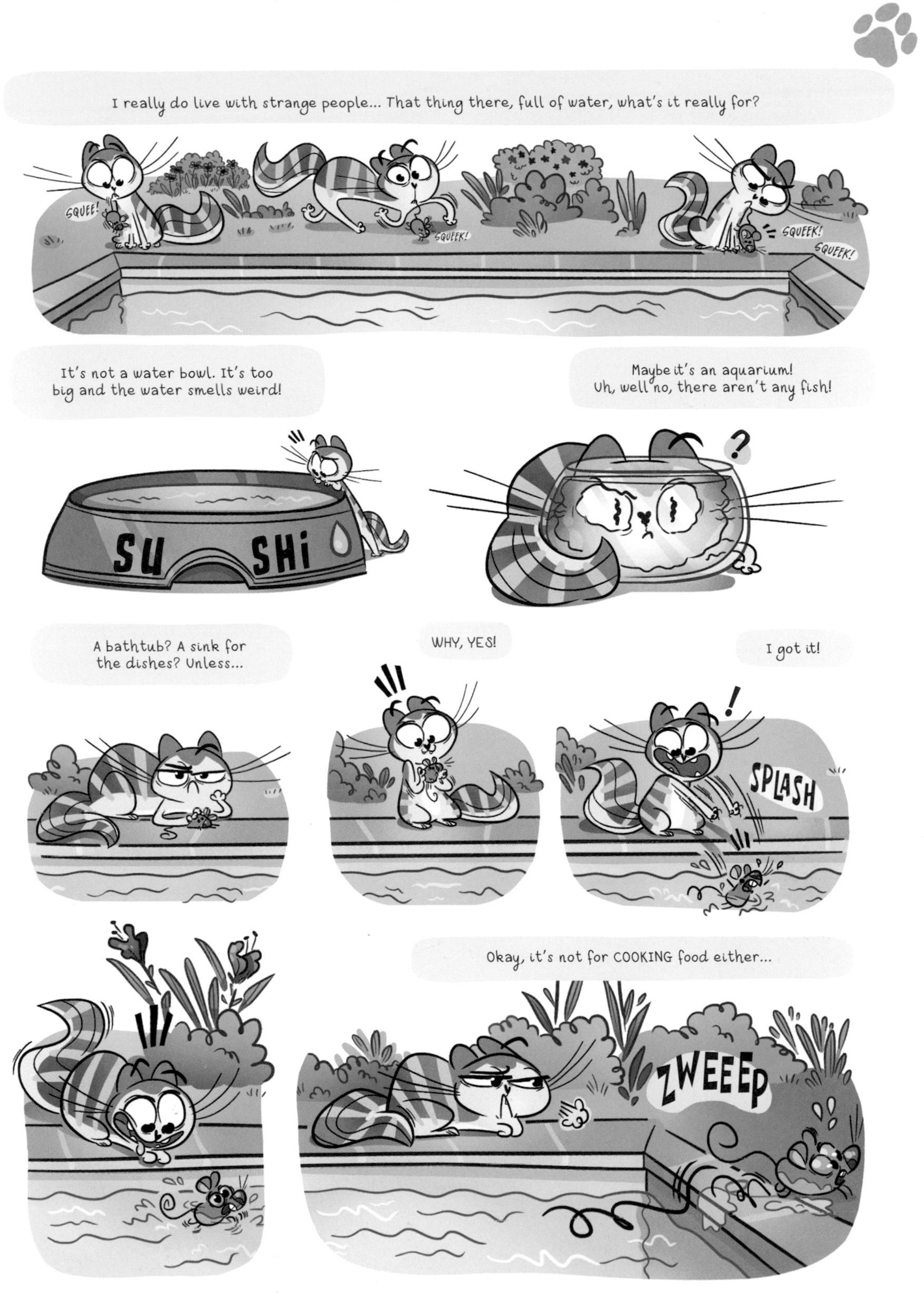
I really do live with strange people... That thing there, full of water, what's it really for?
SQUEE!
SQUEEK!
SQUEEK!
SQUEEK!
It's not a water bowl. It's too big and the water smells weird!
SU SHi
Maybe it's an aquarium! Uh, well no, there aren't any fish!
A bathtub? A sink for the dishes? Unless...
WHY, YES!
I got it!
SPLASH
Okay, it's not for COOKING food either...
ZWEEEP

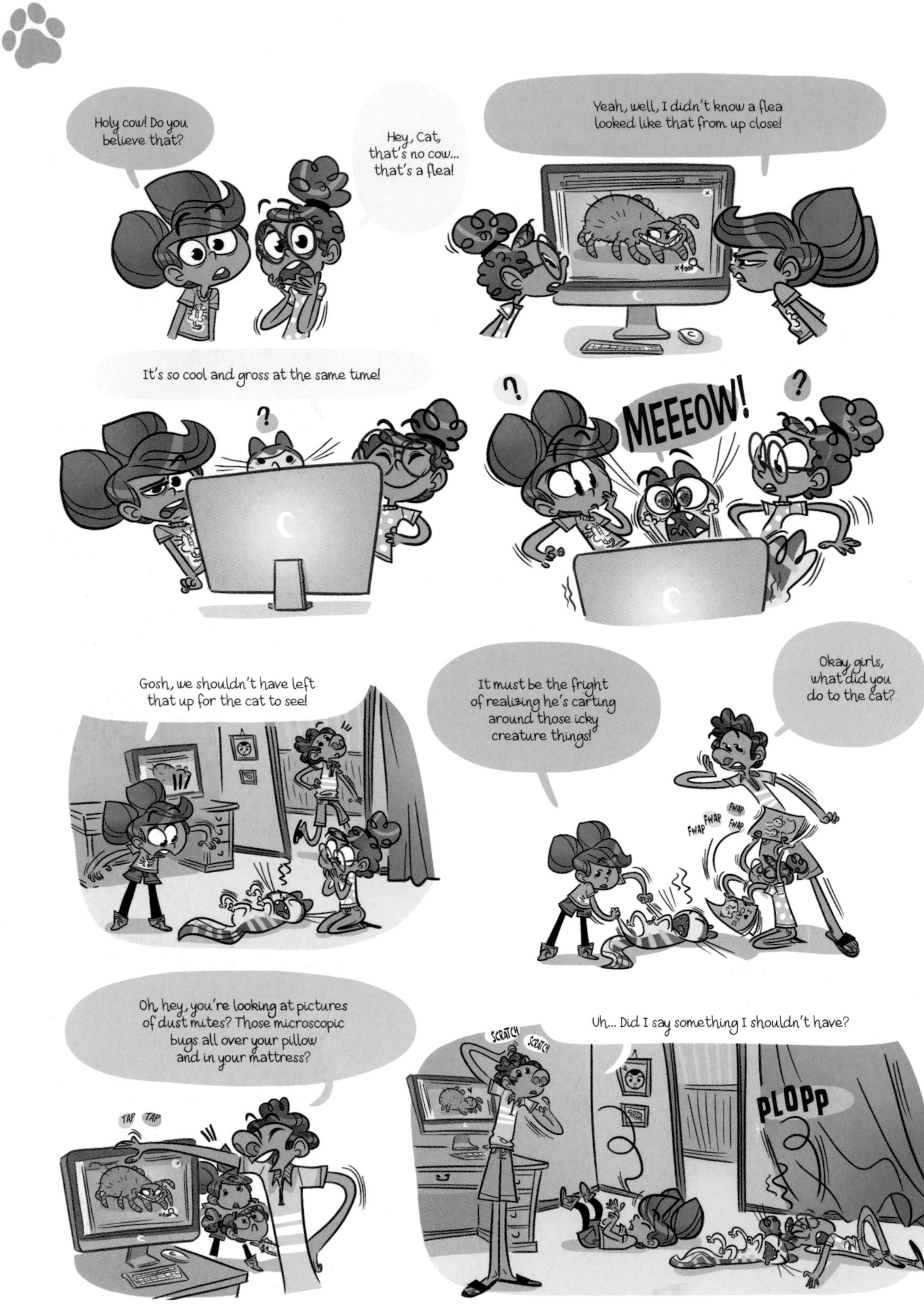
Holy cow! Do you believe that?
Hey, Cat, that's no cow... that's a flea!
Yeah, well, I didn't know a flea looked like that from up close!
It's so cool and gross at the same time!
?
?
?
MEEEOW!
Gosh, we shouldn't have left that up for the cat to see!
It must be the fright of realizing he's carting around those icky creature things!
Okay, girls, what did you do to the cat?
FWAP FWAP FWAP FWAP
Oh, hey, you're looking at pictures of dust mites? Those microscopic bugs all over your pillow and in your mattress?
TAP TAP
Uh... Did I say something I shouldn't have?
SCRATCH SCRATCH
PLOPP

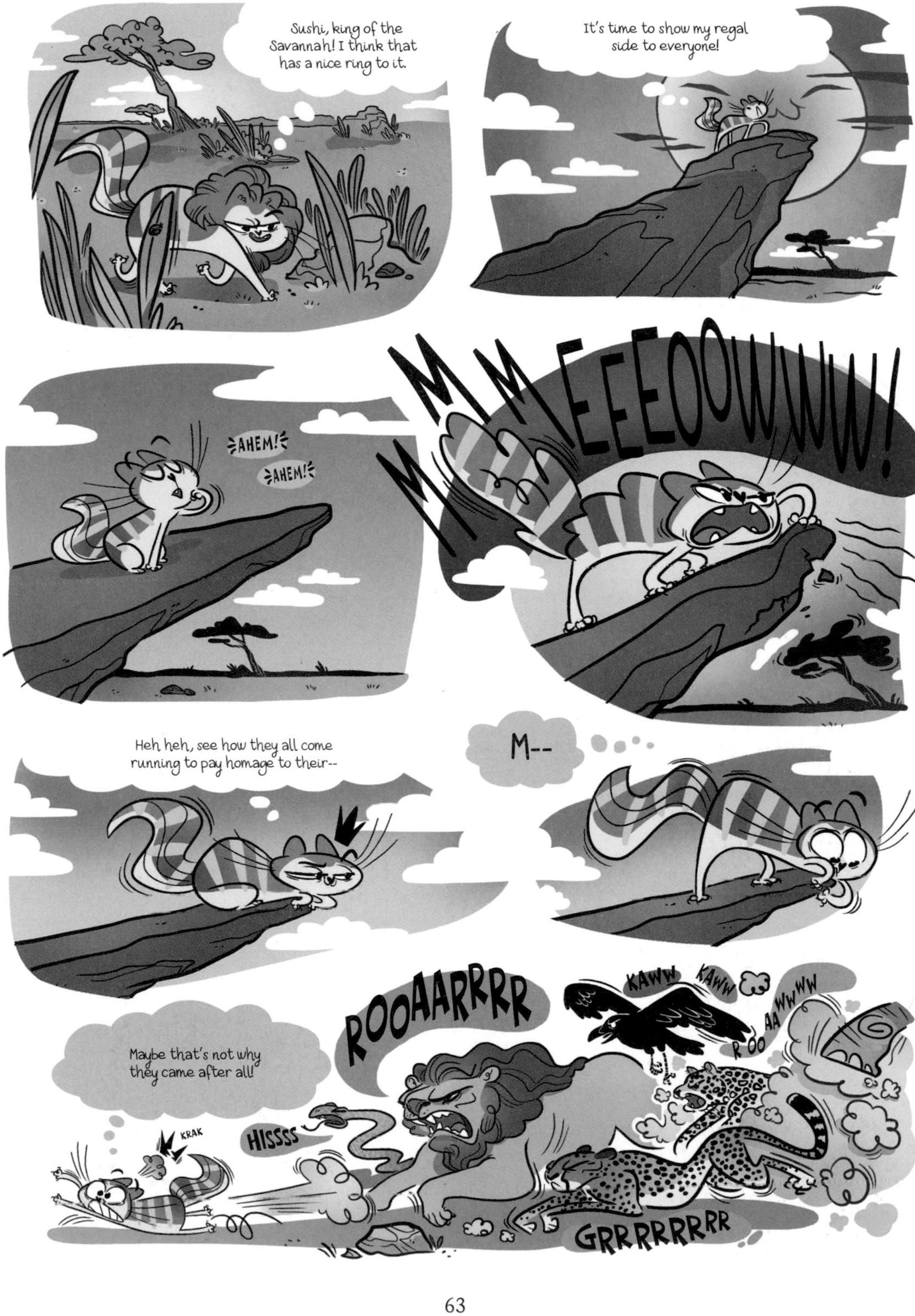
Sushi, king of the Savannah! I think that has a nice ring to it.
It's time to show my regal side to everyone!
AHEM!
AHEM!
MMMEEEOOWWWW!
Heh heh, see how they all come running to pay homage to their--
M--
Maybe that's not why they came after all!
ROOAARRRR
KAWW
KAWW
ROOAAWWWW
HISSSS
KRAK
GRRRRRRRR

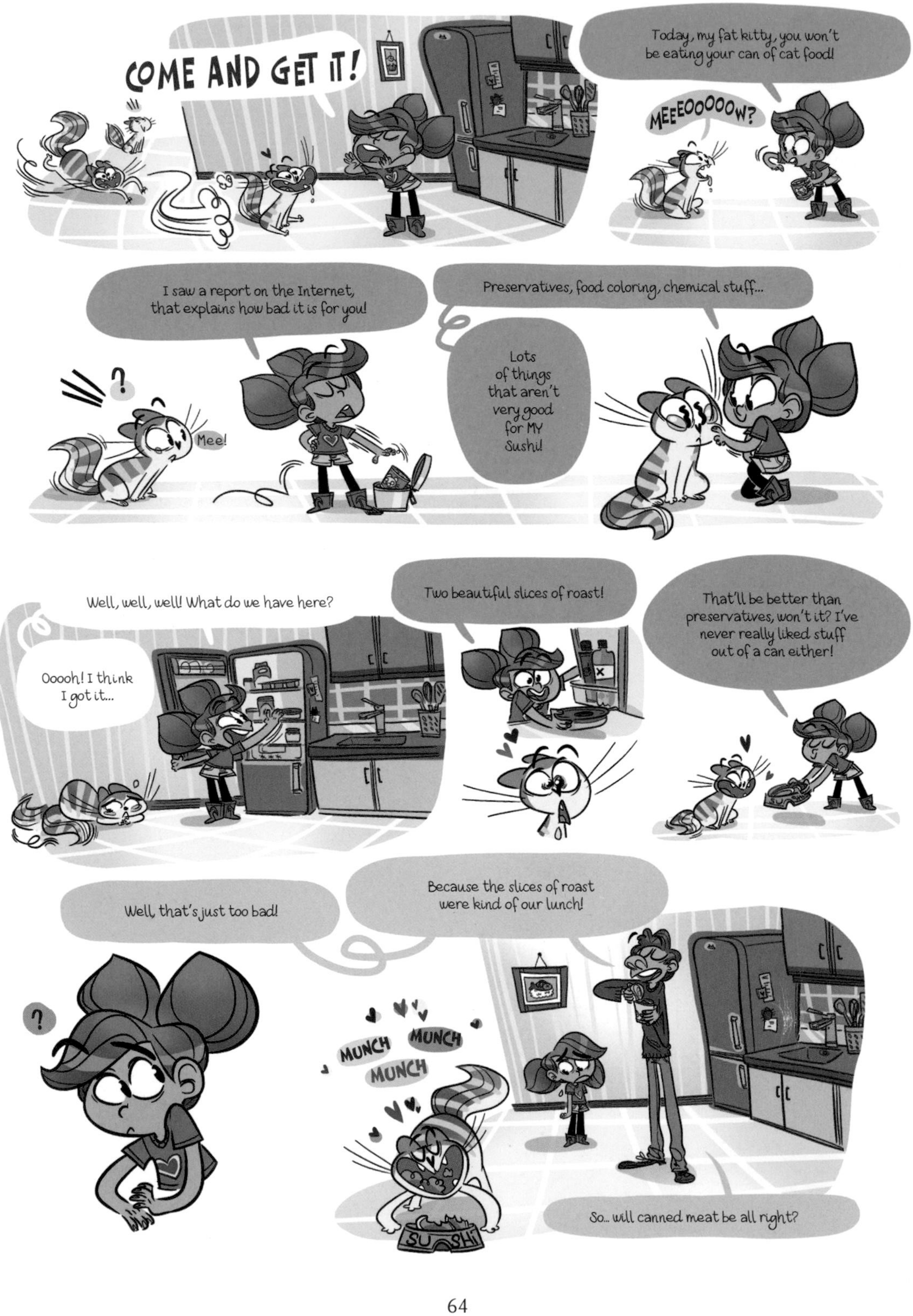
COME AND GET IT!
Today, my fat kitty, you won't be eating your can of cat food!
MEEEOOOOOW?
I saw a report on the Internet, that explains how bad it is for you!
Mee!
Preservatives, food coloring, chemical stuff...
Lots of things that aren't very good for MY Sushi!
Well, well, well! What do we have here?
Ooooh! I think I got it...
Two beautiful slices of roast!
That'll be better than preservatives, won't it? I've never really liked stuff out of a can either!
Well, that's just too bad!
Because the slices of roast were kind of our lunch!
MUNCH MUNCH MUNCH
SUSHI
So... will canned meat be all right?

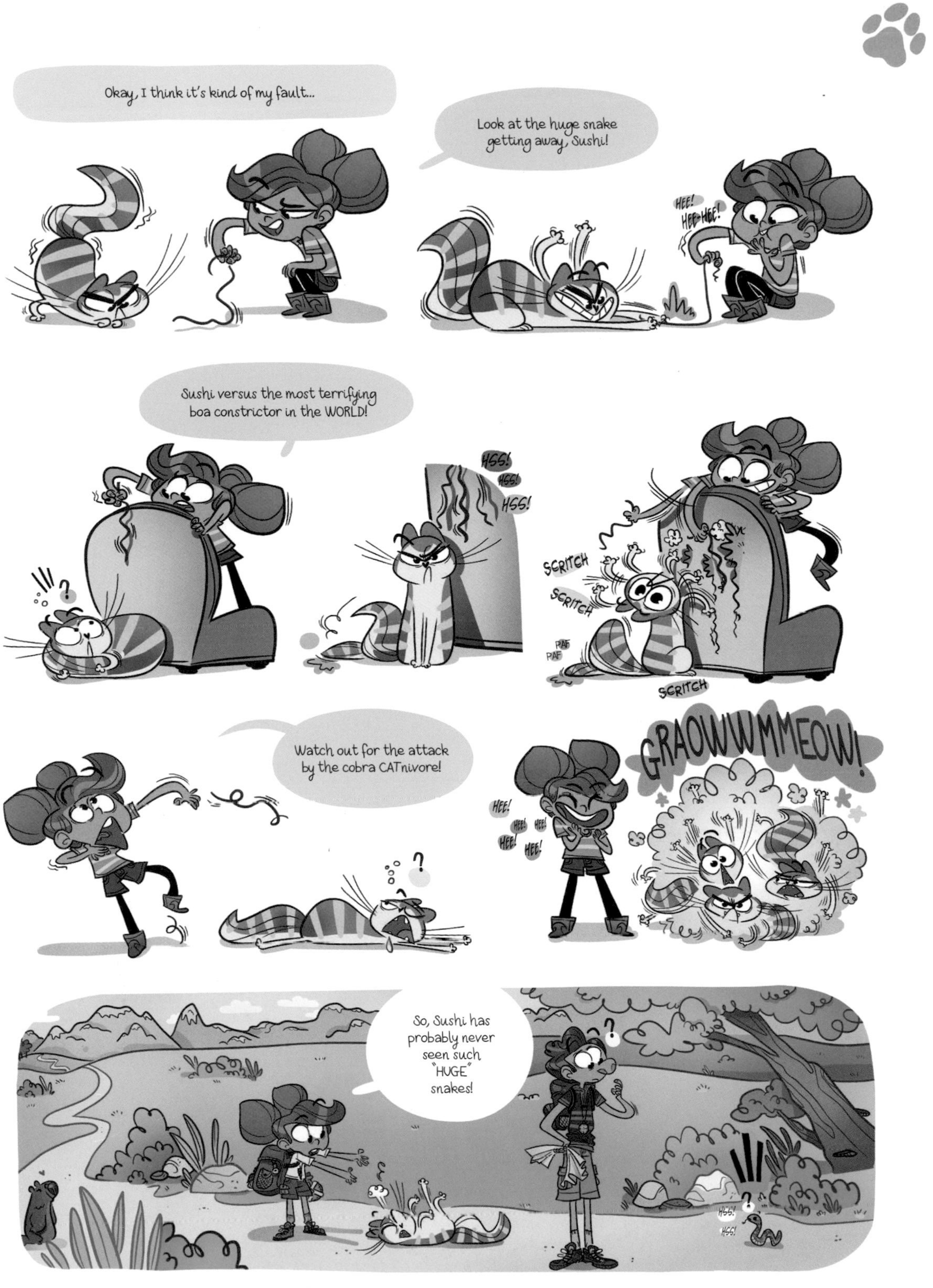
Okay, I think it's kind of my fault...
Look at the huge snake getting away, Sushi!
HEE! HEE-HEE!
Sushi versus the most terrifying boa constrictor in the WORLD!
HSS! HSS! HSS!
SCRITCH
SCRITCH
PAF PAF
SCRITCH
Watch out for the attack by the cobra CATnivore!
GRAOWWMMEOW!
HEE! HEE! HEE! HEE! HEE!
So, Sushi has probably never seen such "HUGE" snakes!
HSS! HSS!

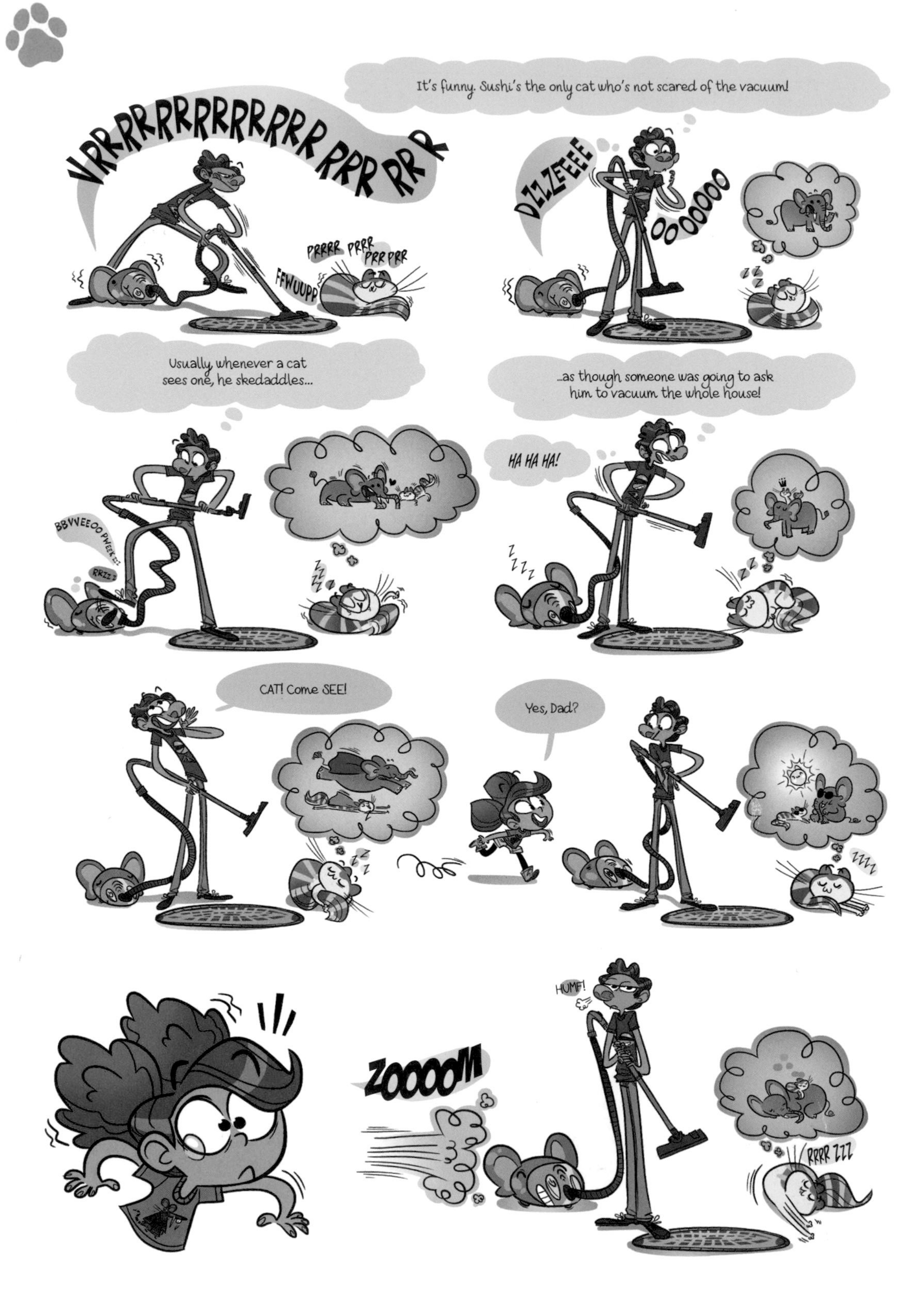

It's funny. Sushi's the only cat who's not scared of the vacuum!
VRRRRRRRRRRRRRR RRR RR R
PRRRR PRRR PRR PRR
FFWUUPP
DZZZEEEE
OOOOOOO
Usually, whenever a cat sees one, he skedaddles...
...as though someone was going to ask him to vacuum the whole house!
BBVVEEOO PWEEK
RRZZ
HA HA HA!
CAT! Come SEE!
Yes, Dad?
ZOOOOM
HUMF!
RRRR ZZZ

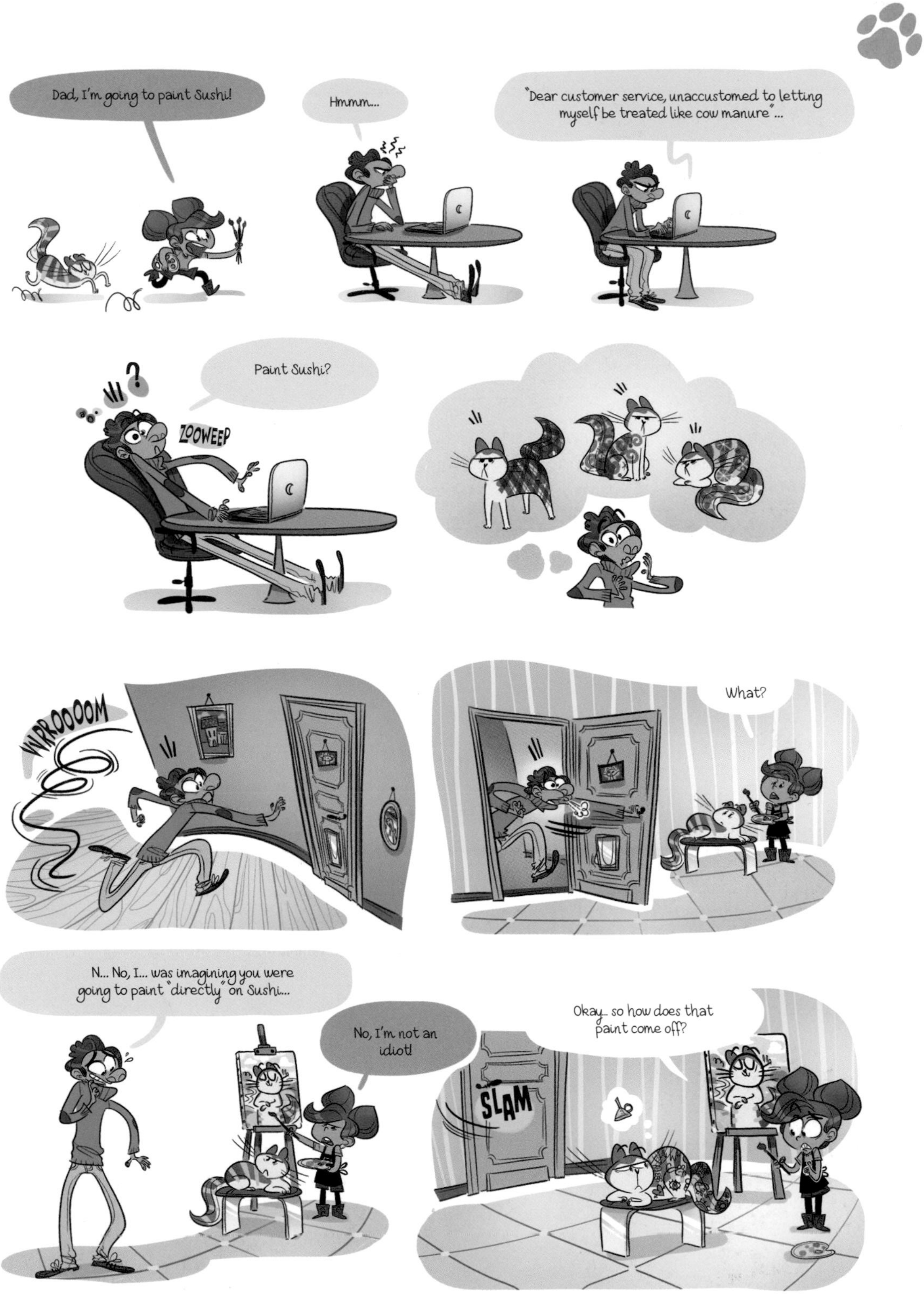
Dad, I'm going to paint Sushi!
Hmmm...
"Dear customer service, unaccustomed to letting myself be treated like cow manure"...
Paint Sushi?
ZOOWEEP
WRROOOOM
What?
N... No, I... was imagining you were going to paint "directly" on Sushi...
No, I'm not an idiot!
SLAM
Okay... so how does that paint come off?

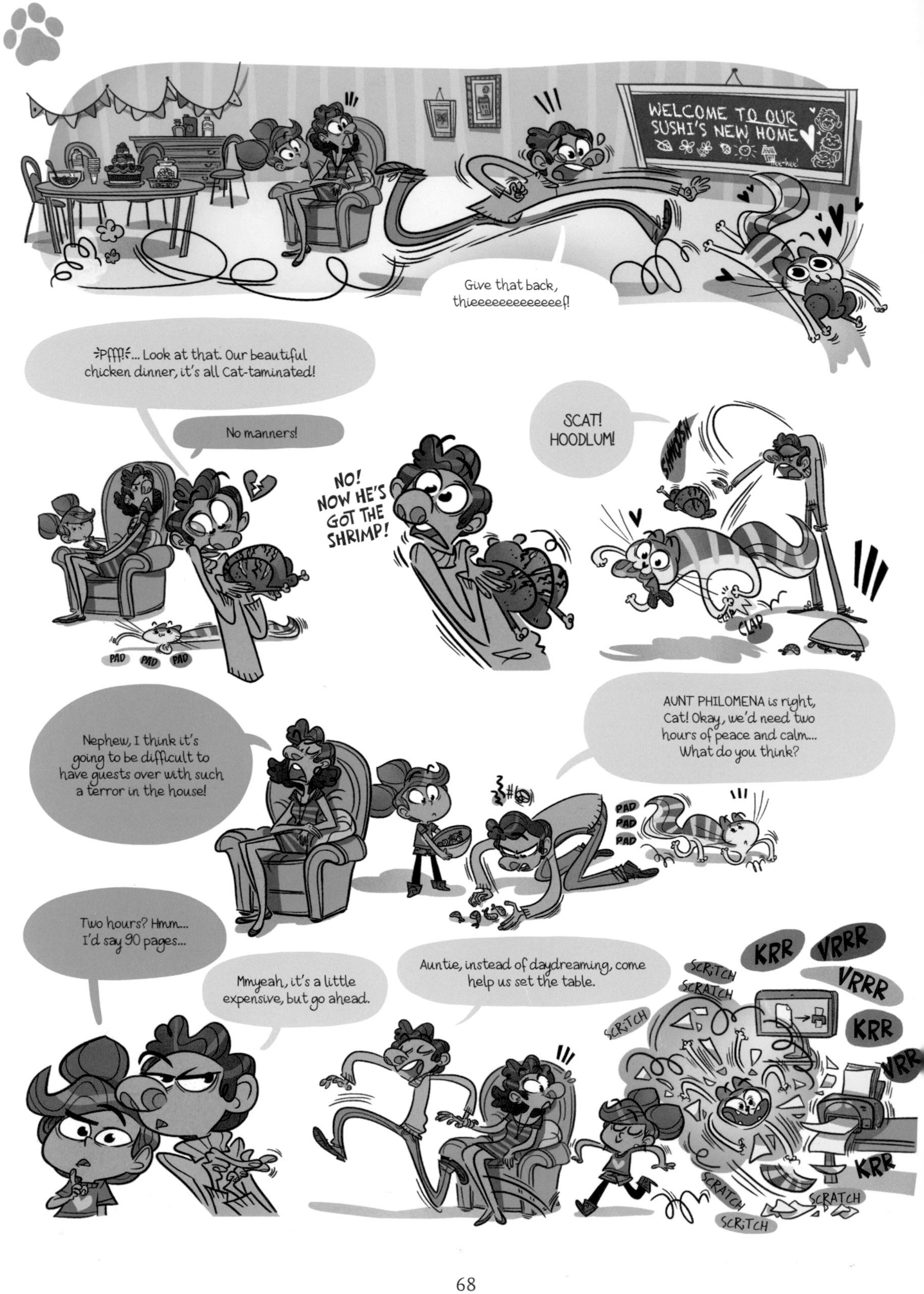
WELCOME TO OUR SUSHI'S NEW HOME
Give that back, thieeeeeeeeeeeeef!
Pfff!... Look at that. Our beautiful chicken dinner, it's all Cat-taminated!
No manners!
PAD PAD PAD
NO! NOW HE'S GOT THE SHRIMP!
SCAT! HOODLUM!
SWOOSH
CLAP
CLAP
Nephew, I think it's going to be difficult to have guests over with such a terror in the house!
AUNT PHILOMENA is right, Cat! Okay, we'd need two hours of peace and calm... What do you think?
PAD PAD PAD
Two hours? Hmm... I'd say 90 pages...
Mmyeah, it's a little expensive, but go ahead.
Auntie, instead of daydreaming, come help us set the table.
SCRITCH
SCRATCH
SCRITCH
KRR
VRRR
VRRR
KRR
VRR
KRR
SCRATCH
SCRITCH
SCRATCH

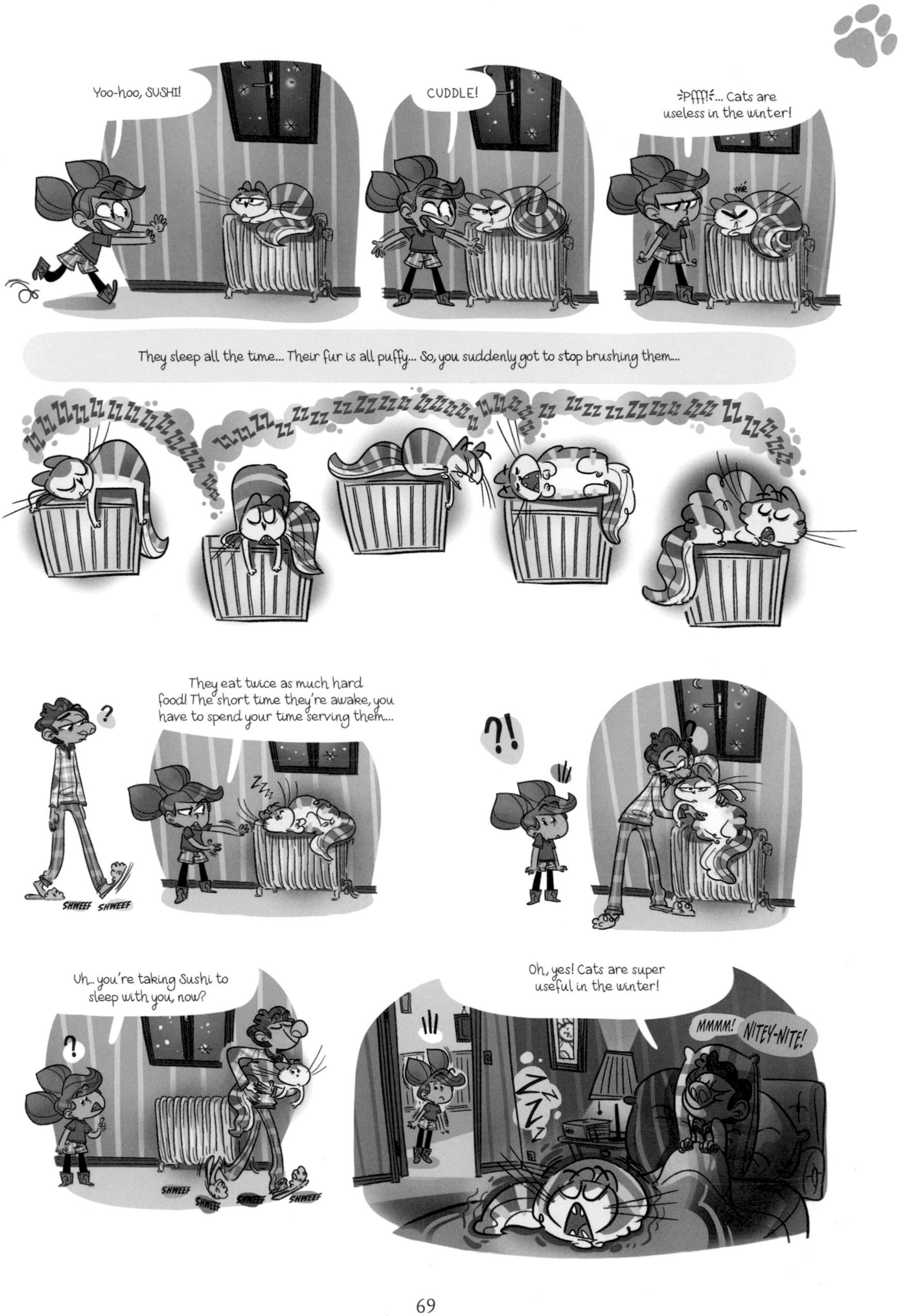
Yoo-hoo, SUSHI!
CUDDLE!
PFFF!... Cats are useless in the winter!
They sleep all the time... Their fur is all puffy... So, you suddenly got to stop brushing them...
?
They eat twice as much hard food! The short time they're awake, you have to spend your time serving them...
SHWEEF SHWEEF
?!
Uh... you're taking Sushi to sleep with you, now?
?
SHWEEF
SHWEEF
SHWEEF
SHWEEF
Oh, yes! Cats are super useful in the winter!
MMMM!
NITEY-NITE!

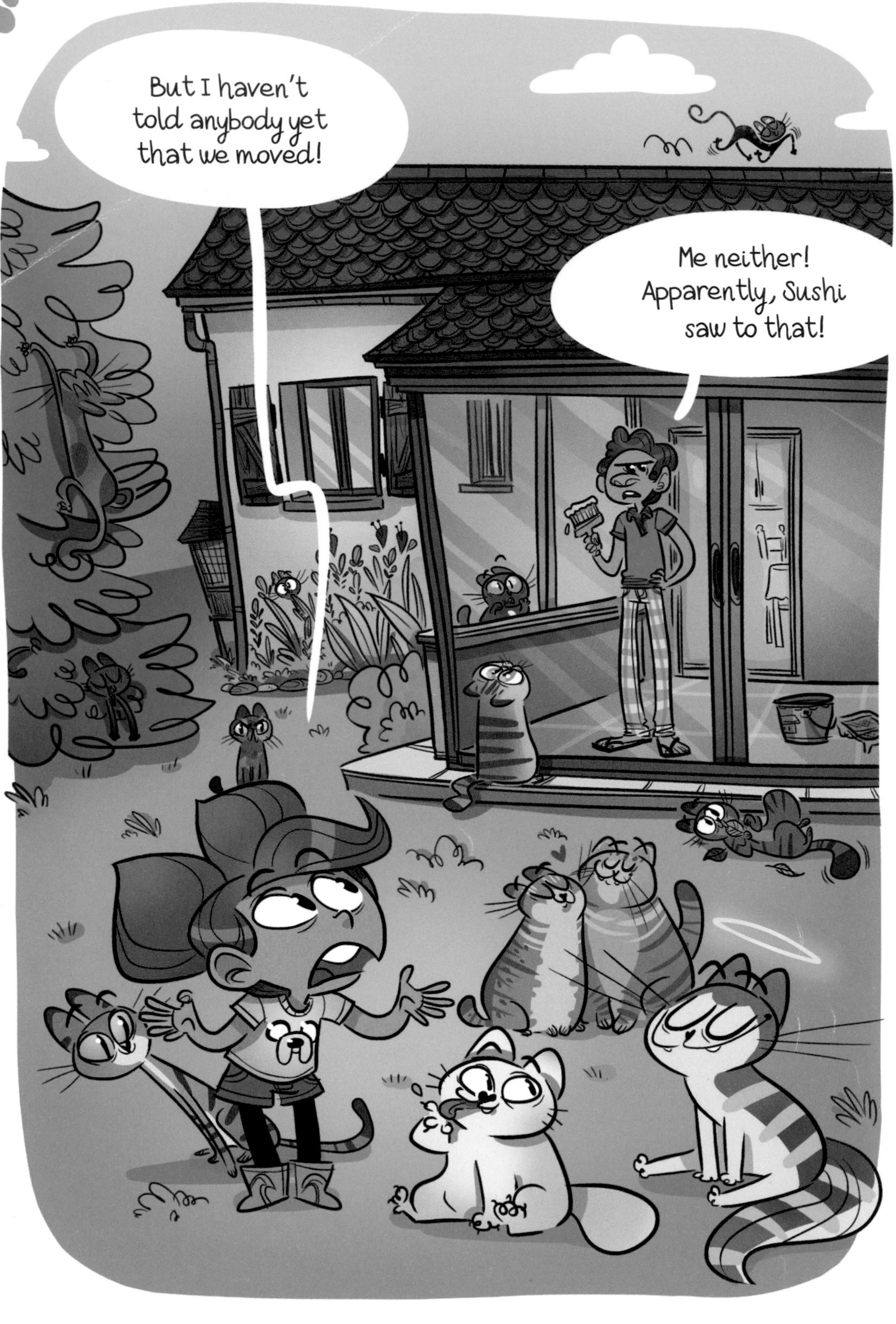
But I haven't told anybody yet that we moved!
Me neither! Apparently, Sushi saw to that!

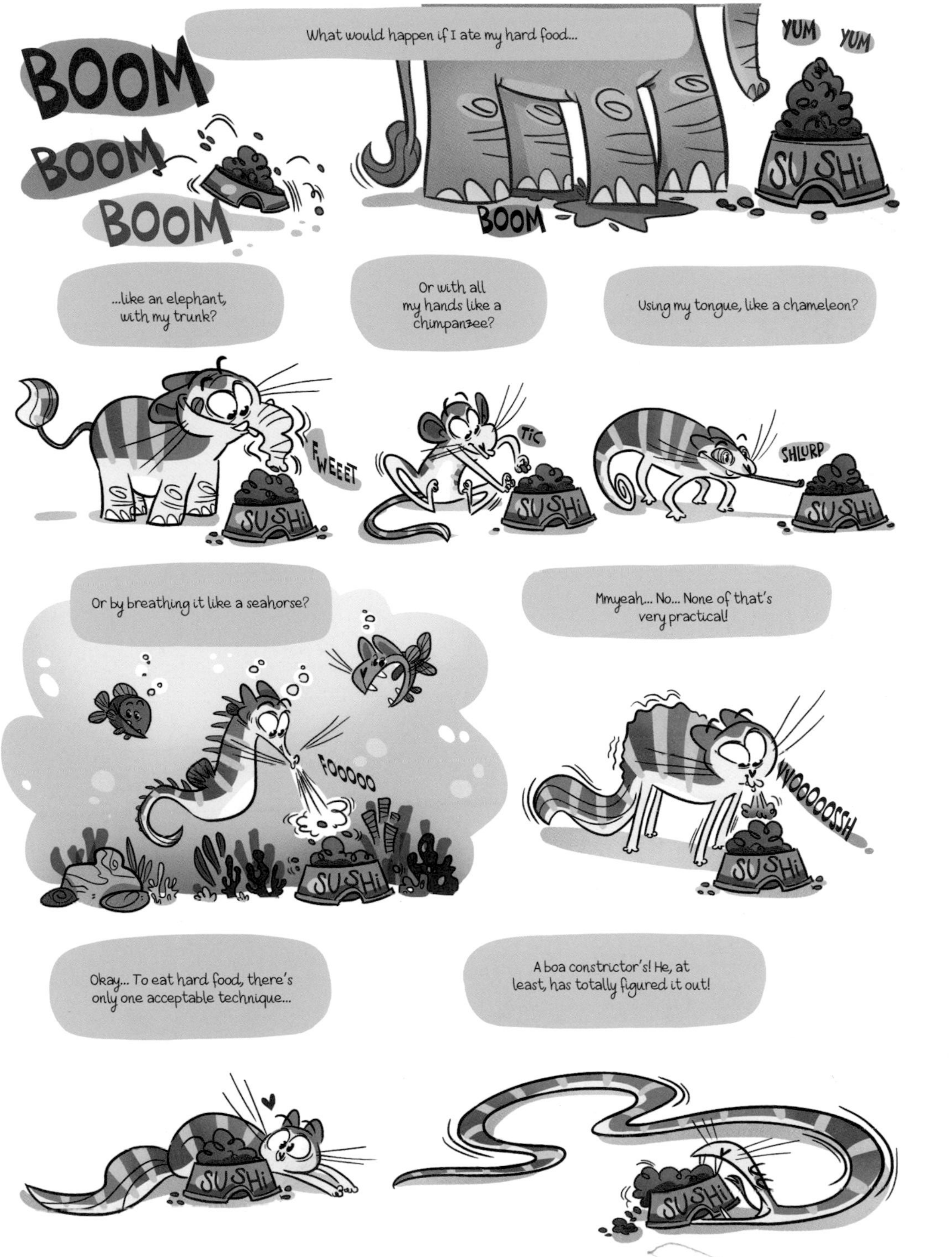
What would happen if I ate my hard food...
BOOM
BOOM
BOOM
BOOM
YUM
YUM
SUSHi
...like an elephant, with my trunk?
Or with all my hands like a chimpanzee?
Using my tongue, like a chameleon?
FWEEET
TIC
SHLURP
Or by breathing it like a seahorse?
FOOOOO
Mmyeah... No... None of that's very practical!
WOOOOOOSH
Okay... To eat hard food, there's only one acceptable technique...
A boa constrictor's! He, at least, has totally figured it out!

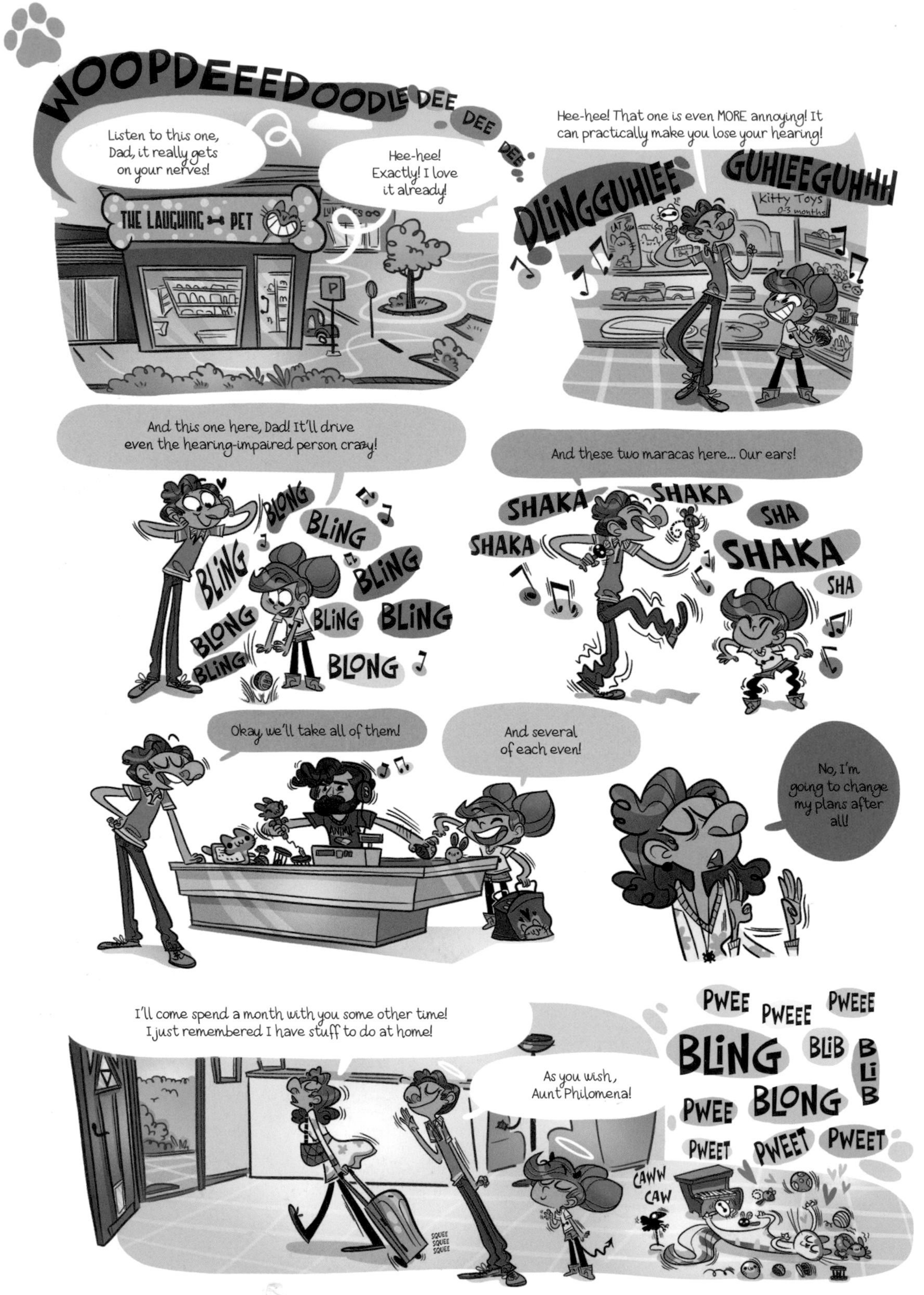

WOOPDEEEEDOODLE DEE DEE DEE
Listen to this one, Dad, it really gets on your nerves!
Hee-hee! Exactly! I love it already!
THE LAUGHING PET
Hee-hee! That one is even MORE annoying! It can practically make you lose your hearing!
DLINGGUHLEE
GUHLEEGUHHH
Kitty Toys 0-3 months
And this one here, Dad! It'll drive even the hearing-impaired person crazy!
BLONG BLING BLING BLING BLING BLONG BLING BLING BLING BLONG
And these two maracas here... Our ears!
SHAKA SHAKA SHAKA SHA SHAKA SHA
Okay, we'll take all of them!
And several of each even!
No, I'm going to change my plans after all!
I'll come spend a month with you some other time! I just remembered I have stuff to do at home!
As you wish, Aunt Philomena!
PWEE PWEEE PWEEE
BLING BLIB BLIB
PWEE BLONG
PWEET PWEET PWEET
CAWW CAW
SQUEE SQUEE SQUEE

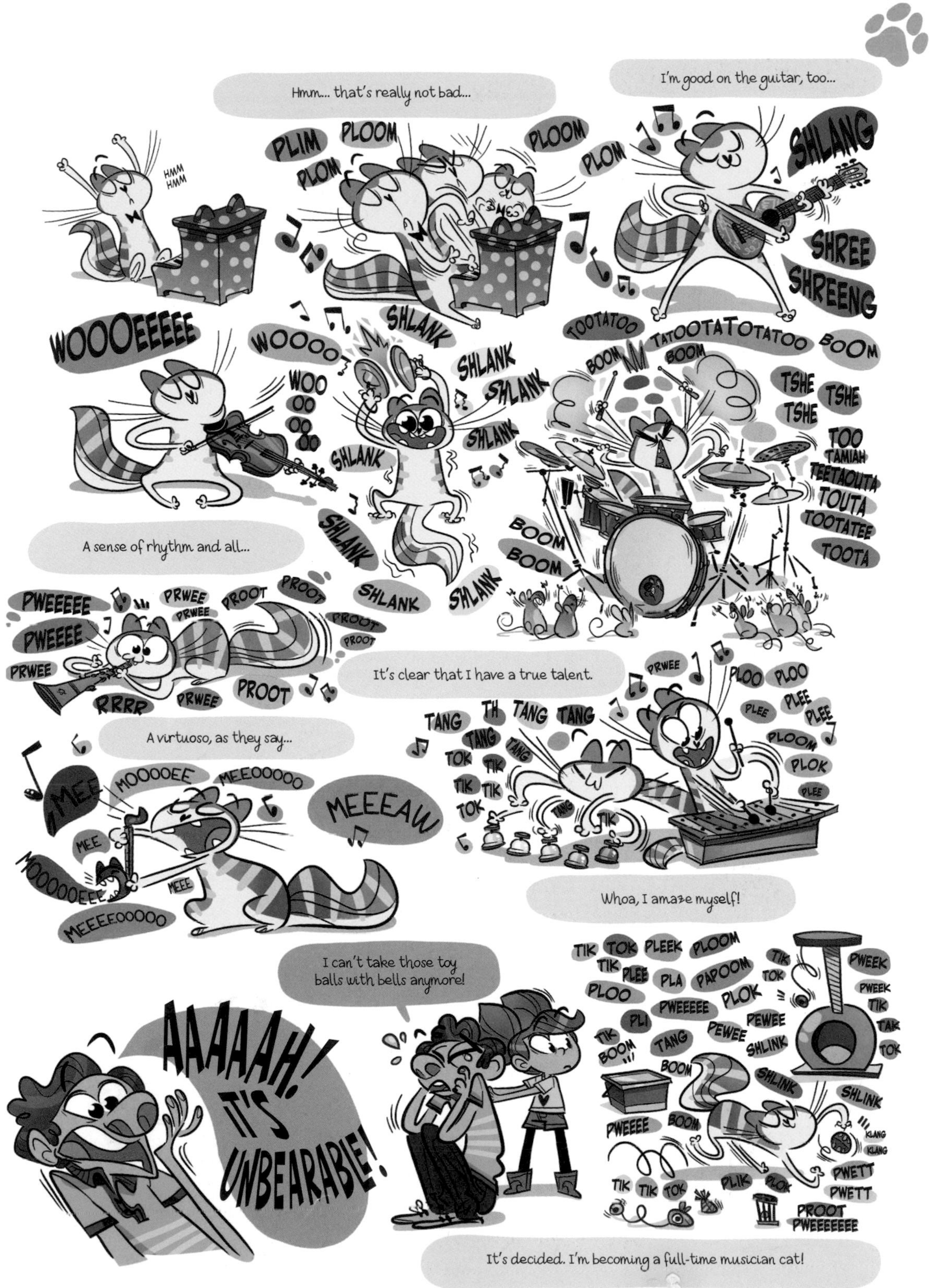

Hmm... that's really not bad...
HMM HMM
PLIM PLOOM PLOM PLOOM PLOM
I'm good on the guitar, too...
SHLANG
SHREE SHREENG
WOOOEEEEE
WOOOO WOO OO OO
SHLANK SHLANK SHLANK SHLANK SHLANK SHLANK SHLANK
TOOTATOO TATOOTATOTATOO BOOM BOOM BOOM
TSHE TSHE TSHE
TOO TAMIAH TEETAOUTA TOUTA TOOTATEE TOOTA
BOOM BOOM
A sense of rhythm and all...
PWEEEEE PWEEEE PRWEE PRWEE PRWEE PROOT PROOT PROOT PROOT
PRWEE RRRR PRWEE PROOT
It's clear that I have a true talent.
A virtuoso, as they say...
MEE MOOOOEE MEEOOOOO MEEEAW MEE MOOOOOEEE MEEE MEEEEOOOOO
PRWEE PLOO PLOO PLEE PLEE PLEE PLOOM PLOK PLEE
TANG TH TANG TANG TANG TANG TOK TIK TIK TIK TOK TANG TIK
Whoa, I amaze myself!
I can't take those toy balls with bells anymore!
AAAAAH! IT'S UNBEARABLE!
TIK TOK PLEEK PLOOM TIK PLEE PLA PAPOOM TIK TOK PWEEK PWEEK TIK TAK TOK
PLOO PWEEEEE PLOK PLI PEWEE PEWEE SHLINK TIK BOOM TANG BOOM SHLINK SHLINK
PWEEEE BOOM KLANG KLANG PWETT PWETT
TIK TIK TOK PLIK PLOK PROOT PWEEEEEEE
It's decided. I'm becoming a full-time musician cat!

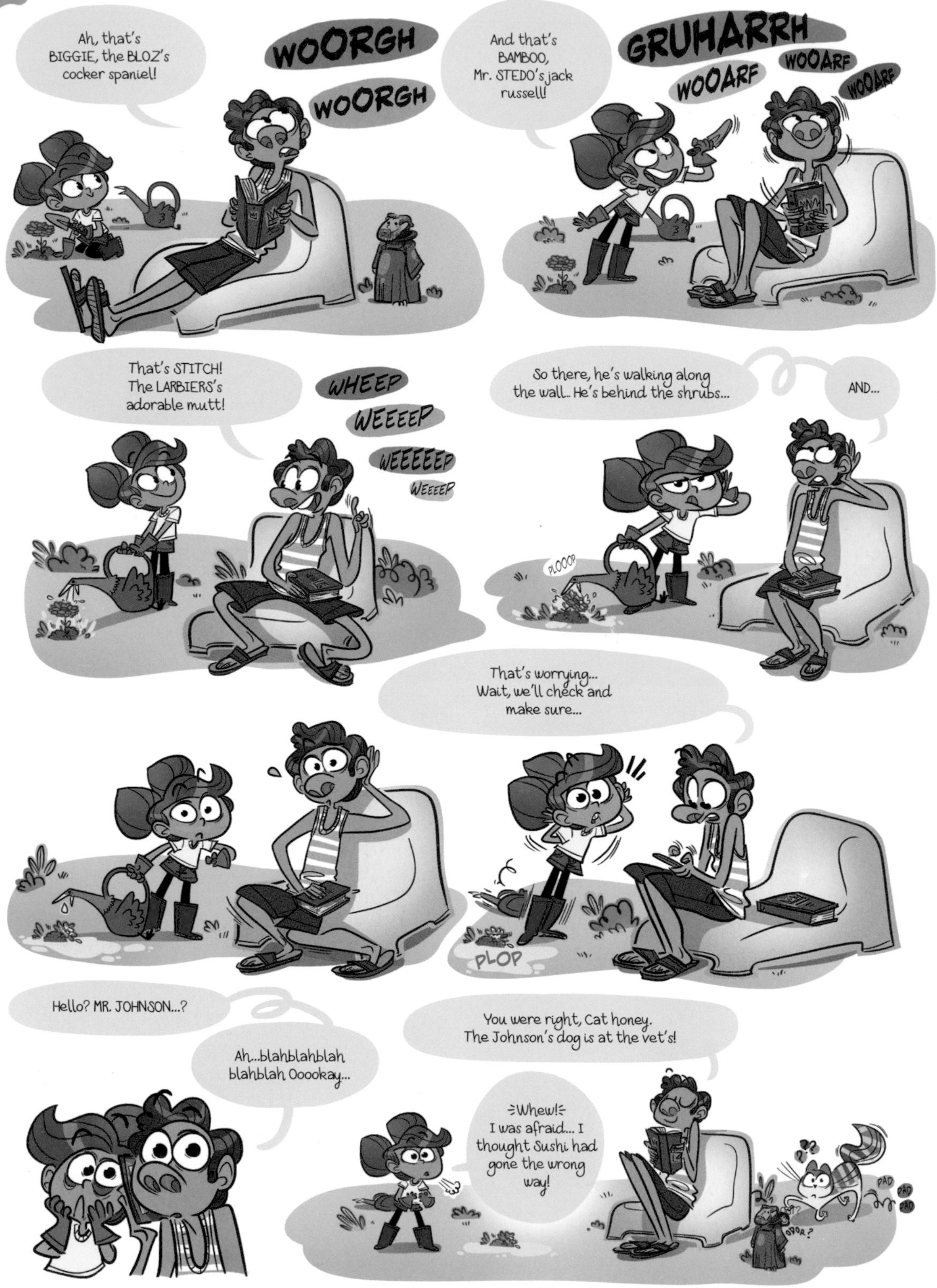
Ah, that's BIGGIE, the BLOZ's cocker spaniel!
WOORGH
WOORGH
And that's BAMBOO, Mr. STEDO's jack russell!
GRUHARRH
WOOARF
WOOARF
WOOARF
That's STITCH! The LARBIERS's adorable mutt!
WHEEP
WEEEEP
WEEEEEP
WEEEEP
So there, he's walking along the wall.. He's behind the shrubs...
AND...
PLOOOP
That's worrying... Wait, we'll check and make sure...
PLOP
Hello? MR. JOHNSON...?
Ah...blahblahblah blahblah Ooookay...
You were right, Cat honey. The Johnson's dog is at the vet's!
Whew! I was afraid... I thought Sushi had gone the wrong way!
PAD
PAD
PAD

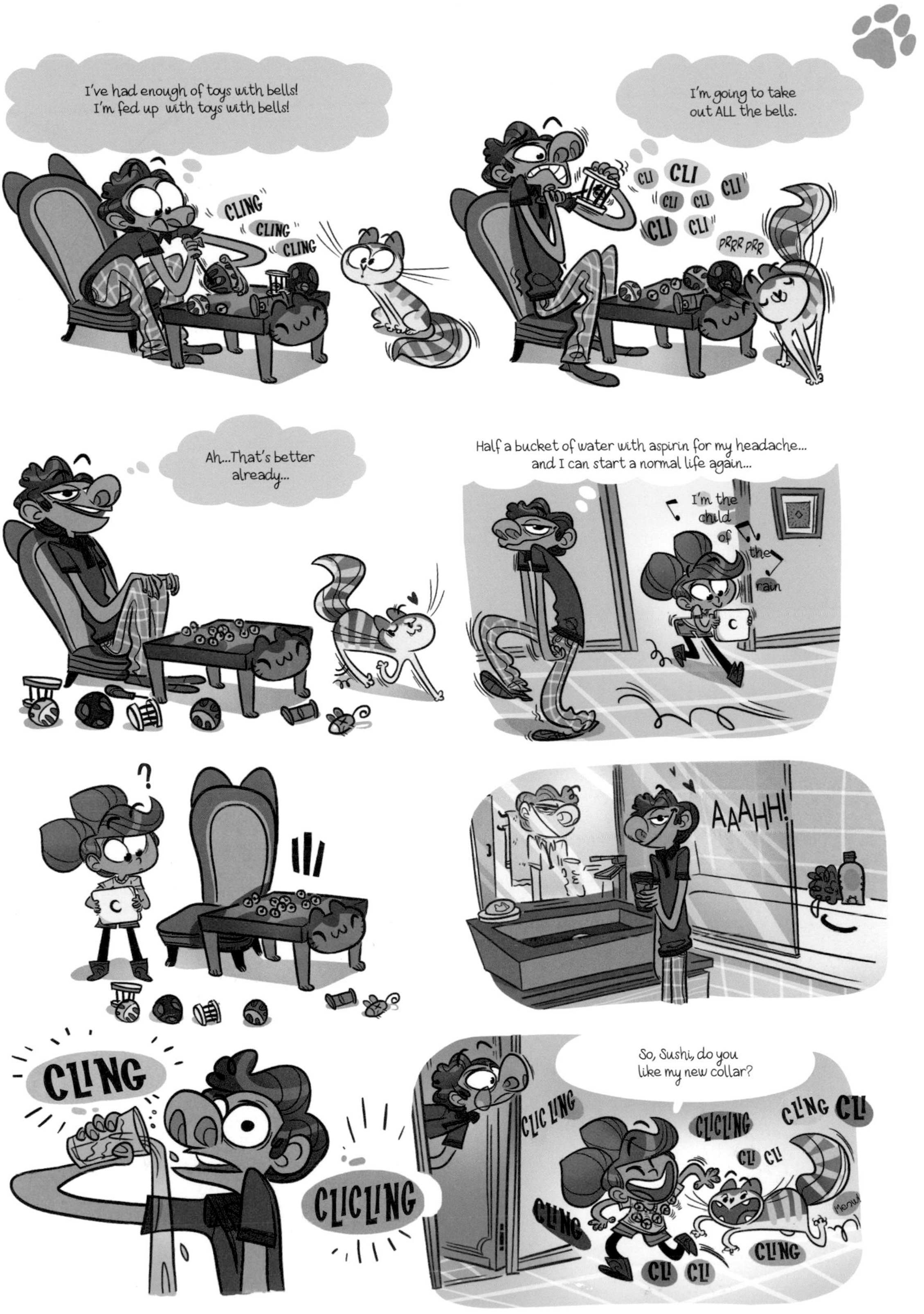
I've had enough of toys with bells!
I'm fed up with toys with bells!
CLING
CLING
CLING
I'm going to take out ALL the bells.
CLI CLI CLI CLI CLI CLI CLI
PRRR PRR
Ah...That's better already...
Half a bucket of water with aspirin for my headache... and I can start a normal life again...
I'm the child of the rain
?
AAAHH!
CLING
CLICLING
So, Sushi, do you like my new collar?
CLIC LING
CLICLING
CLING CLI
CLI CLI
CLING
CLING
CLI CLI

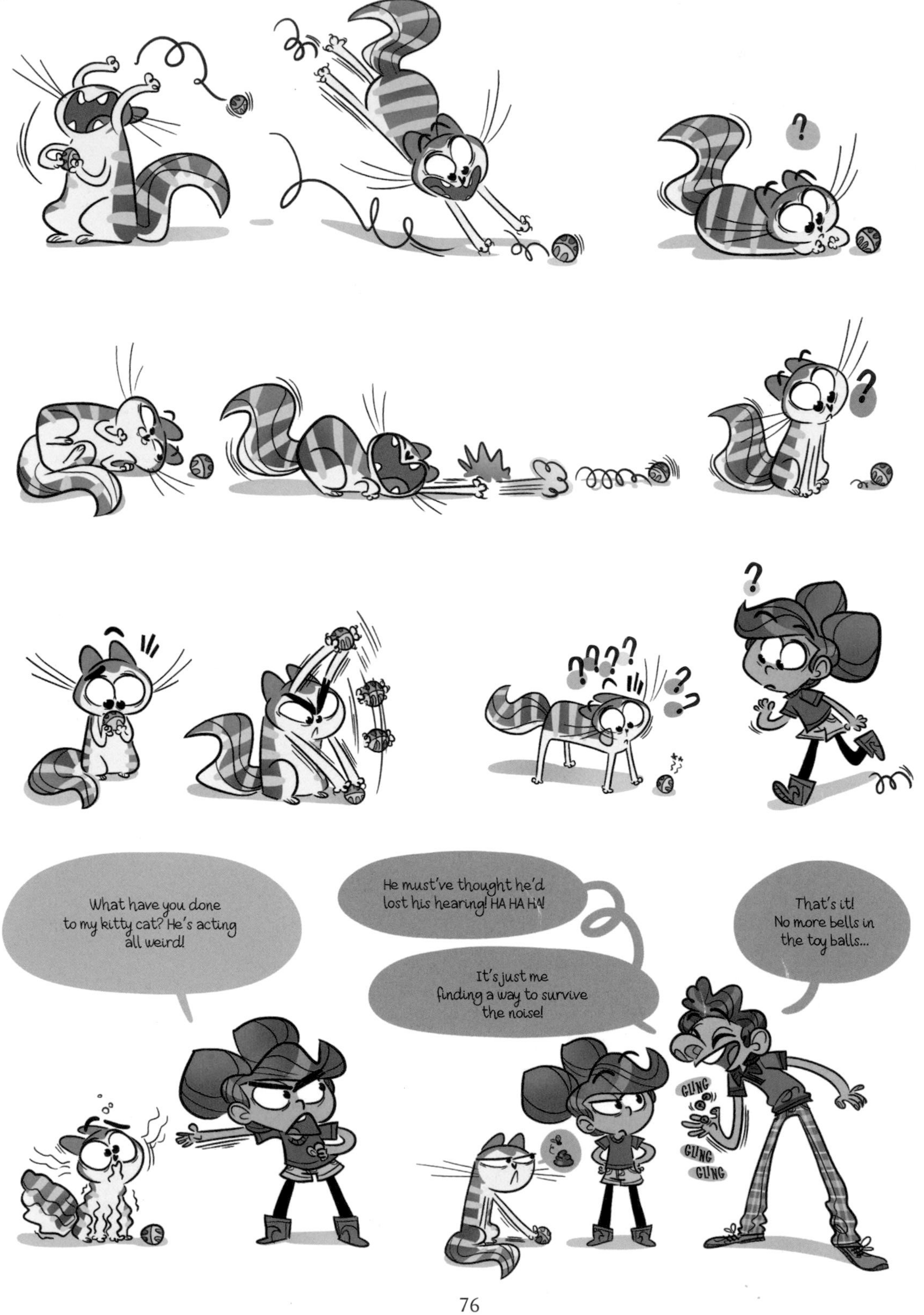
What have you done to my kitty cat? He's acting all weird!
He must've thought he'd lost his hearing! HA HA HA!
It's just me finding a way to survive the noise!
That's it! No more bells in the toy balls...
GLING
GLING
GLING

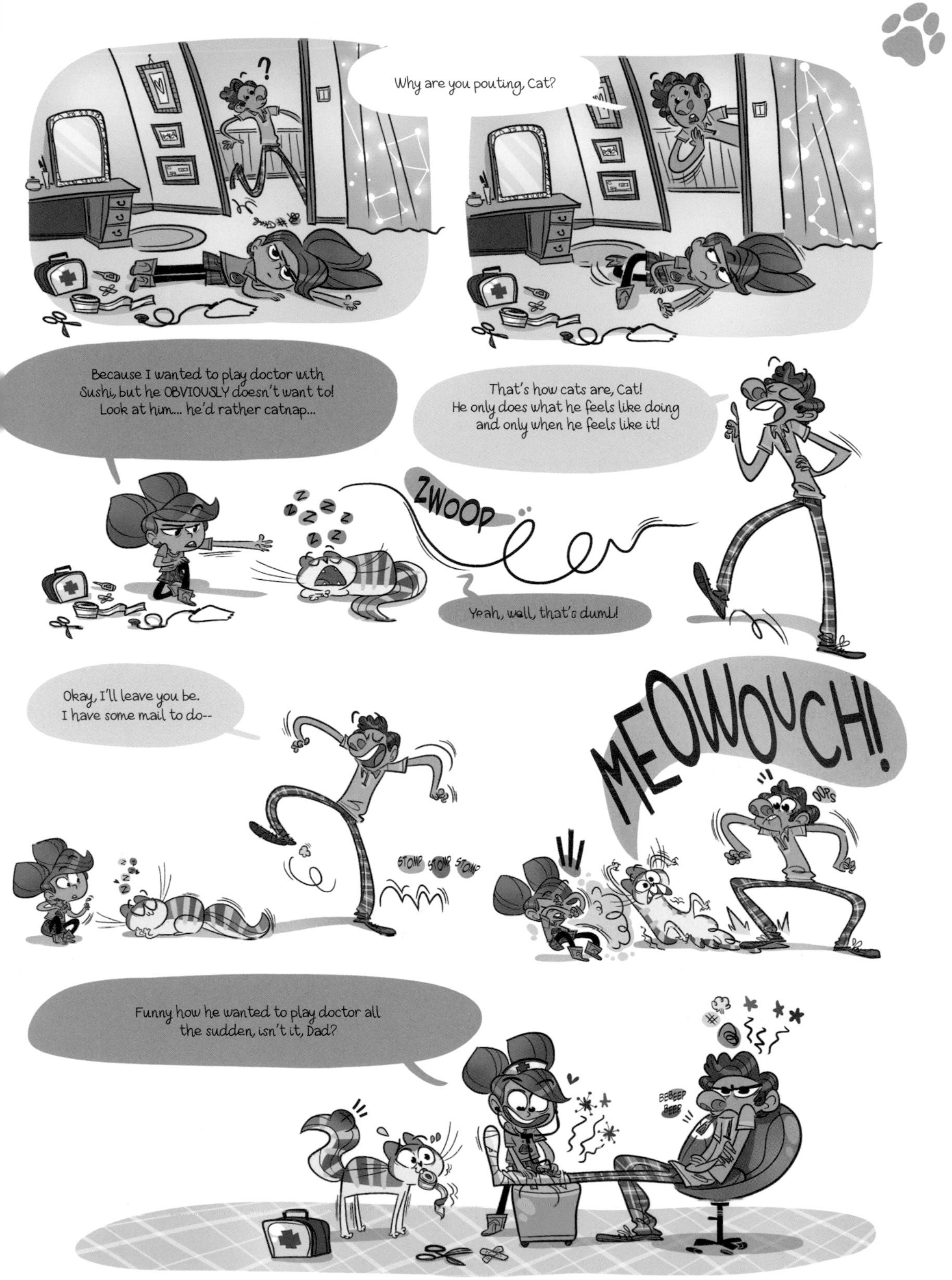
Why are you pouting, Cat?
Because I wanted to play doctor with Sushi, but he OBVIOUSLY doesn't want to! Look at him... he'd rather catnap...
That's how cats are, Cat! He only does what he feels like doing and only when he feels like it!
ZWOOP
Yeah, well, that's dumb!
Okay, I'll leave you be. I have some mail to do--
STOMP STOMP STOMP
MEOWOUCH!
OOPS
Funny how he wanted to play doctor all the sudden, isn't it, Dad?
BEBEEP BEEP

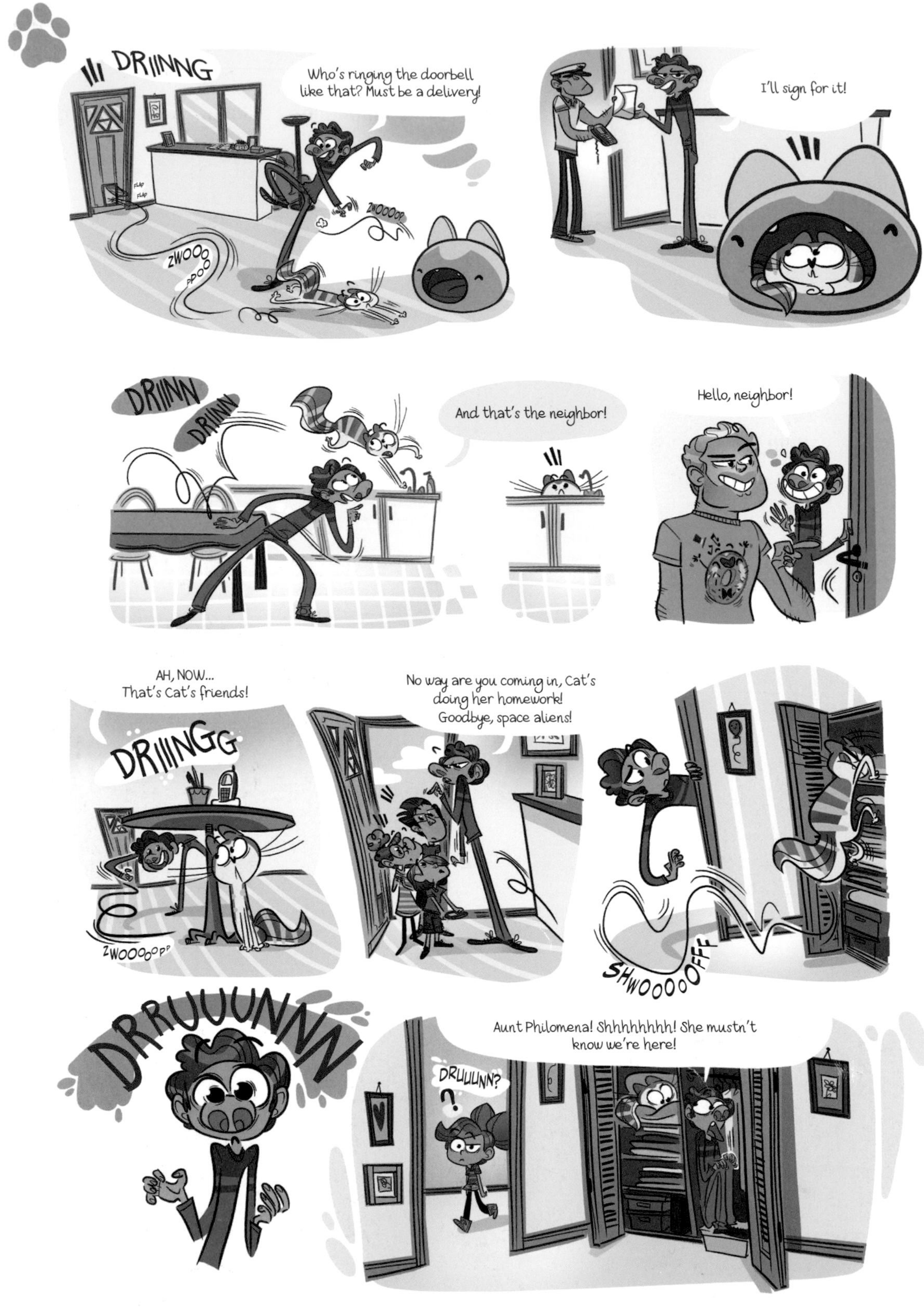
DRIINNG
Who's ringing the doorbell like that? Must be a delivery!
FLAP FLAP
ZWOOOOP
ZWOOOPPOO
I'll sign for it!
DRIINN
DRIINN
And that's the neighbor!
Hello, neighbor!
AH, NOW... That's Cat's friends!
DRIIINGG
ZWOOOOOPP
No way are you coming in, Cat's doing her homework! Goodbye, space aliens!
SHWOOOOOFFF
DRUUUNNN
Aunt Philomena! Shhhhhhhh! She mustn't know we're here!
DRUUUNN?

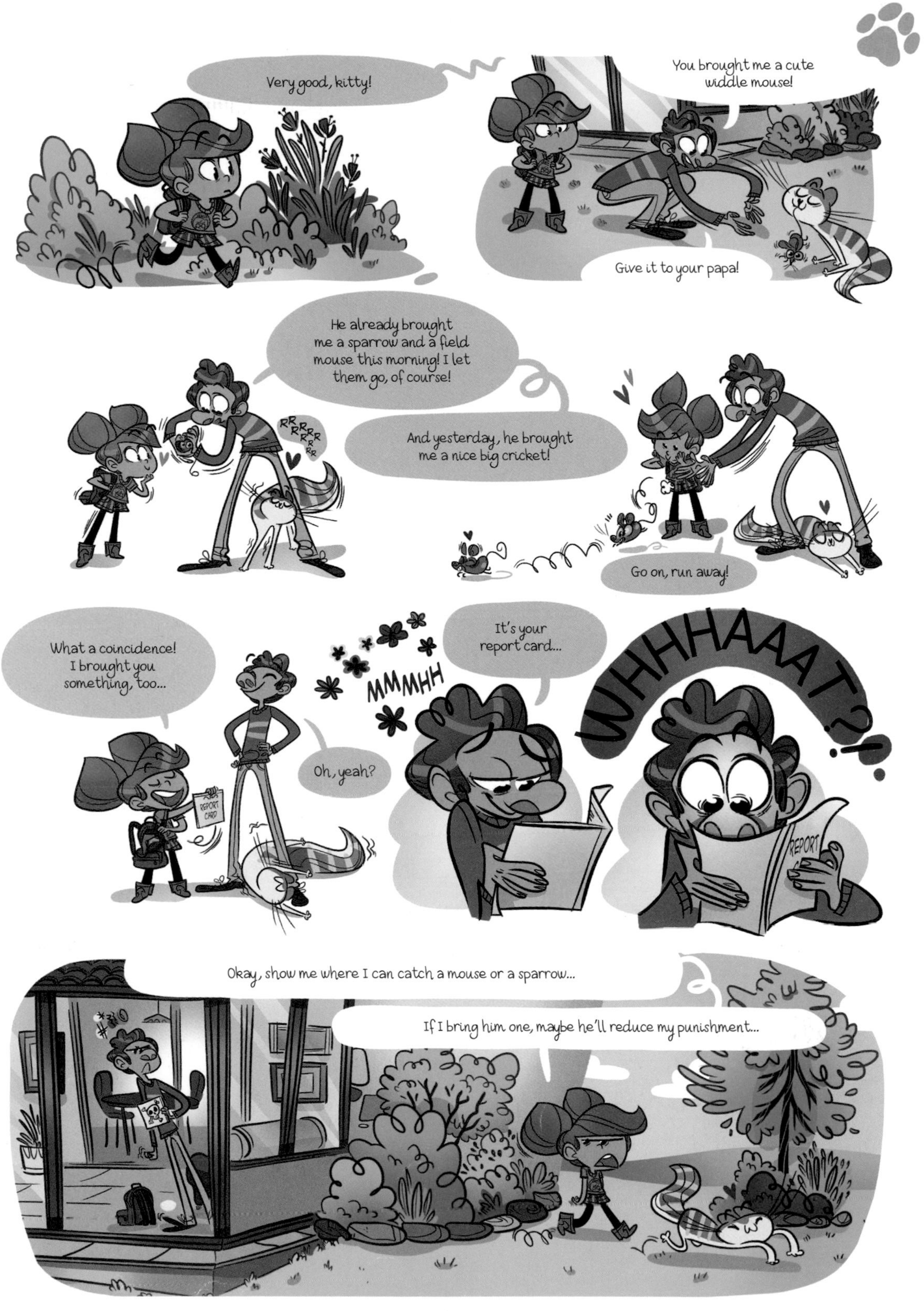
Very good, kitty!
You brought me a cute widdle mouse!
Give it to your papa!
He already brought me a sparrow and a field mouse this morning! I let them go, of course!
RRRRRRRR
And yesterday, he brought me a nice big cricket!
Go on, run away!
What a coincidence! I brought you something, too...
REPORT CARD
Oh, yeah?
MMMHH
It's your report card...
WHHHAAAT?!
REPORT
Okay, show me where I can catch a mouse or a sparrow...
If I bring him one, maybe he'll reduce my punishment...

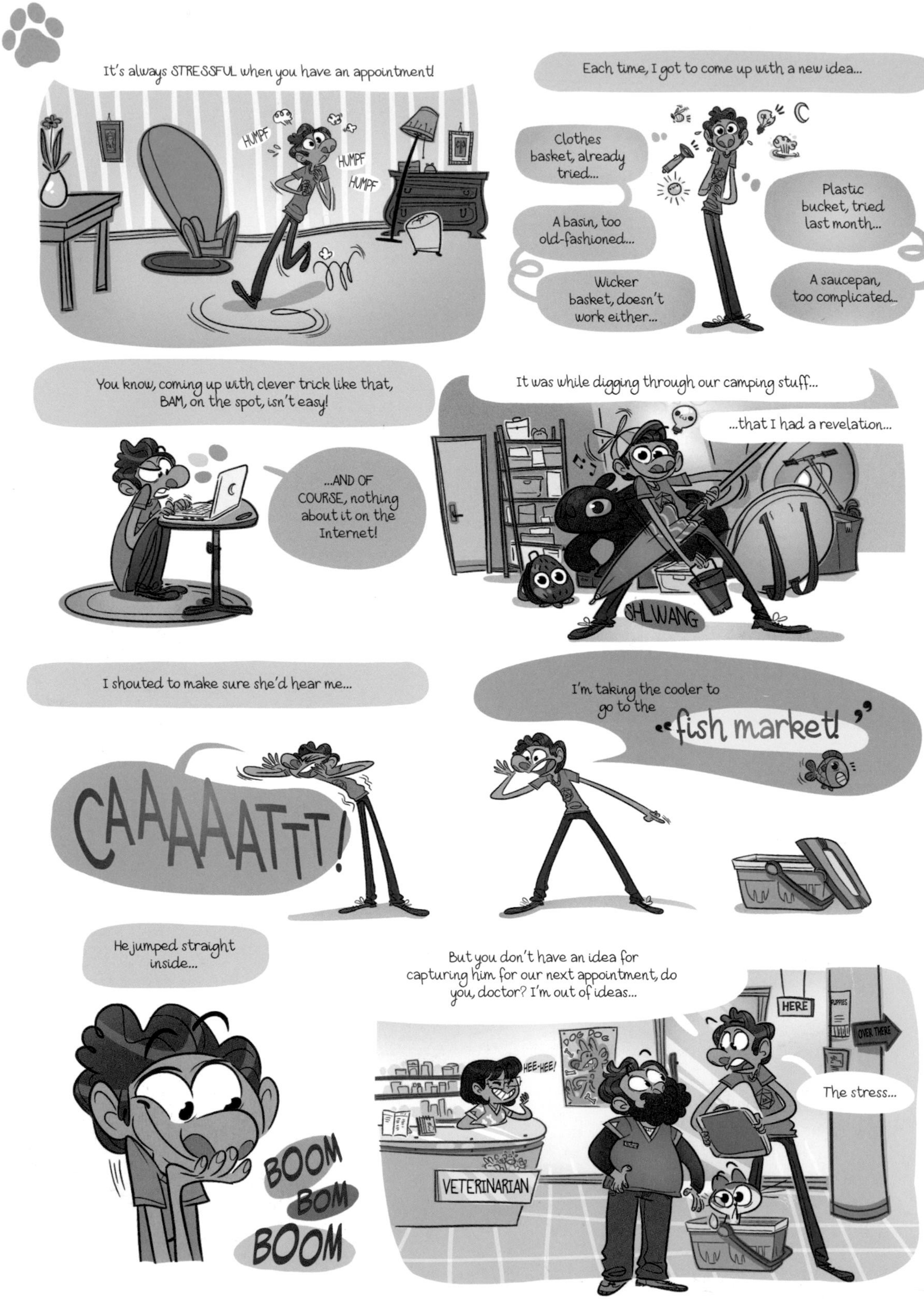
It's always STRESSFUL when you have an appointment!
HUMPF
HUMPF
HUMPF
Each time, I got to come up with a new idea...
Clothes basket, already tried...
A basin, too old-fashioned...
Wicker basket, doesn't work either...
Plastic bucket, tried last month...
A saucepan, too complicated...
You know, coming up with clever trick like that, BAM, on the spot, isn't easy!
...AND OF COURSE, nothing about it on the Internet!
It was while digging through our camping stuff...
...that I had a revelation...
SHLWANG
I shouted to make sure she'd hear me...
CAAAAATTT!
I'm taking the cooler to go to the "fish market!"
He jumped straight inside...
BOOM
BOM
BOOM
But you don't have an idea for capturing him for our next appointment, do you, doctor? I'm out of ideas...
HEE-HEE!
HERE
OVER THERE
VETERINARIAN
The stress...

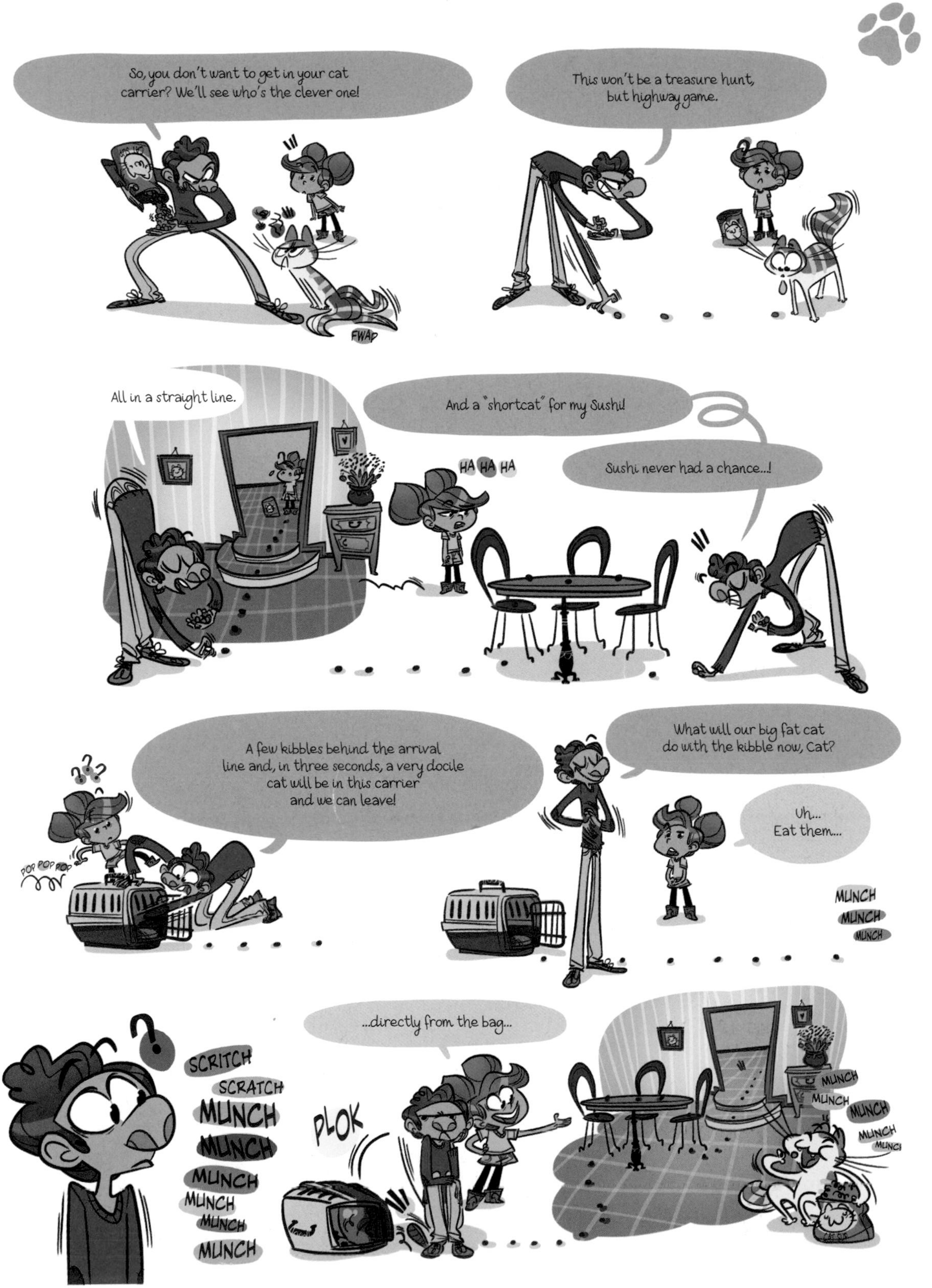

So, you don't want to get in your cat carrier? We'll see who's the clever one!
FWAP
This won't be a treasure hunt, but highway game.
All in a straight line.
And a "shortcat" for my Sushi!
HA HA HA
Sushi never had a chance...!
A few kibbles behind the arrival line and, in three seconds, a very docile cat will be in this carrier and we can leave!
POP POP POP
What will our big fat cat do with the kibble now, Cat?
Uh... Eat them...
MUNCH
MUNCH
MUNCH
SCRITCH
SCRATCH
MUNCH
MUNCH
MUNCH
MUNCH
MUNCH
MUNCH
...directly from the bag...
PLOK
MUNCH
MUNCH
MUNCH
MUNCH

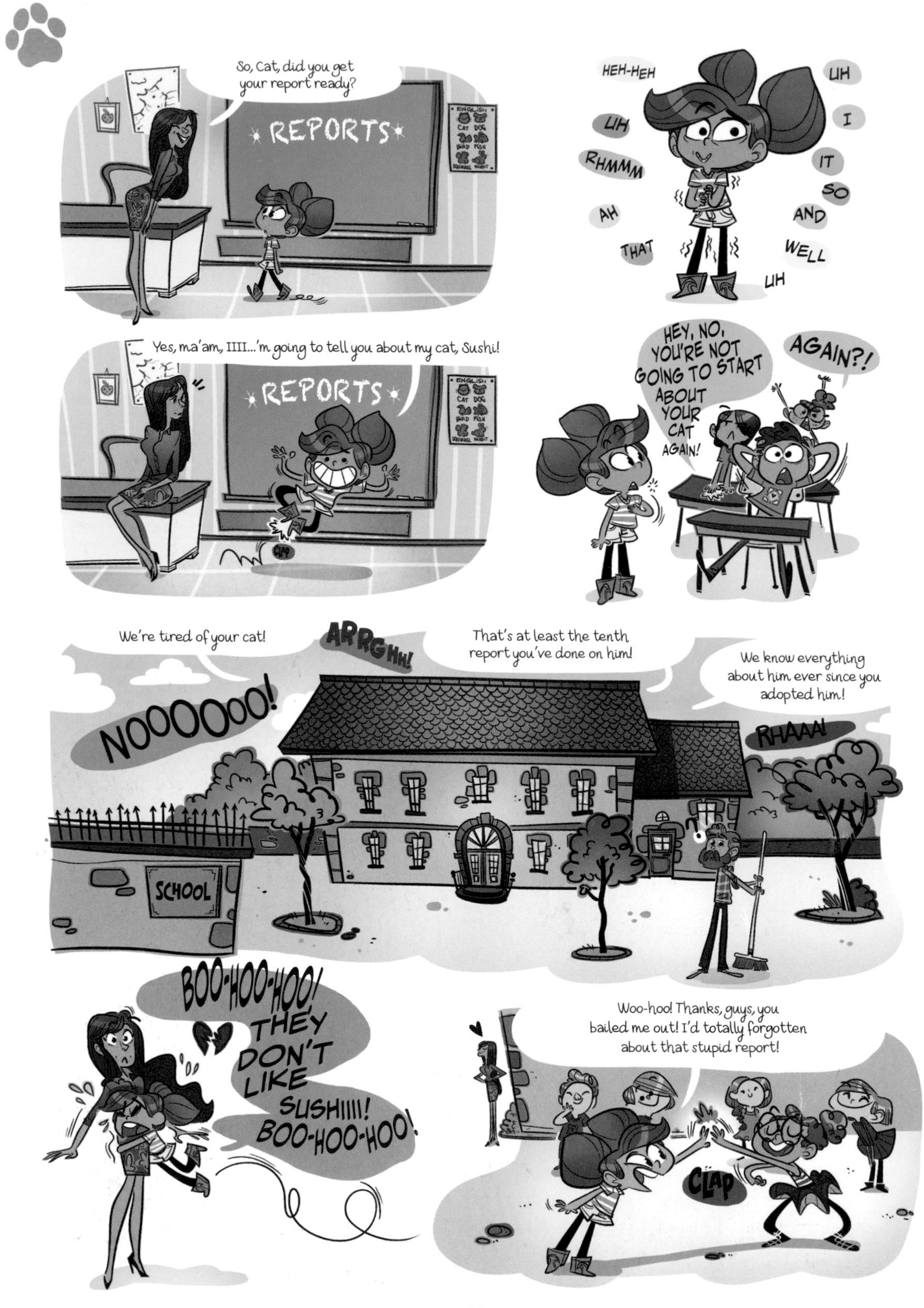

So, Cat, did you get your report ready?
REPORTS
HEH-HEH
UH
UH
I
RHMMM
IT
SO
AH
AND
THAT
WELL
UH
Yes, ma'am, IIII...'m going to tell you about my cat, Sushi!
REPORTS
CLAP
HEY, NO, YOU'RE NOT GOING TO START ABOUT YOUR CAT AGAIN!
AGAIN?!
We're tired of your cat!
ARRGHH!
That's at least the tenth report you've done on him!
We know everything about him ever since you adopted him!
NOOOOOO!
RHAAA!
SCHOOL
BOO-HOO-HOO! THEY DON'T LIKE SUSHIIII! BOO-HOO-HOO!
Woo-hoo! Thanks, guys, you bailed me out! I'd totally forgotten about that stupid report!
CLAP

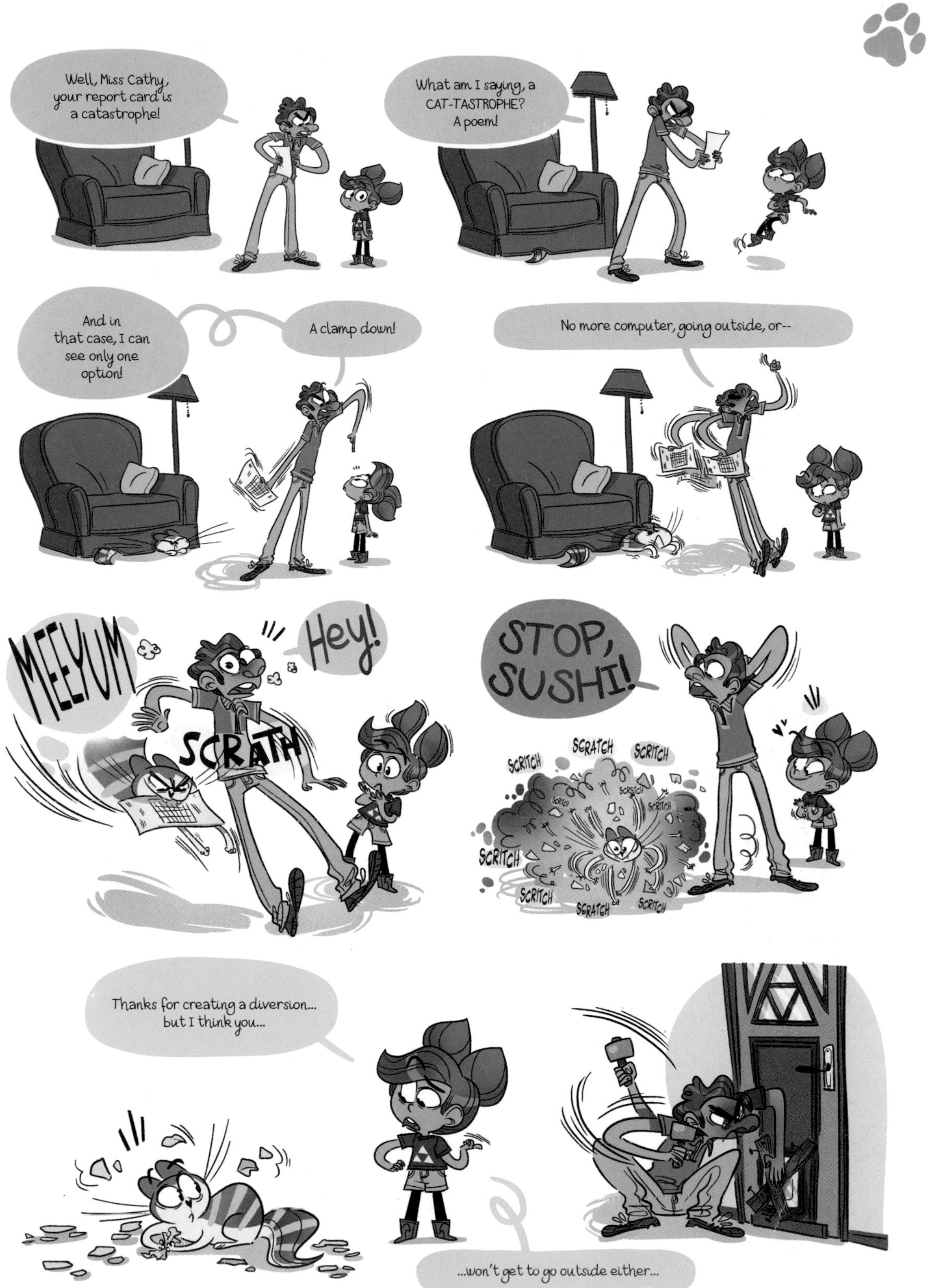

Well, Miss Cathy, your report card is a catastrophe!
What am I saying, a CAT-TASTROPHE? A poem!
And in that case, I can see only one option!
A clamp down!
No more computer, going outside, or--
MEEYUM
SCRATH
Hey!
STOP, SUSHI!
SCRITCH
SCRATCH
SCRITCH
SCRITCH
SCRITCH
SCRATCH
SCRITCH
Thanks for creating a diversion... but I think you...
...won't get to go outside either...

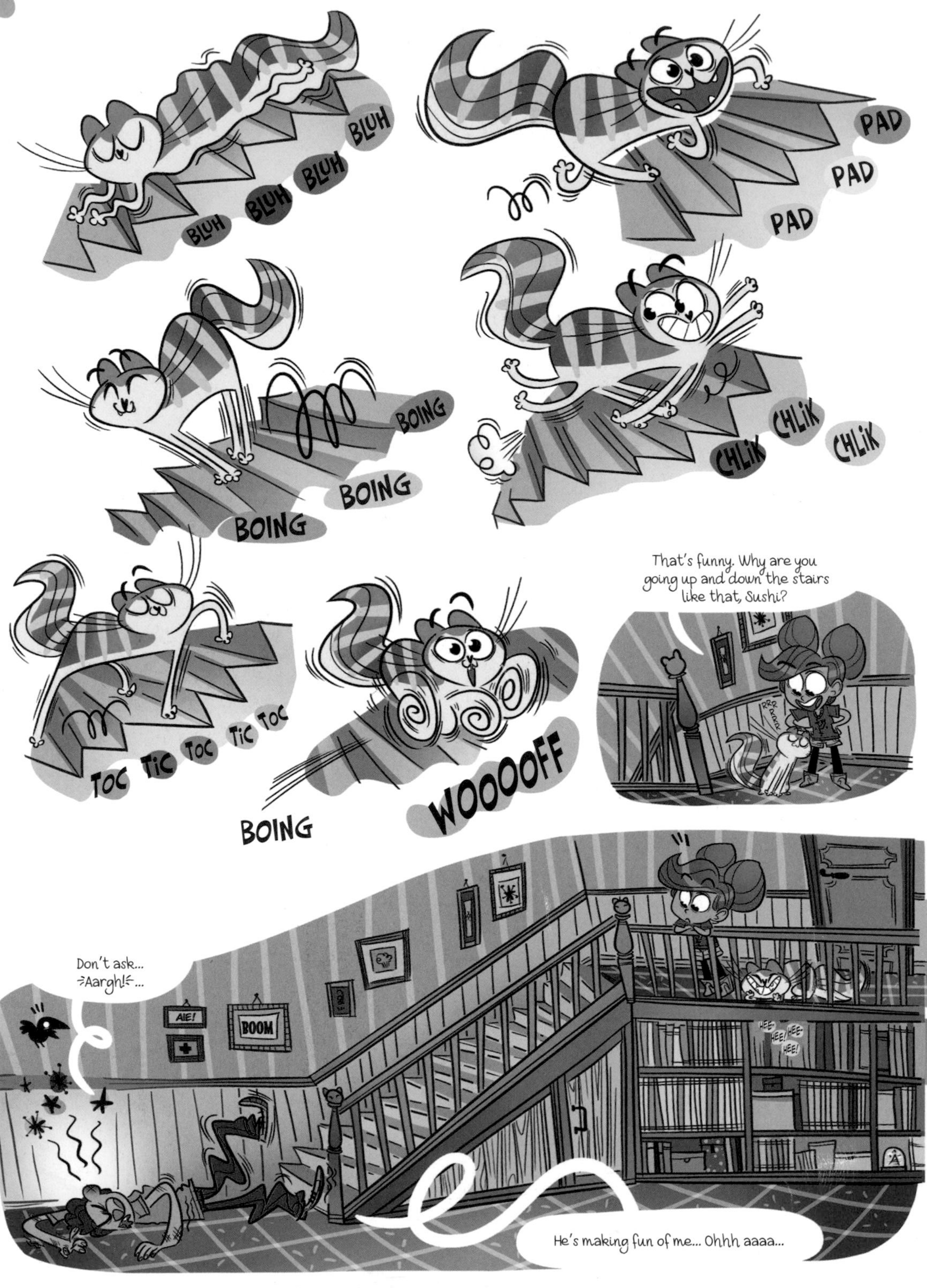
BLUH
BLUH
BLUH
BLUH
PAD
PAD
PAD
BOING
BOING
BOING
CHLIK
CHLIK
CHLIK
TOC
TIC
TOC
TIC
TOC
BOING
WOOOOFF
That's funny. Why are you going up and down the stairs like that, Sushi?
Don't ask... ⇉Aargh!⇇...
AIE!
BOOM
HEE! HEE! HEE! HEE!
He's making fun of me... Ohhh aaaa...

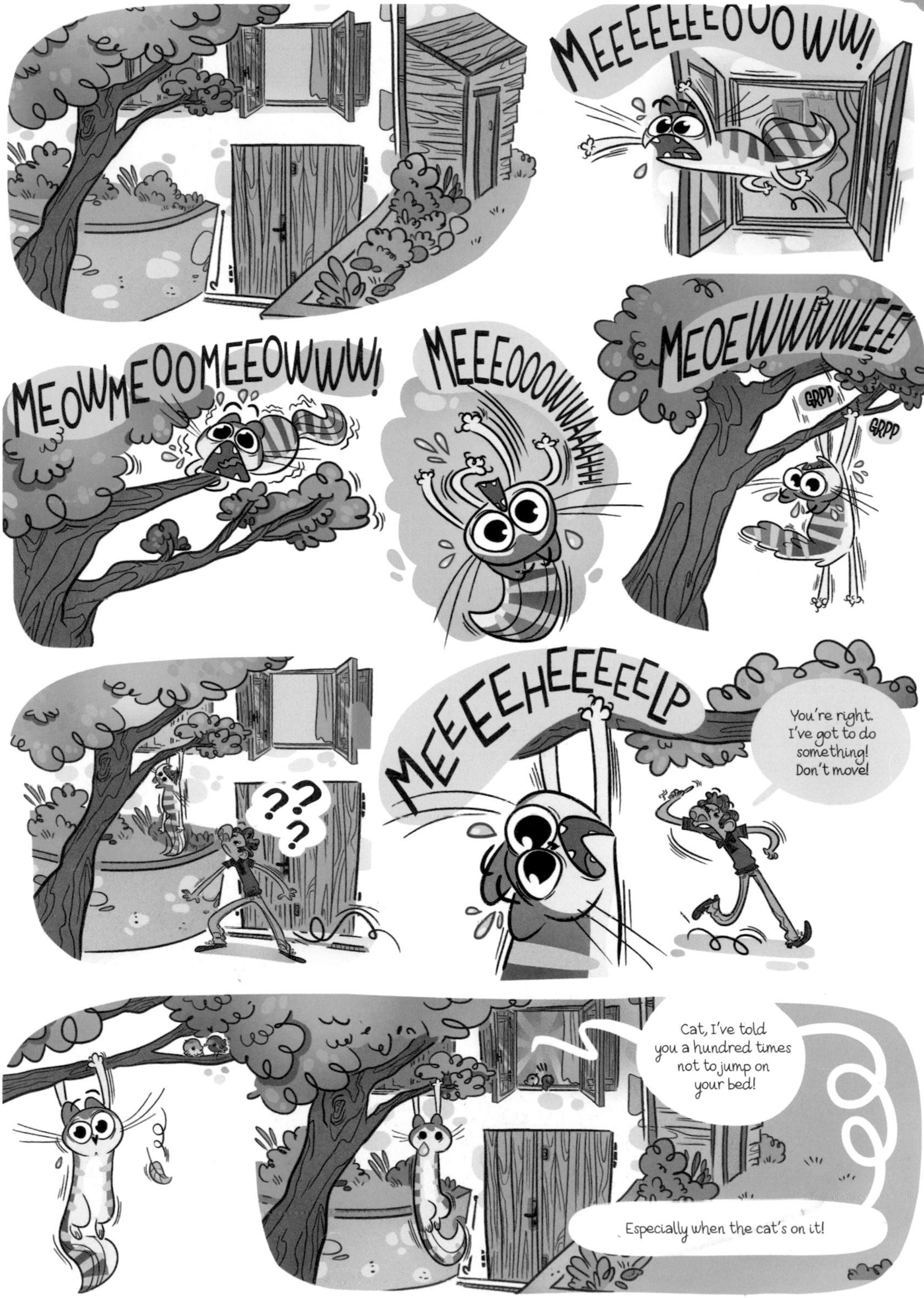
MEEEEEEEOOOWW!
MEOWMEOOMEEOWWW!
MEEEOOOWWAAHH!
MEOEWWWWEEE!
GRPP
GRPP
??
?
MEEEEHEEEEELP
You're right. I've got to do something! Don't move!
Cat, I've told you a hundred times not to jump on your bed!
Especially when the cat's on it!

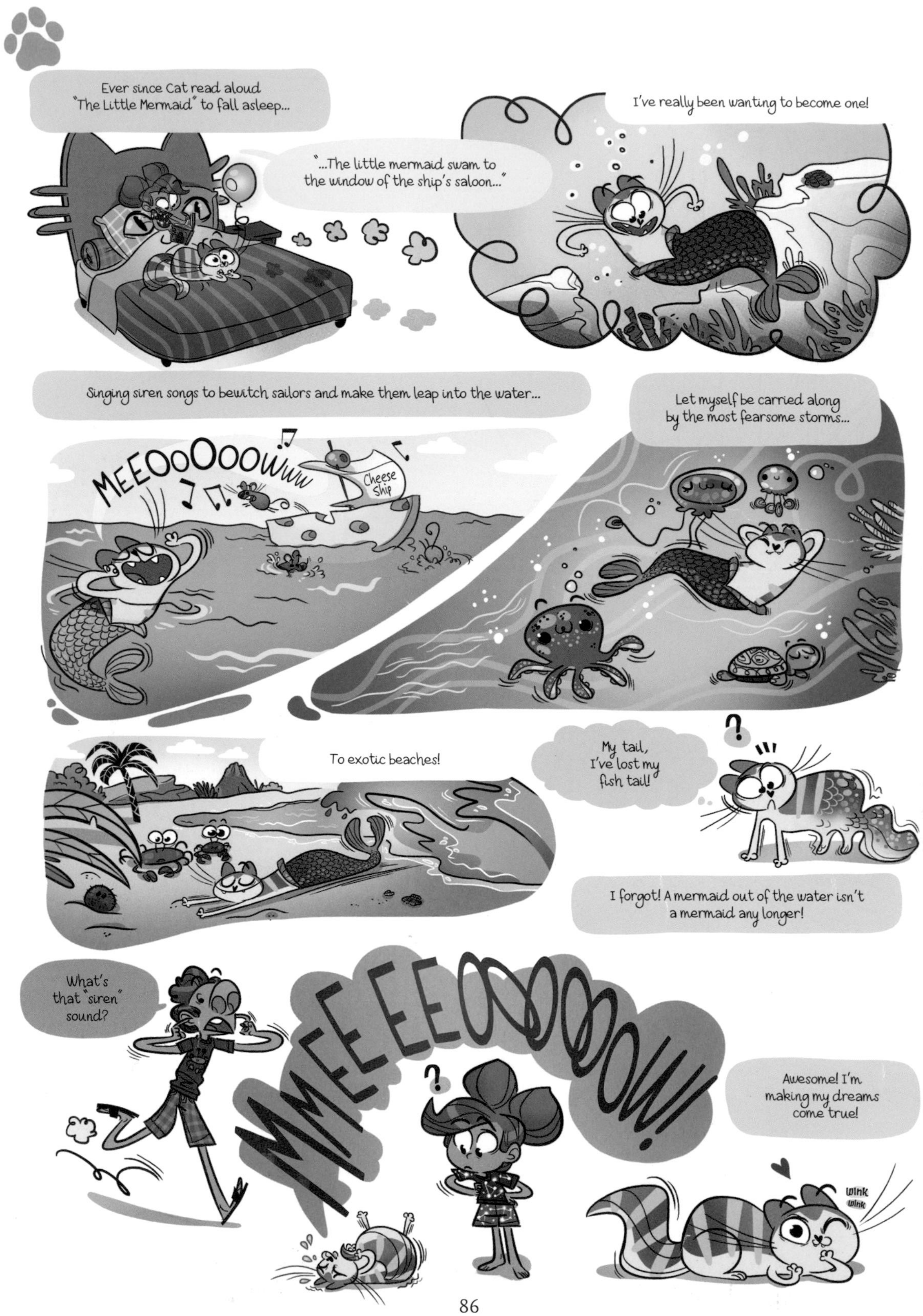
Ever since Cat read aloud "The Little Mermaid" to fall asleep...
"...The little mermaid swam to the window of the ship's saloon..."
I've really been wanting to become one!
Singing siren songs to bewitch sailors and make them leap into the water...
MEEOoOOoOWWW
Cheese Ship
Let myself be carried along by the most fearsome storms...
To exotic beaches!
My tail, I've lost my fish tail!
I forgot! A mermaid out of the water isn't a mermaid any longer!
What's that "siren" sound?
MMEEEEOOOOOW!!
Awesome! I'm making my dreams come true!
wink wink

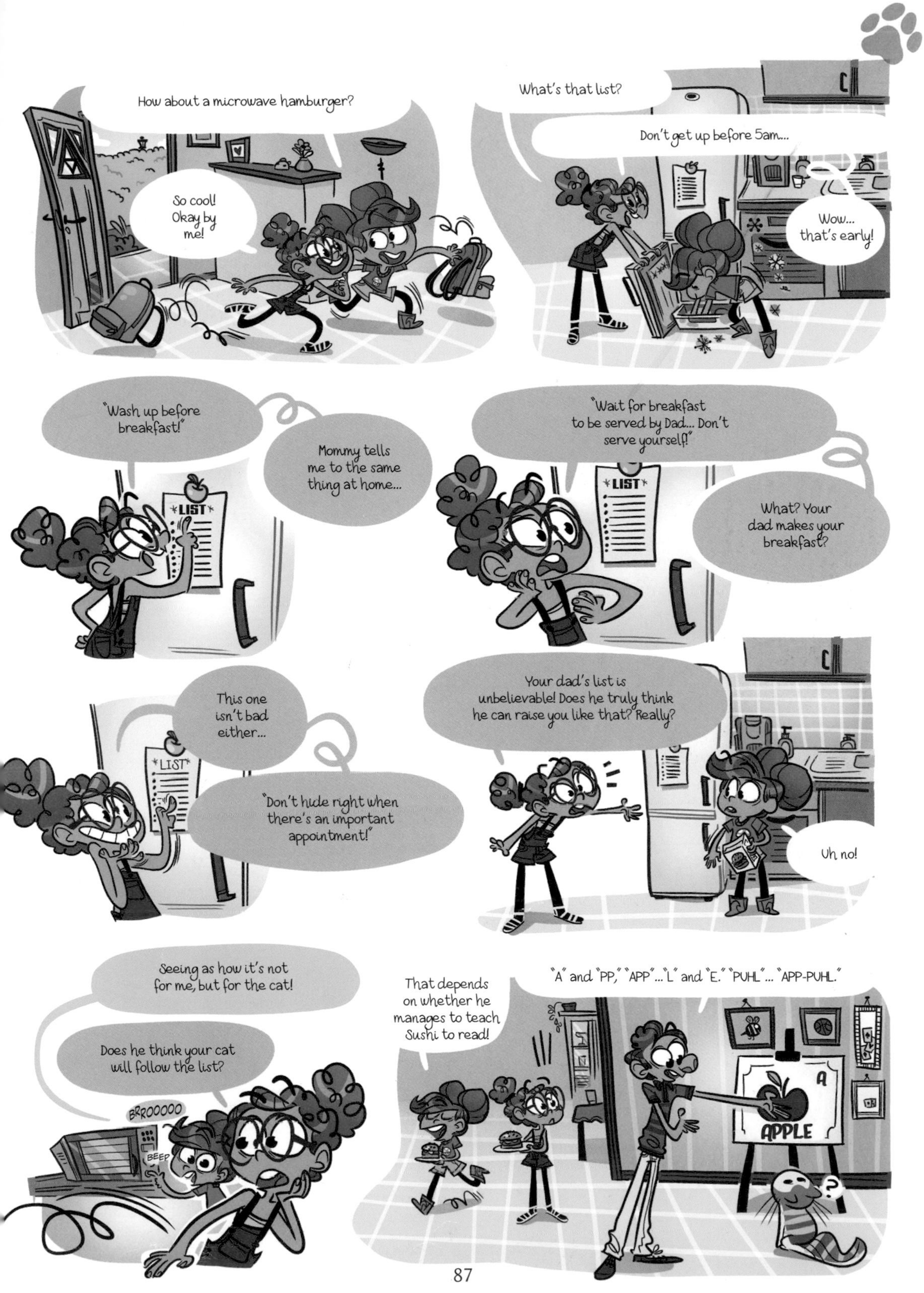
How about a microwave hamburger?
So cool! Okay by me!
What's that list?
Don't get up before 5am...
Wow... that's early!
"Wash up before breakfast!"
Mommy tells me to the same thing at home...
"Wait for breakfast to be served by Dad... Don't serve yourself!"
What? Your dad makes your breakfast?
This one isn't bad either...
"Don't hide right when there's an important appointment!"
Your dad's list is unbelievable! Does he truly think he can raise you like that? Really?
Uh no!
Seeing as how it's not for me, but for the cat!
Does he think your cat will follow the list?
BRROOOOO
BEEP
That depends on whether he manages to teach Sushi to read!
"A" and "PP," "APP"... "L" and "E." "PUHL"... "APP-PUHL."
A
APPLE

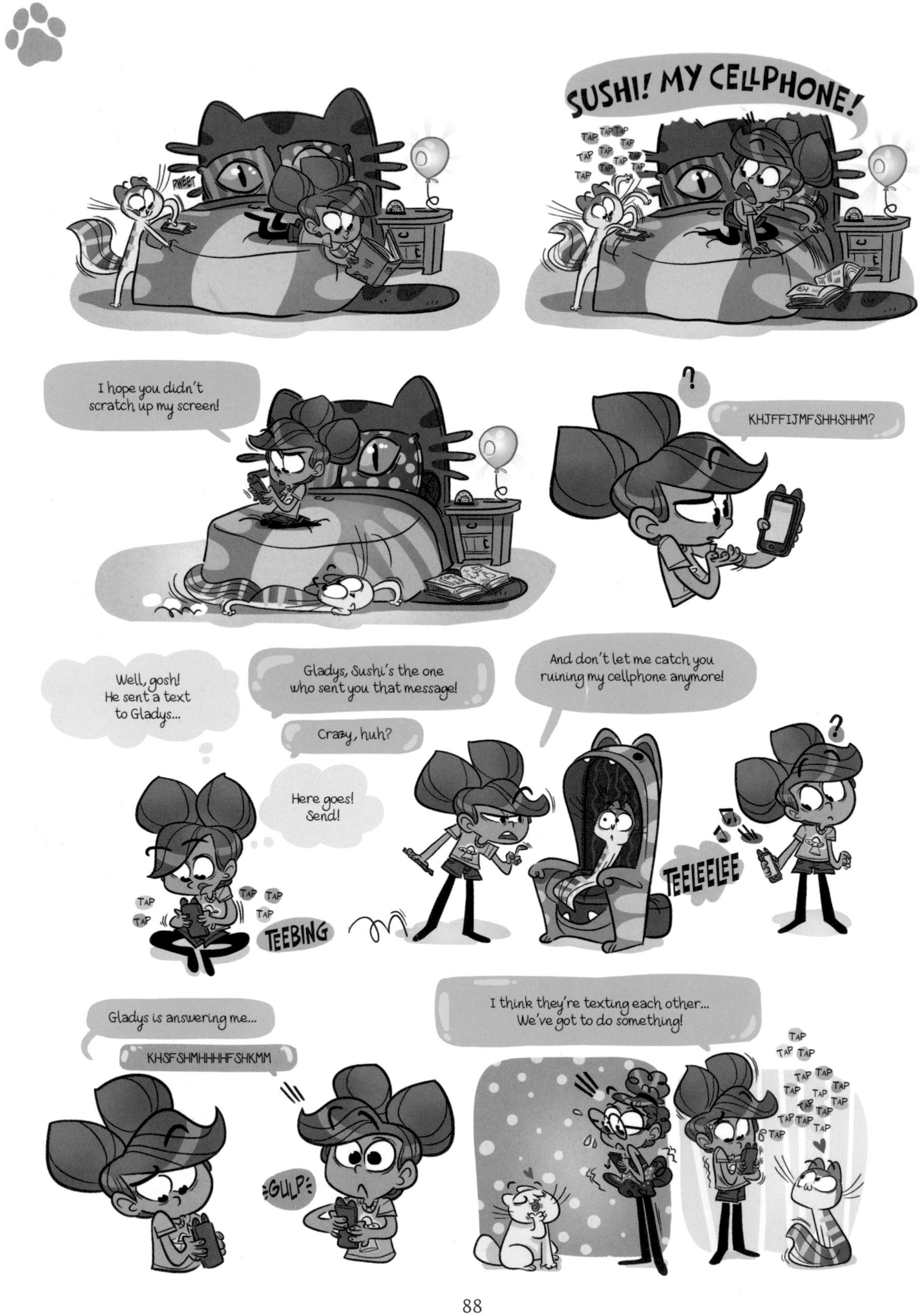
PWEET
SUSHI! MY CELLPHONE!
TAP TAP TAP TAP TAP TAP TAP TAP TAP TAP TAP
I hope you didn't scratch up my screen!
?
KHJFFIJMFSHHSHHM?
Well, gosh! He sent a text to Gladys...
Gladys, Sushi's the one who sent you that message!
Crazy, huh?
Here goes! Send!
TAP TAP TAP TAP TAP
TEEBING
And don't let me catch you ruining my cellphone anymore!
TEELEELEE
?
Gladys is answering me...
KHSFSHMHHHHFSHKMM
GULP
I think they're texting each other... We've got to do something!
TAP TAP TAP TAP TAP TAP TAP TAP TAP TAP TAP TAP TAP TAP

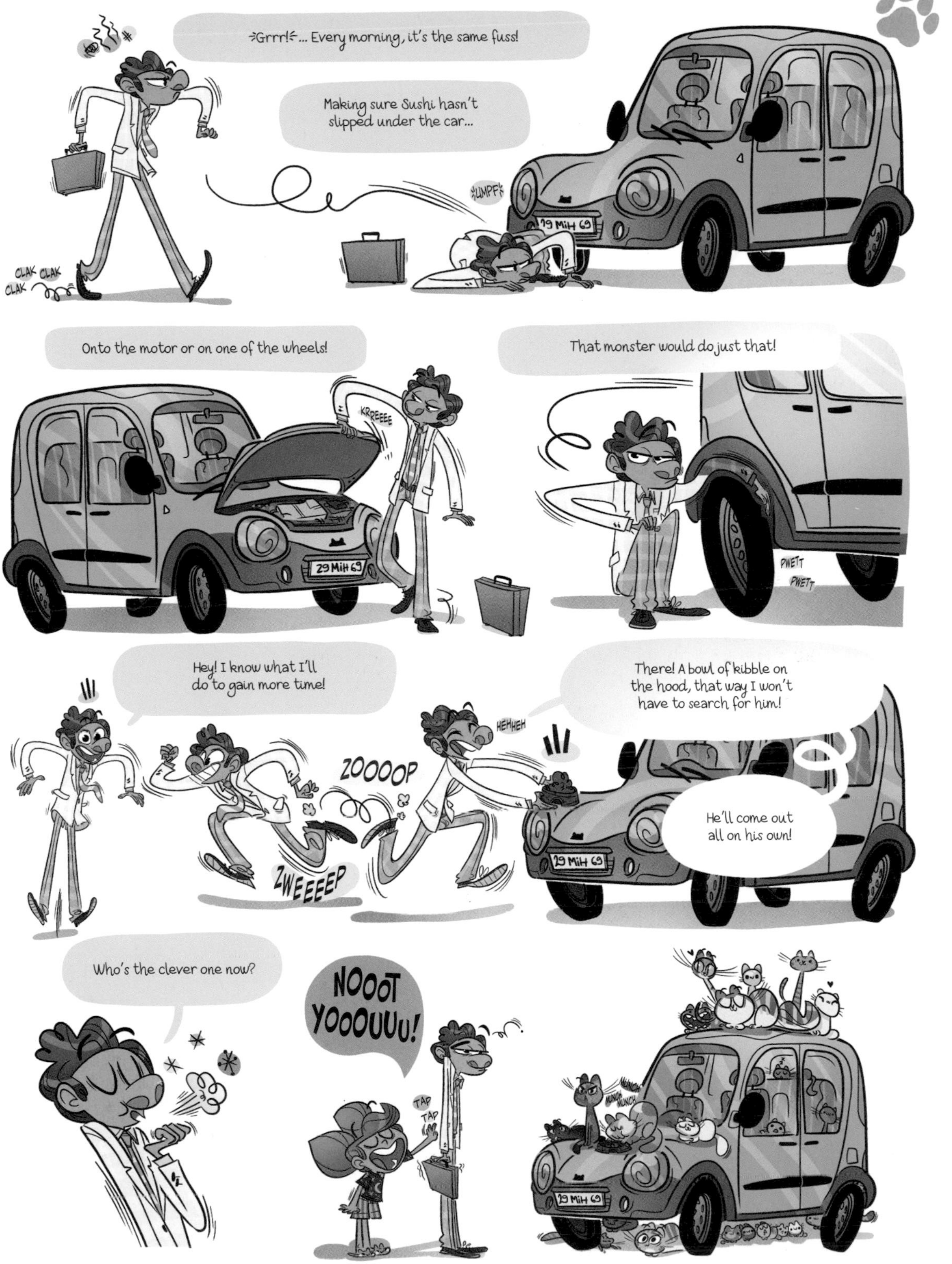
Grrr!... Every morning, it's the same fuss!
Making sure Sushi hasn't slipped under the car...
CLAK CLAK CLAK
UMPF
Onto the motor or on one of the wheels!
KRREEEE
That monster would do just that!
PWETT PWETT
Hey! I know what I'll do to gain more time!
ZOOOOP
ZWEEEEP
HEHHEH
There! A bowl of kibble on the hood, that way I won't have to search for him!
He'll come out all on his own!
Who's the clever one now?
NOOOT YOOOUUU!
TAP TAP
MUNCH MUNCH MUNCH

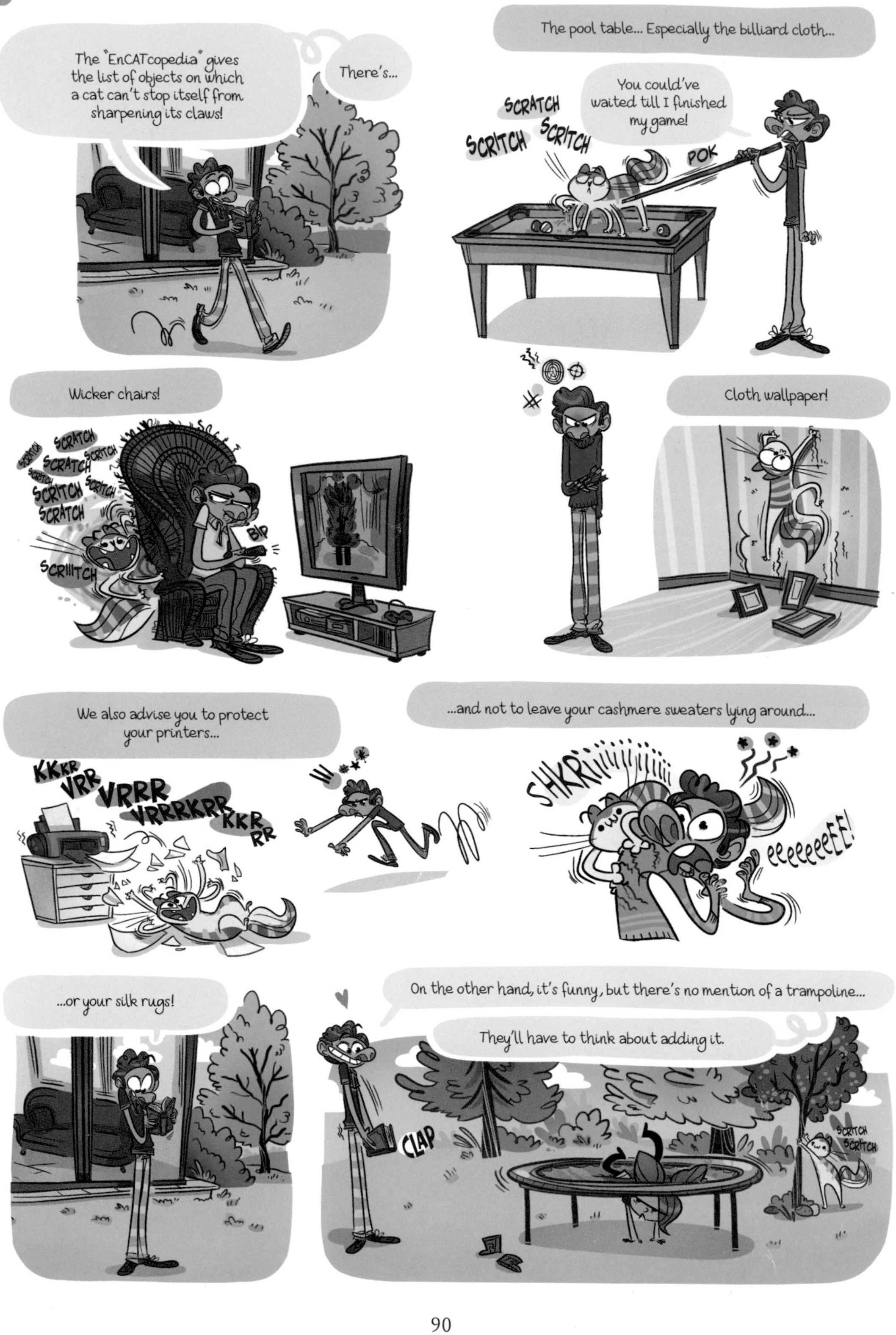

The "EnCATcopedia" gives the list of objects on which a cat can't stop itself from sharpening its claws!
There's...
The pool table... Especially the billiard cloth...
SCRATCH
SCRITCH
SCRITCH
You could've waited till I finished my game!
POK
Wicker chairs!
SCRATCH
SCRATCH
SCRITCH
SCRATCH
SCRITCH
SCRIIITCH
BIP
Cloth wallpaper!
We also advise you to protect your printers...
KKKR
VRR
VRRR
VRRRKRR
KKRR
RR
...and not to leave your cashmere sweaters lying around...
SHKRIIIIIIIII
eeeeeeeeEE!
...or your silk rugs!
On the other hand, it's funny, but there's no mention of a trampoline...
They'll have to think about adding it.
CLAP
SCRITCH
SCRITCH

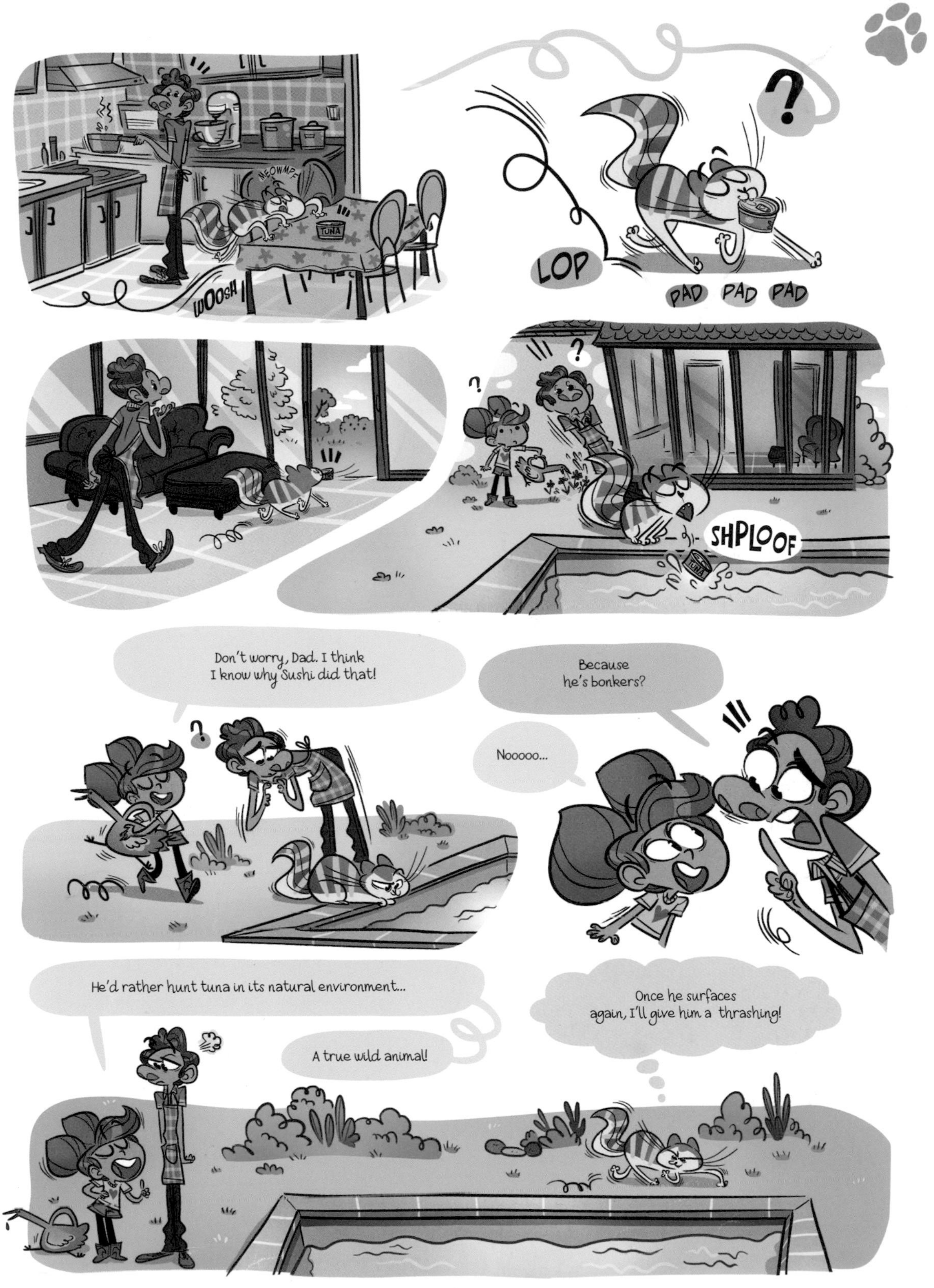
MEOWMPF
TUNA
WOOSH
?
LOP
PAD PAD PAD
?
?
SHPLOOF
TUNA
Don't worry, Dad. I think I know why Sushi did that!
Because he's bonkers?
?
Nooooo...
He'd rather hunt tuna in its natural environment...
A true wild animal!
Once he surfaces again, I'll give him a thrashing!

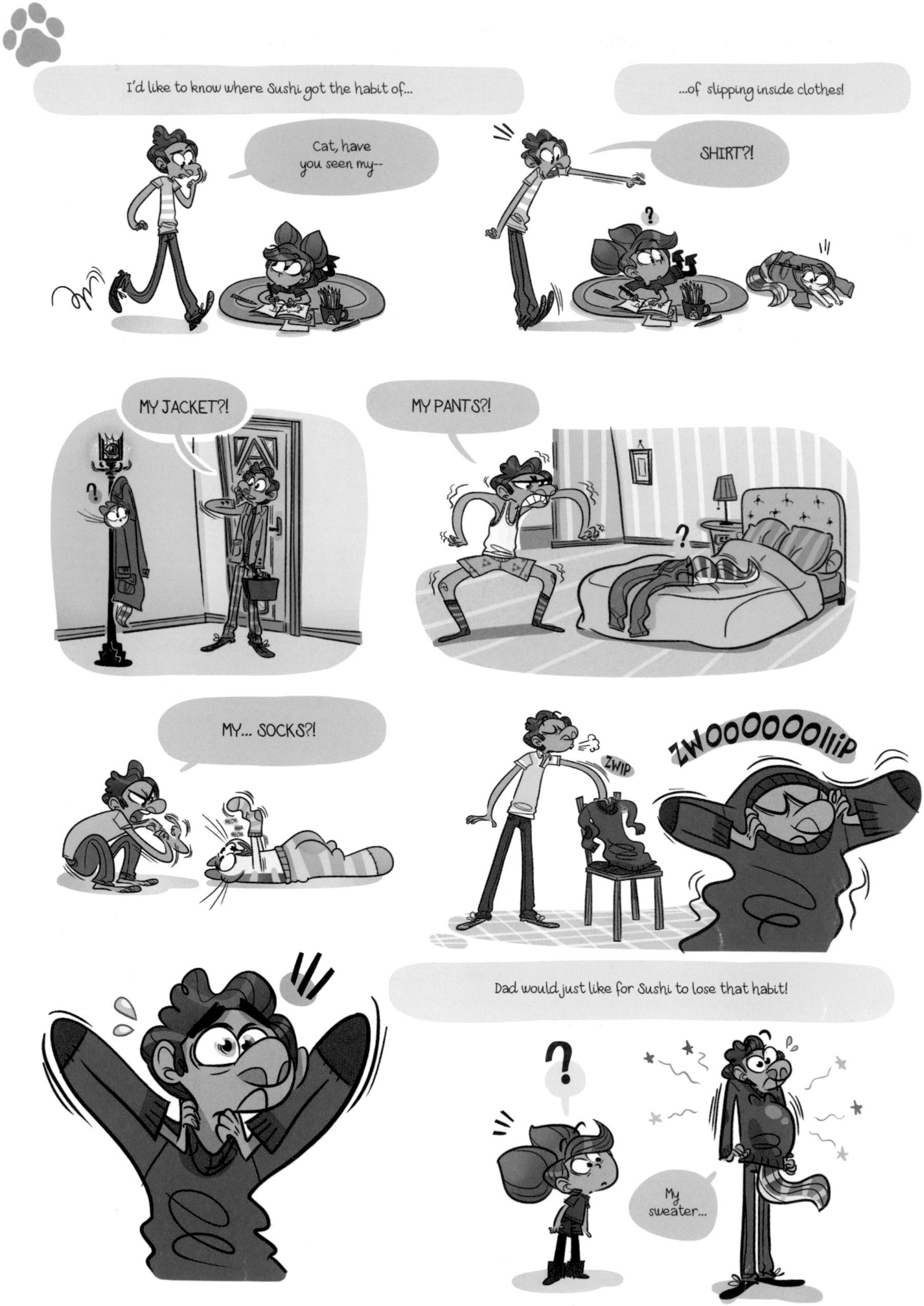
I'd like to know where Sushi got the habit of...
Cat, have you seen my--
...of slipping inside clothes!
SHIRT?!
MY JACKET?!
MY PANTS?!
MY... SOCKS?!
ZWIP
ZWOOOOOOllliP
Dad would just like for Sushi to lose that habit!
My sweater...

WATCH OUT FOR PAPERCUTZ

Welcome to the second washed up graphic novel of CAT AND CAT, by Christophe Cazenove and Hervé Richez, writers, and Yrgane Ramon, artist, from Papercutz, those crazy cat-video connoisseurs dedicated to publishing great graphic novels for all ages. I'm Jim Salicrup, the Editor-in-Chief and Keeper of the Kitty Litter. In CAT AND CAT #1 (which is still available at libraries and booksellers everywhere), I told you how cat-crazy we are at Papercutz and listed many of the Papercutz graphic novels that featured our favorite felines. Well, in the interest of equal time for canines, we wanted to mention there's an absolutely adorable little doggie in an exciting new series available from Papercutz right now. The dog's name is Dogmatix, and the series is called ASTERIX. It's a really big deal that Papercutz is publishing it, as ASTERIX is one of the biggest-selling graphic novel series in the world. This was big news and was even reported in *The New York Times* and *The Hollywood Reporter*. But regarding Dogmatix, while he does appear briefly—for one whole panel—in ASTERIX #1, it isn't until ASTERIX #2, where he starts to play a bigger role in the series.
Now some of you may not have heard of this Asterix fella, so let's take a quick journey in the Papercutz time machine...

We're back in the year 50 BC in the ancient country of Gaul, located where France, Belgium, and the Southern Netherlands are today. All of Gaul has been conquered by the Romans... well, not all of it. One tiny village, inhabited by indomitable Gauls, resists the invaders again and again. That doesn't make it easy for the garrisons of Roman soldiers surrounding the village in fortified camps.
So, how's it possible that a small village can hold its own against the mighty Roman Empire? The answer is this guy...

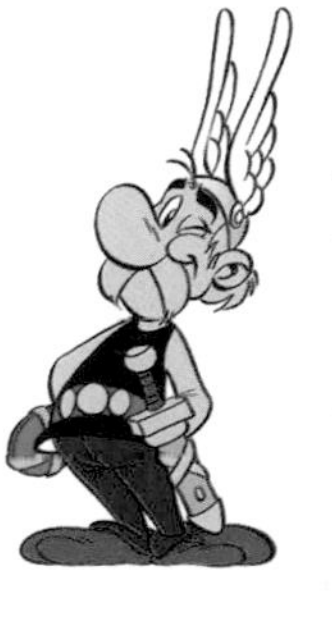

This is **Asterix**. A shrewd, little warrior of keen intellect... and superhuman strength. Asterix gets his superhuman strength from a magic potion. But he's not alone.

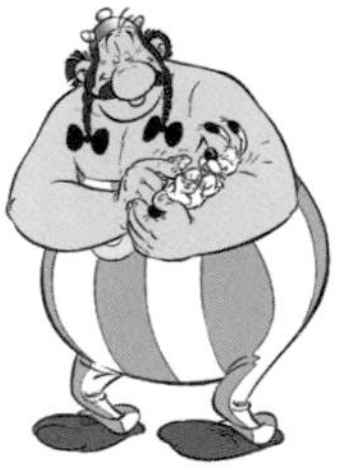

Obelix is Asterix's inseparable friend. He too has superhuman strength. He's a menhir (tall, upright stone monuments) deliveryman, he loves eating wild boar and getting into brawls. Obelix is always ready to drop everything to go off on a new adventure with Asterix. His constant companion (starting with ASTERIX #2) is Dogmatix, the only known canine ecologist, who howls with despair when a tree is cut down.

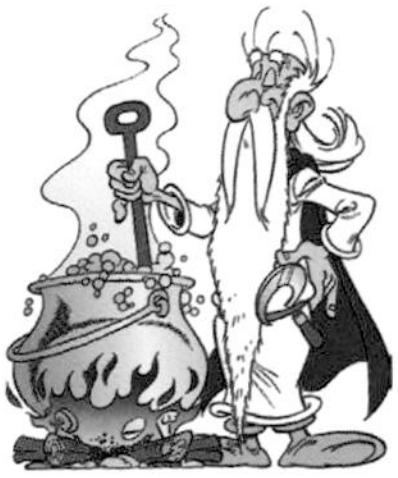

Panoramix, the village's venerable Druid, gathers mistletoe and prepares magic potions. His greatest success is the power potion. When a villager drinks this magical elixir he or she is temporarily granted super-strength. This is just one of the Druid's potions! And now you know why this small village can survive, despite seemingly impossible odds.

It's time we get back to the palatial Papercutz offices and wrap this up. Now, where did we park our time machine? Oh, there it is!

We're back. Of course, you may find dogs in other Papercutz titles — Charles in THE LOUD HOUSE and Puppy in THE SMURFS, for just a couple examples — but we're so excited about ASTERIX, we couldn't resist sharing the news with you.
And if you still consider yourself more of a cat person and love Sushi (the cat, not the food), be sure not to miss the next CAT AND CAT graphic novel coming your way soon.

Thanks, JIM

STAY IN TOUCH!

EMAIL: salicrup@papercutz.com
WEB: www.papercutz.com
TWITTER: @papercutzgn
INSTAGRAM: @papercutzgn
FACEBOOK: PAPERCUTZGRAPHICNOVELS
FANMAIL: Papercutz, 160 Broadway, Suite 700, East Wing, New York, NY 10038

SPECIAL PREVIEW OF ASTERIX #1

IN 50 BC, THE GAULS WERE CONQUERED BY THE ROMANS AFTER A LONG STRUGGLE...
LEADERS SUCH AS VERCINGETORIX WERE FORCED TO LAY DOWN THEIR ARMS AT CAESAR'S FEET...
YEOW!
CLANG
PEACE WAS ESTABLISHED, DISTURBED BY A FEW QUICKLY REPULSED ATTACKS BY THE GERMANS...
BUT ACHTUNG!(1) VE'LL BE BACK!
ALL RIGHT! VE'RE LEAFING!
ALL OF GAUL IS OCCUPIED...
Armorica
Celtica
Aquitania
Provincia Romana
ALL OF IT?... NO! FOR THERE'S ONE AREA VIGOROUSLY RESISTING THE INVADER, A SMALL AREA SURROUNDED BY ENTRENCHED ROMAN CAMPS...
AQUARIUM
LAUDANUM
BUTTERDRUM
ALL EFFORTS TO CONQUER THESE PROUD GAULS HAVE BEEN FUTILE, AND CAESAR WANTS TO KNOW...
QUID?(2)
HERE'S WHERE WE MEET OUR HERO, THE WARRIOR ASTERIX, WHO'S OFF TO ENJOY HIS FAVORITE SPORT: HUNTING.
YOU COMING BACK SOON, ASTERIX?
I'LL BE BACK FOR LUNCH, OBELIX...
THERE HE IS!
WE'LL GET HIM!
IPSO FACTO!(3)
SIC!(4)
POW
YEEOOW!
BAMM
OWW!
THE ROMANS CAN'T MAKE HEADS OR TAILS OF ANYTHING!
VAE VICTUS...!(5)
WHAT'S HE SAYING?
A1

(1) GERMAN FOR "ATTENTION." (2) LATIN FOR "WHAT (THEN)?" (3) LATIN FOR "BY THE VERY FACT..." (4) LATIN FOR "THAT IS SO." (5) LATIN FOR "WOE TO THE VANQUISHED."

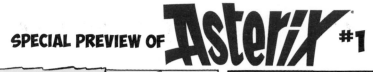

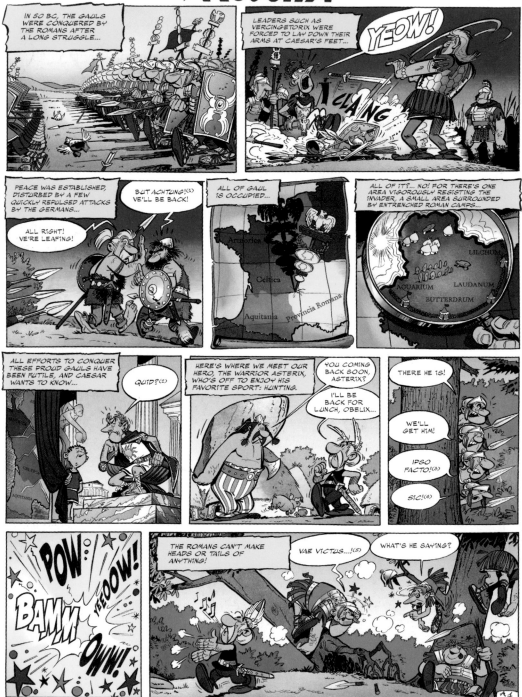

INVADE WHEREVER FINE BOOKS ARE SOLD AND PICK UP ASTERIX #1 TODAY!

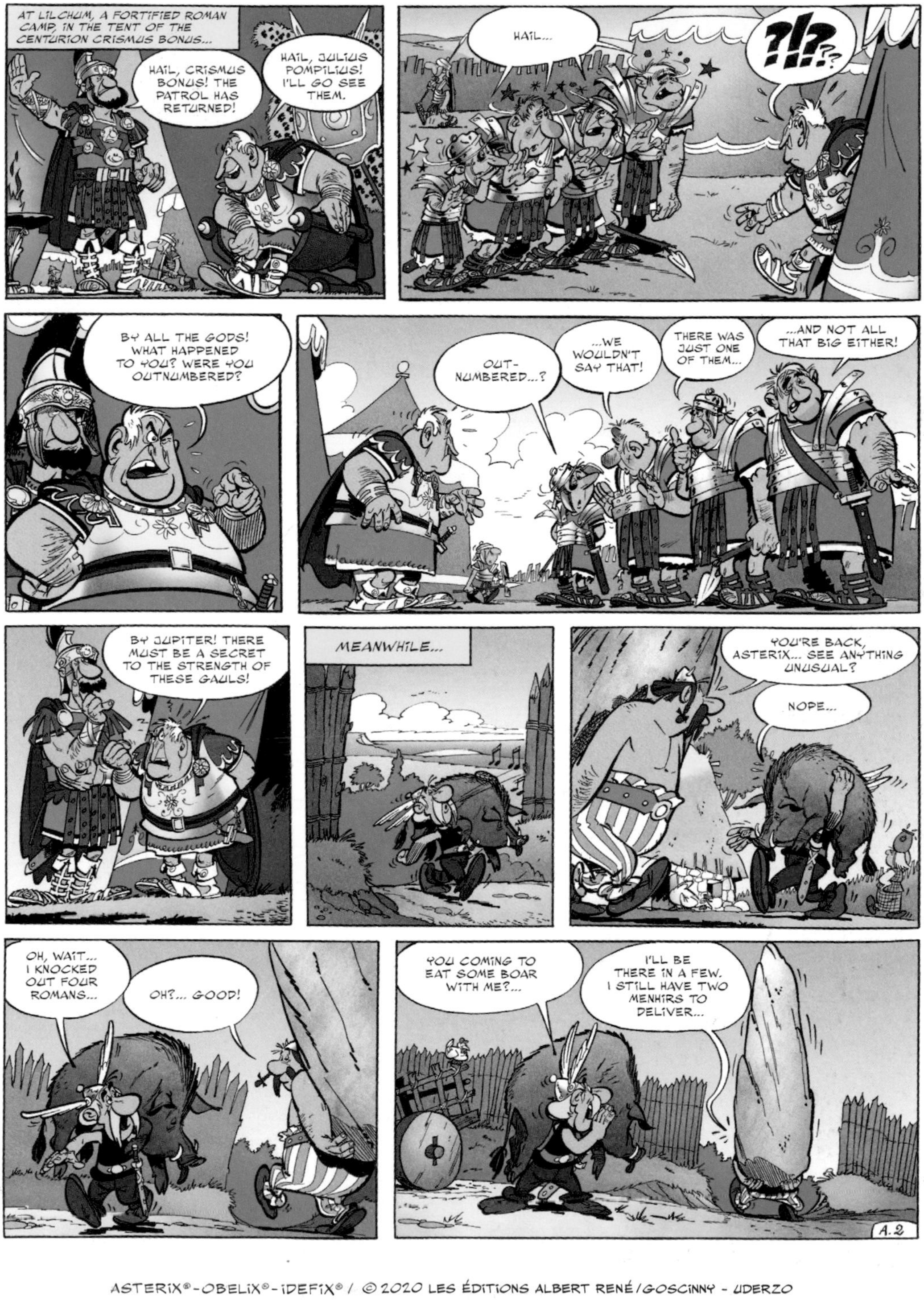
AT LILCHUM, A FORTIFIED ROMAN CAMP, IN THE TENT OF THE CENTURION CRISMUS BONUS...
HAIL, CRISMUS BONUS! THE PATROL HAS RETURNED!
HAIL, JULIUS POMPILIUS! I'LL GO SEE THEM.
HAIL...
?!?? ?
BY ALL THE GODS! WHAT HAPPENED TO YOU? WERE YOU OUTNUMBERED?
OUT-NUMBERED...?
...WE WOULDN'T SAY THAT!
THERE WAS JUST ONE OF THEM...
...AND NOT ALL THAT BIG EITHER!
BY JUPITER! THERE MUST BE A SECRET TO THE STRENGTH OF THESE GAULS!
MEANWHILE...
YOU'RE BACK, ASTERIX... SEE ANYTHING UNUSUAL?
NOPE...
OH, WAIT... I KNOCKED OUT FOUR ROMANS...
OH?... GOOD!
YOU COMING TO EAT SOME BOAR WITH ME?...
I'LL BE THERE IN A FEW. I STILL HAVE TWO MENHIRS TO DELIVER...
A. 2